Looking for the Durrells

HarperInspire, an imprint of
HarperCollins Christian Publishing
1 London Bridge Street
London SE1 9GF

www.harpercollins.co.uk

www.harperinspire.co.uk

First published by HarperCollins 2021
Copyright © Melanie Hewitt 2021

The author asserts her moral right,
including the right to be identified as the author of this work.

A catalogue record for this book is available from the British Library

ISBN: 9780310130451 (TPB)
ISBN: 9780310130468 (ebook)
ISBN: 9780310130475 (Audio)

Typeset by e-Digital Design

Printed and bound in the UK by CPI Group (UK) Ltd, Croydon CR0 4YY

MIX

Paper from responsible sources

FSC FSC™ C007454

Looking for the Durrells

Some summers change
us forever

Melanie
Hewitt

INSPIRE

About the Author

After deciding she wanted to be a book illustrator, Melanie went to art college at the age of 18. Halfway through the year, she changed her mind and secured a place at Swansea University to study English. However, after eighteen months, she left, moved home, and started looking for work as a nanny in London.

A local job advert for a reporter changed her life and career. She took up the post at the Doncaster Advertiser, later became Editor, and then worked in PR. She now works in education as Communications Lead for the XP Schools Trust based in Yorkshire, and is a Fellow of the Royal Society of Arts.

Looking for the Durrells is her first novel.

For my family and all the animals we've loved, and love.

In Memory of:

Brian Cartlidge, my father (1931–1998). An artist and reader of a million books, who loved the Durrells, Greece, and us.

Nikos Louvros (1947–2021). A Corfiot who shared his beloved island with those he knew instinctively needed its magic and would, in return, cherish it, as he did.

Prologue

The weak winter sunlight squeezed itself through the hospice blinds and fell in pale stripes on the bed. The squeaking wheels of a trolley being pushed along the corridor, beyond the closed door, made Penny pause.

She had been reading aloud. A paperback lay open on the bed, her hand grasped her dad's, until she realized with mild interest that her hand was starting to feel a little numb. Reluctant to let go of him for more than a second, she pulled her hand away, flexed it a few times and then placed it back.

Cold hands, warm heart. She wondered how many times he'd said that to her as he'd helped her put on her woollen mittens as a child. Now, it was winter again, but it could have been any season beyond the confines of this small hospice room. Their roles were reversed too – all the help to put on anything, eat, wash had come from her for a while now.

She winced, feeling the decline of the last months in a single spasm of mental and physical pain. Things had never been the same since the day he had come out of the consultant's room and confirmed, 'It's cancer'.

It had been just the two of them as she'd grown up, but this news had isolated her, as though she was at the top of a high mountain, looking down on the world below. Detached from the normal flow of life below, elevated from the here and now.

The countdown to Christmas was denoted by the regular delivery of presents, usually tins of biscuits dropped at the nurses' station, and the dusting-off of slightly garish and faded decorations from a dusty stockroom. The hospice existed as a world within a world and Penny and her dad had been citizens of it for over a week now.

The door opened suddenly. Penny looked up and smiled at Carol, the nurse who had begun to feel like an extended family member; a companion in arms in this fight against pain and its inevitable end.

'Would you like a cup of tea?' Carol walked across the room gathering up the plates of half-eaten sandwiches and a couple of untouched cakes, almost apologetic in their overly bright paper cases.

Penny wondered whether the kind and comforting Carol had heard the raised voices, before Bruce, his anger barely controlled, had walked out of the building a few minutes earlier. Her fiancé had, for a few days, been the darling of the nurses' station, but the fact that his casual and sometimes devastating charm had soon worn off, like the rolled gold on costume jewellery, did not surprise her.

How could they actually fall out in a hospice, as her dad lay dying, arguing about . . . what was it? . . . whether it was possible – realistic even – for her to travel to Italy and back every weekend, while Bruce settled in there, if he was offered the new job he had applied for. Why did he always have to almost bully her into submission, win every point or argument? Discussion seemed to be a long-forgotten and abandoned part of their relationship.

'That would be great, thanks,' she answered Carol absent-mindedly.

'Are you okay?' Carol paused at the door, looking at Penny and then across at the unconscious, grey and drawn man in the bed.

Penny nodded, afraid that if she used her voice, it would break and then so would she. There was something of the art of brinkmanship about waiting for someone to die; so many moments when the temptation to let go was overwhelming; to stop holding in, holding back, and give in to the hopelessness and pain. To let her heart and all the love trickle through her fingers. But what if it was too soon and there was nothing left to carry her through the days ahead?

She turned back to the book and, remembering that Carol had said that her dad might still be able to hear her, Penny began to read again.

After a while, she paused and flicked the book over, looking for the hundredth time, at the dragonfly on the cover of the old favourite book in her hands – *My Family and Other Animals* by Gerald Durrell.

As a child, she'd listened in awe to tales of tortoises and tempests, sun-scorched days and star-laden nights. She and her dad had talked then, and in later years, of visiting Corfu for themselves and discovering the magical island where the book was set. School, then university, followed by work and the hurry of life in general, had resulted in other plans.

Twenty years earlier, her dad had read the novel to her. Now he was dying. Only yesterday he had still been semiconscious, rising above the waves for a moment of clarity and connection, before sinking again into the sea of morphine.

He was only 60 years old, but looked ancient in this fading afternoon light. Like a carved, stone Grail knight, coming to life, if only for a brief moment.

As long as there was still a chance that some of the golden

words might reach him, this book had felt like the perfect choice. It had always transported both of them somewhere else, into a world of sparkling seasons and rich anecdotes.

It was easier, strangely, to carry on now *without* Bruce here. When he was around, she had to admit reluctantly that it felt like looking after two people. Bruce had to be managed, his dislike of hospitals palpable and ever-present.

Now, after yet another argument about nothing and everything, he had grabbed his car keys and, no doubt pulling out of the car park too fast in his fury, had left.

The situation was tiresome and tiring. His handsome face, which she had once sometimes watched as he slept, had lost its fascination. His sullen moods muted and soured the impact of the good looks that made people take notice when he entered a room.

They'd been together for three years, moved in together after a year and, for the last six months, as she'd helped her dad cope with a vicious cancer diagnosis and decline, Penny realized she'd begun to dislike Bruce. The knowledge flashed across her consciousness and disappeared just as swiftly, but it left its mark.

Any love and tenderness between them, she thought, was now more about something lost than the reality of something genuine or current.

She shook her head as though to clear her mind, overloaded with too much to compute or resolve, and began to look again at the words on the page. They danced, elusive and jumbled, then suddenly blurred.

A tear fell onto the yellowing page. She swallowed in a vain attempt to rid herself of the lump in her throat, and continued aloud.

Back to a moonlight swim with the Durrells on Corfu, with its balmy air, fragranced with the sea and sun-ripened flowers, laughter and languor filling the night with memories to catch and bottle.

'Here we go, Dad,' she said softly. 'We're climbing into the little wooden boat. You can trail your hand in the water. It's so relaxing and peaceful. All you have to do is be in the moment, let the boat take you to the bay with the silver sands.'

Chapter 1

Six months later

The summer had barely begun. After two days of scudding white clouds, a light breeze, and erratic sun creating a patchwork landscape of light and shade, the promising weather had reverted to scowling dark skies and a stiff breeze seemed to come straight from a cruel Arctic landscape.

Train stations in England felt cold at any time of year. The airport was only a short journey away, thank goodness, and in a few hours she would walk down the steps of the plane and experience for herself the magical transition from the capricious weather of an England in late June to the confident, established heat of a Greek-island summer.

Penny's anticipation of this spontaneous and possibly indulgent adventure was tempered by a heaviness in her heart and stomach. Some days it felt like another era, sitting in the hospice at her father's bedside, watching him slip away. Other days it was as sharp and vivid as something that had happened a moment ago.

The outcome had been inevitable and in a world of narrowing choices, how it all ended – to make the parting the best it could be – had enveloped everything. Imaginings of what might have been shared and said in the last days were far from the reality of what had happened. But somehow that didn't matter. There was nothing more to say that could have been said.

His passing marked the end of thirty-three years of love, learning, and safety. He had always made her feel safe.

It puzzled her that she was still breathing, making plans, and waking up every morning. How could her heart, mind, and body deal with so much pain, such grief and still work, still function?

Penny checked herself as she pulled her suitcase onto the train. She didn't like the idea of inviting interest or sympathy by letting the pain out in public.

Once wedged into the window seat, and boundaries established with her fellow passengers above and around the unforgiving table between them, she stared passively as the patchwork fields and small towns rolled by. Eyes half-closed, she fell back slowly into the film playing out in her head: the endless dialogue, regrouping, replaying scenes from the last months, years.

This new world would take some getting used to. This planet that didn't have her father on it. She was also now facing whatever lay ahead as a newly single woman, with an ex-fiancé.

The past came back, like a familiar tune played time and time again, as she unravelled how this had come about in the end. The endless back and forth of who had said what in the final days before the packing up and the moving out. It had made more sense for her to be the one who moved, with her childhood home now empty, and the flat they'd shared to go on the market eventually if Bruce got his new post – which he had.

How strange, she thought, that she'd be flying so close to his new home in Italy. So close and yet so far. It was hard to imagine him at a new university she'd never seen or heard of before. It wasn't hard though to think of how he would fit in.

Bruce had always had an innate sense of style and confidence, with the white shirt, the heirloom watch, the hair that behaved. If she was honest, this had sometimes made her feel a little inadequate, if not eccentric, in her choice of clothes. particularly on painting days in the studio, when a large apron with pockets and a baggy shirt with rolled-up sleeves formed her uniform – more nineteenth century than twenty-first.

Penny smiled at herself for a moment, feeling the smooth material of her retro summer dress between her fingers. The old cotton looked a little faded, but for her this only added to its beauty. When she'd found it in a vintage shop a few years before, it had felt like meeting an old friend. The roses in neat rows, and the bands of blue that framed them in hoops around the skirt, enchanted her.

She'd never worn it until today though. There had never been the right time. It was a dress that needed to be taken on an adventure, although wearing it didn't necessarily guarantee the courage she felt she needed. And when her best friend Lizzie had dropped her off at the station, she had, just for an instant, wished she was getting back in the car and going home.

Why am I heading for Corfu, on my own, for a month? Why do I do these things to myself? It had seemed like such a terrific idea at the time, a glass or two into a girls' night in with Lizzie. The conversation had turned, as it often did, to the last days of her dad's life in the hospice and her farewell to Bruce in the days that followed . . . the things she and her dad had promised they'd do – the trip to Corfu, the Durrells' pilgrimage.

'Why not go, while you can? No ties, no children, no one to stop you.' Lizzie had got excited about the idea in a heartbeat and became carried away with her own vision of this trip to paradise. 'I'd come with you if it wasn't a madly busy time with the business, and then there's the after-school stuff with the twins, before you even factor in the rest of the random happenings that make up my life.'

As she'd listened, Penny, sitting cross-legged on the floor in the sitting room that she'd known since a small child, glanced up at a painting on the wall.

It was at that moment, noticing for the first time in years the painting of Corfu she'd drawn from imagination as a child, and which her dad had treasured, framed, and put in pride of place, that she realized why she was going, why she had to go.

How many times had she dreamed of walking into that picture as it magically came to life like a scene from a children's film?

Now, on this packed and stuffy train, rushing almost recklessly towards the airport, she knew that whatever the next four weeks might bring, this trip had to be made. It was unfinished business, a part of the journey to healing, or whatever it was she needed right now. To mend the hollowness of the grief and hurt left by the loss of one man and the departure of another; even if Bruce's exit had felt, at the time, like a release.

Chapter 2

For Penny, the thrill of flying had always been tempered with a sense of the possibility of something going horribly wrong. As Lizzie had once said to her, 'It's not the flying that worries me; it's the crashing.'

Her dad had hated it. Whenever they flew, he would barely move, as though afraid he would tip the plane if he leant forward or turned his head. He used to say it was like being trapped in a metal corridor at 30,000 feet. This memory made her smile as she moved into the window seat and started to browse through the duty-free catalogue.

The soothing tone of the pilot's voice told everyone they were on time, no turbulence expected, and in Corfu that morning it was already 32 degrees.

For the hundredth time in as many days Penny opened Gerald Durrell's *Corfu Trilogy* and started to read. The beginning, the description of the first sight of Corfu, always enchanted her. Now, as the Homeric wine-dark sea, infused with turquoise and lilac, drew closer, there was a warming rush of anticipation and for the first time in a very long time, a sense of peace.

Two hours, a glass of rosé and something that had masqueraded as a goat's-cheese baguette later, the plane, having soared gloriously over the Alps, began its run down the Italian coast. The sea, now crystalline and blue, dazzled thousands of feet below.

Looking to her left at the seat occupied by a stranger rather than Bruce, she felt a pang of regret and arguing inwardly with herself, a misplaced longing. He was somewhere there on the ground, no doubt striding purposefully, but ever so slightly self-consciously, between lectures, the tan leather belt on his carefully chosen casual trousers matching his loafers, the sunglasses understated but making a statement.

It was easy to dismiss him for his ultimate shallowness, his vanity, but even after six months of the single, Bruce-free life, older memories of when they'd first met and all was golden sometimes caught her off-guard. There had been no one in her life quite like him; so vibrant, so confident. She'd tried to paint him once, but hadn't been happy with the result. He wasn't one of her book illustrations, created so meticulously. He was real and even now she could not, as a professional artist, dilute his handsomeness, even though it would have helped her to move on.

Corfu's runway stretched out across the old lagoon at the edge of the sea; a spectacular site reached at the end of a slow, breathtaking descent along a coastline of great beauty. Green, felt-textured hills and peaks, with rocks that appeared white where they broke the surface. Pale houses and white-rimmed island contours appeared and then finally the plane swooped down so close that the sea could be seen rippling in the gentle cross winds.

Mouse Island – in legend, Ulysses' ship turned to stone – and the southern end of Kanoni welcomed the passengers lucky enough to be able to look out of a window. To the west, if one approached from the south, were the Chessboard Fields Gerry Durrell had visited as a boy; a matrix of ancient waterways and home to many creatures.

It was really Gerry's writing, the adventures of a ten-year-old boy recounted twenty years later, that had brought her here. A miraculous experience, which had begun when he'd been lifted from Bournemouth and replanted in the richness of the land and life of Corfu, along with his family: his mother Louisa, Leslie and Margo, all following Gerry's eldest brother Larry, who was already there with his wife Nancy.

Nothing ever stayed the same, whether a person or an island. Would Corfu still smell and sound the same as it had for the Durrells when they had lived there in the 1930s? Would the air shimmer with waves of nostalgia and remembrance, like radio signals bringing the lost past into the present, powerful echoes she might feel travelling through time? Or would there just be sadness for those no longer there, with memory conjuring melancholy on an island saturated with sunshine and sun-seekers.

As the plane bounced down onto the runway Penny hoped that a month would be enough time to find all the answers to the questions in her heart and head. Or would a month be too long? Would disappointment – or the discovery that this was a silly, indulgent idea –leave her morose and lost?

As she stood at the top of the plane steps blinking against the light and feeling the warm, heavy, pine-and-herb-scented air of Corfu for the first time, Penny knew one thing for certain – she wished her dad was with her more than anything in the world.

Chapter 3

Guy Frobisher had already had a difficult day and it was only noon. The airport was getting hotter by the second, one of the luggage carousels had broken down, and there were two people who he had sent off to their transfer coach three times, who kept bouncing back. How difficult could finding Bay 22A be?

After ten weeks the novelty and perks of being a holiday rep had almost vanished for the university student, who had imagined freer, finer, and altogether more glamorous things. To add to the day's woes, he'd also just had to say goodbye to a tearful Ellie from Newcastle, to whom he had promised regular text messages and perhaps more.

His day brightened at the thought of the possible arrival of another 'Ellie' on the next flight. After all, he mused, who could resist the significant charms of his slightly plummy accent, entertaining stories, and blue-eyed, floppy-haired handsomeness?

At 20, Guy thought he had peaked and his irresistible personality and pulling power were not to be squandered. It would be wrong, he thought, not to share his gifts with an ever-changing cast of female leads in the *Guy Frobisher Show*.

A smitten college friend had once told Guy that he looked a little like Rupert Brooke, the war poet, and from that moment he often brandished an embossed leather notebook and a silver fountain pen, just in case the muse came upon him.

'Guy, which bay is the Gouvia bus in?' A small blond lad with an impish face puzzled over a collection of papers taped clumsily to a clipboard that bore the legend *Greektime* in pseudo-Greek lettering, on a bright blue and yellow background. A happy sun with large white-gloved hands in the thumbs-up position, wearing sunshades, dominated the logo.

Guy responded with a casually raised arm and pointed vaguely to the right. 'Over there, Rich, but it doesn't seem to matter today, my friend, because wherever you send 'em, they keep coming back in droves and telling me the bus or the bay doesn't exist.'

Richard Leigh smiled, aware in his quiet and accepting way that Guy wasn't in the best mood. They had arrived together on Corfu, feeling lucky and happy to be on the same island for their summer job, as they were pals and roommates at university. For their final year they planned to share a small flat, in which Guy had already claimed the en-suite bedroom.

In spite of the bus and bay confusion outside the airport, within thirty minutes all the coaches were full and Guy and Rich were heading south. Between them they looked after five resorts, some lively, others more sedate. The last stop on the journey was St George South and as the air-conditioning began to soothe everyone's nerves, the noise level on the coach dropped and minds turned to thoughts of beaches, bars, and relaxation.

In a few hours, thought Guy, the rest of the day will be all mine. Corfu Town was calling and as the following day only involved a couple of welcome meetings, he would no doubt be out until dawn – or his money ran out.

As he handed out welcome packs to the passengers, he caught the eye of a young woman travelling with friends and smiled. She smiled back and Guy immediately channelled Mr Brooke as he took out his antiquated notebook with a flourish and – not too ostentatiously – looked thoughtful and began to write.

After waiting for the carousel to behave, Penny emerged from the airport with the right suitcase and looked for a Greektime rep. The bright yellow uniform was easy to spot and within seconds she arrived in a bus bay, directed by a small lad with a clipboard, who seemed to be part of a double act with a tall floppy-haired chap of about the same age.

Morecambe and Wise, Pete and Dud, Stan and Ollie? Penny wasn't sure which iconic duo they reminded her of, but there was something comic about their interaction that made her smile. When the pair joined her coach they handed out welcome packs and the driver slowly navigated the road from the airport. As they doubled back to follow the coast road, from the left-hand side of the coach, she saw another plane floating above the sea as it began its elegant descent. The Greek mainland glowed green, grey, and blue in the distance, the channel between the island and the mainland narrower than Penny had imagined.

The local radio station delivered its eclectic soundtrack of Greek and international pop music, as the film set of the road south rolled by the bus window. Past Perama, site of the Durrell's first home, the Strawberry Pink Villa, and on through Gastouri, famous for its charming donkeys with a distinctive white circle around their eyes.

Benitses, Moraitiki, Messonghi . . . on they went, stopping

occasionally to decant holidaymakers at their hotels and apartments. As they turned inland the roads became narrower and the corners tighter. Gnarled and ancient olive trees, their nets folded in the lower branches, featured at the side of the roads. Chickens and a goat or two worried the soil in the welcome shade, their surroundings bleached by the relentless sun. Painted shutters of china blue, now looked washed-out and pale, the grass patchy between each village, apologetic and sparse.

Eager to absorb every inch of the journey's unfolding story, Penny closed her eyes every few minutes as though trying to imprint an image on her mind's eye. The camera inside her head clicked away and treasured every single view that presented itself, beautifully composed and framed. Picture-perfect.

To her surprise, unbidden and unexpected, Bruce pushed himself again into that same space inside her head. She straightened her back in her seat, as though preparing for an argument or a difficult conversation – an old, familiar sensation.

She had acknowledged when they broke up that far from being the man she had thought he was, Bruce had also failed in her eyes to be the human being she'd hoped most people could be. As her father had become more confined and frustrated by his cancer, Bruce had competed childishly for her attention. He commented in a passive-aggressive way on the time Penny spent in her old family home, creating an unwelcome, exhausting layer of conflict and appeasement. An opportunity for him to work in Italy had brought things to a head. He had to go as it was the opportunity of a lifetime, he'd explained: 'You have to understand, Penny, this is a top university. A professorship at my age doesn't happen every day.'

What Bruce didn't realize was that she'd already stepped away from him by the time he shared the news of the job in Brindisi. A phrase, a sentence, a collection of words had begun this process, but the impact had been profound: 'I don't like hospitals,' he declared as she pushed her father, who was in acute pain, in a wheelchair down a busy hospital corridor. Bruce's petulance, after a sudden call from Penny asking him to meet her at the local infirmary, had surfaced in an ugly but ultimately timely way.

She had realized at that moment and in the weeks that followed that this was not – as her father used to say – 'someone who's wagon you would want to hitch your star to'. Bruce had sent a short letter of condolence when her father had died, informing her he was about to move abroad, but that he was thinking about her as he knew how much her dad had meant to her.

She imagined him now just across the water in Italy, still disliking hospitals and still happily believing that the world should revolve around him.

The bus stopped suddenly and, pulled back into the present, Penny saw a tourist in a hire car reversing frantically to let the bus through. A sign on the bend in the road declared, 'Welcome to St George South'.

She had made it. For the next month this would be home.

Chapter 4

St George South spread out to the left and right, radiating from a small picturesque harbour; a safe haven that day for four boats, anchored neatly, waiting patiently for a fisherman or holiday sailor. Restaurants, bars, cafés, several supermarkets, and a jewellery shop followed the shoreline. On the horizon, a tiny island shimmered luminously, as though part of an imaginary world.

A number of small hotels, apartments and tour, and car-hire companies lined the main road through the resort. Individual homes, some with beautifully manicured gardens, colour and fragrance escaping over the low whitewashed walls, made up the rest of the street landscape. To the north, the beach widened out into sculptured sand dunes.

The true secret of St George's success however, as with most places, resided with its people. Visitors returned each year as dear friends or extended family, building relationships and showered with warm, welcoming Greek hospitality. For decades, generations of residents had welcomed thousands of sun-seeking, tired, frazzled, and expectant families and individuals to this little piece of paradise. Most came looking for something prosaic or profound, or days by the pool with suntan oil and swimming costumes, or sometimes a need for rest, release, or hope.

The answer each found at the end of their week or fortnight stay was, quite often, one that they hadn't expected. Sometimes they felt the positive glow of a week well spent with friends old and new. Others left with a determination to change their lives or lifestyle, to find a better work-life balance or perhaps – with balmy sunset meals still vivid in the memory – just to eat outside in the garden more.

Everyone took back with them a speck or two of the magic Corfiot dust that had settled on every visitor, even before the likes of Nero and Mark Antony had arrived in the harbour at Kassiopi.

It was into this world that Penny stepped as the coach stopped outside the Athena restaurant.

Penny had barely turned around with her suitcase when a small boy, who looked around 7 years of age, approached the bus. Guy and Rich greeted him with the easy familiarity of established friends and shared some banter with their young pal, who showed them a small kitten, before Rich guided Penny across the road and along a lemon-tree- and honeysuckle-lined path. It was early afternoon, hazily hot, and the small lizards that populated this little lane hid in shady gaps in the wall. One poked its nose out for a moment to take a closer look at Penny. They would emerge in the cooler evening, she thought.

Two double-storey villas came into view, each painted pale blue with creamy yellow shutters and divided into four separate apartments, with one bedroom, an en-suite bathroom, and a small kitchen and living area. A small balcony or veranda, depending which floor you were on, accommodated a circular table and two chairs.

Deep pink, abundant bougainvillea softened the stucco. To the right a few intrepid residents braved the high sun, as they melted slowly beside a small pool. The heat would defeat them soon and a late-afternoon nap would beckon in their shuttered rooms.

'Here we go,' said Rich as he led Penny up a set of cool marbled stairs. 'You're on the best side of the building, so you get a mountain view and a glimpse of the sea.'

Penny opened the shutters and stepped onto the balcony. A triangle of azure glistened to her left and a plane glided over the green and silver mountain to her right, on its way to the airport.

'I'll leave you to it then. There's a meeting this evening at the Athena across the road at seven. Just a little welcome meeting for all our new arrivals – and a free drink. If you have any questions about anything, that's a good time to ask. See you then!' Rich backed out of the room and closed the door behind him.

Penny sat down on the bed closest to the balcony windows, the mustard-coloured bedspread soft between her fingers as she smoothed it down. For a second, she felt more alone than she'd ever done in her life.

She lay back on the bed, lifting her feet from the cool floor, and closed her eyes for a moment. Her left hand stretched out across the blanket, as though looking for human contact. Six months of sleeping alone and she still hadn't got used to it. She turned her head on the pillow, eyes open now, and fixed her gaze on the empty space beside her.

A mosquito enjoying the shelter of the room buzzed around laconically. Penny watched it cross the ceiling and settle on the light fitting. Getting up, she opened her suitcase mechanically and found the mosquito plug-in she'd bought the day before. Laughing quietly at herself – the ever-practical, ever-organized Penny – she plugged it in and acknowledged that her sense of loneliness, if accompanied by itching bites, would definitely make things worse. There was always something she could do to help herself, some small thing to help lift her mood, until the low passed.

He dad had said that nothing stayed the same. Good, bad, indifferent, it all moved on, whether we wanted it to or not. Change was part of life. Each wind, each tide brought something new. So, she would force herself to the Athena at 7 p.m. and meet her fellow Greektime travellers.

The temptation to wander out now, then shower and change before the meeting, was too great. *The unpacking can wait*, she thought, as the large suitcase stood like a monolith, accusingly in the corner.

This place is only really for sleeping and showering, she told herself, realizing suddenly how eerily quiet a room could feel when you were the only one staying in it.

Grabbing her slightly battered, but jaunty, wide-brimmed sunhat, she took a quick look in the mirror above the dark, wooden set of drawers next to the second bed. *I look hot*, she thought, *but not in a good way*. Picking up the leaflets the reps have given her, she fanned her face for a few seconds and then, dropping her keys in her small rucksack, left the apartment.

Chapter 5

It had been a steady day for Tess, with the usual mini-crises that running a popular restaurant and apartments brought. The heat had been fierce in the middle of the day, but happily she had been mostly in the shade. The air was cooler now and the breeze from the sea made the Athena the perfect place to sit in the early evening.

How lovely, she thought, to stop just for a few minutes, close your eyes, and take in all the sounds and sensations hanging in the air. The low murmur of relaxed chatter competed with the rhythmic sweep of the waves below, muffled laughter, and calls from the kitchen.

Keeping busy was a financial necessity, but also an emotional one. She had lost her husband three years earlier. Theo her son had been 5, and her 40th birthday only days away, when Georgios had stepped out onto the road and a tourist, who had forgotten momentarily which side of the road he was meant to be driving on, had hit him. A helicopter flight to Athens and all the expertise of the team at the hospital had failed to revive him from the coma the head injury had caused.

Her desolation mingled with remorse. That morning she

and Georgios had argued – not an unusual occurrence, but all the more painful now because no more words could be said, and the last ones between them, if not meant, had been harsh and shrill.

She pulled two tables together and rearranged the chairs. The twice-weekly holiday rep welcome meetings at the Athena were a useful advertisement for the restaurant's ambience and perfect setting. But the Athena had no real need for advocacy and signposting. The welcome was warm, the team professional and helpful, the food, created in the cosy kitchen by the indomitable Anna, outstanding. The tables, pale-blue and shabby chic rather than rustic, were well spaced and matched by solid wooden chairs.

The idyllic setting embodied the true secret of the Athena's well-deserved popularity, as it perched on the side of gently sloping rocks, about ten feet from the sea below. To the right was the harbour and beyond it, a cluster of palms and beautiful flowers.

All tavernas and wine bars were now beginning to fill with holidaymakers, anticipating their first glass of wine or lager. Across the sea a large yacht sailed sedately along the coast, reflecting a flash of radiance from the setting sun back to the shore.

Tess felt the warm breeze as she stepped into the outside area of the Athena, its soft stone a gentle contrast with the white-veined, marble floor of the open-sided interior. Clear blinds could be drawn down if the wind whipped up too much, or a summer squall trespassed near the diners.

The bar on the left was quite high and crowded with mementos from visitors and friends: photos, trinkets, tea towels from English seaside resorts, and good-luck charms were all part of the eclectic decor.

For decades, ever since Tess's father-in-law Spiro and

his late wife had opened the taverna in the 1970s, an ever-growing band of Athena superfans had considered the spot to be their own personal holiday paradise. Now there were three members of the Ioannidis family left, one for each generation: Spiro, Tess, and Theo.

Young Theo, now 7, had English grandparents in Devon, so the question, unspoken but already hanging in the air, was would he stay in St George South when he grew up? He should have been called 'Spiro' after his grandfather, but after a difficult birth Tess had wanted to call her new and miraculously delivered son after the doctor who, she felt, had saved them both. Georgios was so grateful to have his wife and child safe, he gave in easily. So, Theo it was.

The chatter of Guy and Richard interrupted her thoughts and she turned, hand on hip, cloth in hand, to greet them. The boys made her smile and Theo, with his menagerie of rescued local flora and fauna, sought out their company whenever he could. There was always an ailing kitten to save, a dog to feed, or a friendly lizard to coax into the house.

Rich and Guy always drew a suitably awed and interested audience. This, along with a dozen other maternal and protective reasons, was why she had, in a few short weeks, grown fond of them.

'Good day, Tess?' Guy flopped down and stretched his legs.

'Fine. You two?'

Rich smiled at Tess and gave her a thumbs-up.

'Bay 22A at the airport still seems to be perplexing people. It's like the Bermuda Triangle of coach terminals: people either can't find it, or they disappear.' Tess enjoyed Guy's exaggerated tall tales, his well-practised mock annoyance and impatience one of the charming things about him.

'So, who are you expecting, gentlemen? How many glasses shall I put out?'

'I make it five,' Rich said. 'A couple who arrived last night, two from this morning, and a woman who arrived earlier. Shall I go and tell Lily, or fetch the glasses from Anna?'

Tess smiled inwardly at his eagerness. Rich's willingness to help her waitress Lily had not gone unnoticed.

'That's great. Thanks, Rich. There should be three jugs ready: ouzo, orange juice, and water. Also, ask Lily if she checked the fridge this morning, would you, please?'

She liked to give him reasons to chat to Lily and help the potential romance along. However, although Rich was lovely, kind, and clever in his quiet way, sadly he was not the man occupying most of Lily's waking thoughts – although, luckily for Rich, Ryan Gosling wasn't likely to pop into the Athena any time soon. So, in that sense he had the advantage.

'Here they come,' drawled Guy as he spotted a middle-aged, sunhatted couple cross the road. 'Showtime!'

Chapter 6

Penny savoured every step, as she walked slowly the few hundred yards to the Athena from her room. The air washed over her in a gentle wave of warmth and calm, laced with rich scents, but not heavy or cloying. The milky yellow, peach-tinged petals of the honeysuckle that grew randomly along the side of the thoroughfare had a subtlety of colour that gave it the quality and texture of a painting. A ginger cat in its sparse shade lazily followed Penny's progress without moving an inch, as cicadas provided a noisy soundtrack.

This tiny snapshot of Corfu at that moment reinforced Penny's earlier impressions from her walk around the harbour and along the beach. Pellucid-blue waters, quicksilver fish, the air heavy with heat, all contributed to this beautiful, serene, if slightly alien environment. If she'd wanted to be in another world, she had surely found it here.

She heard laughter and a loud confident voice as she reached the Athena and took the side entrance where the outside tables stretched to the sea. A small group, including the two holiday reps, had gathered there.

'Hello,' the confident voice greeted her and motioned her to sit down. 'Welcome. What would you like to drink? We have water, ouzo, and orange juice, or any combination of the three.'

Penny smiled at each member of the group in turn, as Guy launched into his hard, but disarming sell of the 'sensational, not-to-be-missed, life-changing' daily excursions by land and sea, delivered so brilliantly by Greektime. Penny's mind wandered.

She already knew that the places she wanted to see and experience did not form part of the regular trips on offer. She intended to take her time, savour, absorb the visits to each location in the order she had planned in her mind for so long. Places made so special by the books she loved. The Strawberry Villa first; then the Daffodil Yellow; and then the Snow White. Finally, in some ways the most anticipated of all because it was a place where she could touch the ancient walls and dine with the same view Larry Durrell had enjoyed . . . the White House, at Kalami.

Each house had acquired an almost mythical quality in Penny's mind, as though they were portals into a secret garden from another time. From behind her sunglasses, she observed her fellow travellers: a middle-aged couple and two older ladies.

Both couples hung on Guy's every word and the women filled any gaps in his monologue by giving the group the benefit of their knowledge of many Greek islands, particularly the location of the best English breakfast and cheapest wine on Corfu.

Only half-listening, but managing to look fully engaged, Penny glanced at the little harbour entrance only a stone's throw from the Athena, to see a small blue and white boat ploughing valiantly through the white wave peaks on its way in. The two dark-haired men on board wore jeans and loose shirts. One had a white cap. As the boat touched the harbourside the hatless one jumped effortlessly onto the quayside and secured the vessel.

Brothers? Friends? she wondered.

'If you have any questions at all, or if you'd like to book now for any of the excursions, Rich and I will be here for the next half hour.' Guy's closing words brought Penny back into the room and she smiled across at the two reps.

'Thank you. I hope you can help me,' she said, 'but my question is more about local knowledge and getting around the island, rather than the trips, if that's okay?' Penny looked across at the other guests and saw they were already getting out their credit cards to pay, so added quickly, 'Please, look after everyone else first. I'll get myself a drink and wait over there.'

Guy nodded and Rich smiled. 'If you're having wine, ask for the house rosé; it's really good apparently,' he told her. It was Lily's favourite drink.

Sitting at the sea's edge Penny had an uninterrupted view of the reddening sun, which looked as though it had stayed out too long under its own rays and was now eager to reach the cooling sea and sink with a sigh beneath the waves. With a glass of rosé in hand, she let her shoulders fall and savoured the sharp and sweet wine, perfectly chilled and smooth. The place, the calm, the peace created a precious moment. Corfu's all-embracing welcome, echoed in the texture of each plant, leaf, and vivid orange and pink flowers and fruit, was already penetrating her skin and soul.

New voices muttered in the background and she turned to see the woman she assumed ran the restaurant talking to the two men from the boat. They sat down at the bar and drinks appeared. An animated conversation followed, punctuated by the older man with sweeping hand movements and a deep, powerful laugh. The son, if that was who his companion was, seemed quieter.

Penny could only see the back of his head, his sunglasses balanced on top, and his dark hair curled into his neck. For the second she caught him in profile, he appeared quiet but not relaxed; as though he didn't want to stay, couldn't settle.

His nose was aquiline and even at this distance, without seeing him face-on, his demeanour possessed a kind of nobility, like a marble sculpture that came to life at night and then forgot how to sit still and behave like a statue.

Restless. Yes, that was it.

She suddenly realized she was staring and turned back to look at the sea. Guy and Rich headed over.

'Thanks for your talk, but I need some local info,' Penny began. 'I'm on a mission and have some specific locations in mind. I'd like to hire a car, but also need someone, who you'd recommend or know personally, who could take me by sea to Kalami from Corfu Town.'

It came out in a rush, but even so she thought she sounded as if she knew what she was doing. Her usual confidence, though buoyed by the welcoming feel of St George, had a tendency these days to ebb and flow.

'I think we can help you there,' Guy said. 'I know you've just arrived,' he continued in an almost comedic theatrical tone, 'but Rich and I are more than happy to act as your *unofficial* guides. Our speciality is the delights of Corfu Town, particularly of an evening.' Penny almost expected a flourish or a bow at the end of this sentence, but Guy just smiled and she smiled back.

He had a winsome, warm energy about him and she suddenly found herself thinking he'd make a smashing younger brother.

'Tess, what time does Spiro open up in the morning?'

'Usually 9 a.m., but Alexia will be there from 8.30.'

'Penny needs a car. For a month?' he asked her.

'Most of the month. There'll be some days when I'll just stay here,' Penny answered. 'I don't know whether there's a way I can book the car for days at a time.'

Tess wandered over from the bar and Guy introduced them. 'Spiro's a sweetheart. Just tell him Tess sent you. His cars are immaculate and you won't find a more reasonable deal on the island.'

Penny smiled her thanks and asked Tess how long she had been in St George South.

'When I arrived here, I was single, no child, and about to meet the love of my life,' Tess began. 'So, be warned.' She smiled. 'What are you planning for your month here? Or are you taking each day as it comes?'

Penny explained the pull of the Durrells' connection, the promise she and her dad had made to visit one day and that, although there was no itinerary, she had a sort of plan. The last location on her list was the White House, at Kalami, which she hoped to travel to by boat from Corfu Town, as she knew Lawrence Durrell had made the trip many times.

'Ah,' said Tess, 'then you need Dimitris. He fishes with his father some days, but has his boat moored at the Old Port and is sometimes available for chartered trips.'

Tess looked over her shoulder. 'He was here a minute ago with his father. I can ask him to speak to you if you like.'

Penny looked across at the bar and the now-empty bar-stool where the restless sculpture had sat, and nodded her thanks to Tess.

'He's gone now, but don't worry – he'll be back. He sometimes stays overnight at his dad's house in the village when they've been fishing.' She paused then added. 'I can detect a little bit of an accent there. Are you from Yorkshire?' Penny, still looking across at the harbour, turned back to Tess.

'Yes, born and bred.'

'I'm a Devon girl myself, originally, but home is really about the people, isn't it, wherever they are, rather than the place?'

Tess looked down at her feet for a moment and then before Penny had a chance to respond someone called her name from the kitchen and with a smile she was gone.

Chapter 7

Stepping out of bed, Penny felt the shock of the chilled tile floor. As her eyes adjusted to the darkness, a faint glow outlined the edges of the shuttered door. She crossed the room carefully, wary of unfamiliar shapes and obstacles, then lifted the steel door latch and pulled the heavy shutters towards her. Light and heat entered instantly. The glass double doors revealed roofs and, beyond and above them, higher land, grey-green hills, and olive trees.

From the small balcony the smells and sounds of St George washed over her as she glimpsed a blue triangle of sea and the small island across the bay – a lozenge of loveliness, that looked as though it had been dropped clumsily on its way to another place.

The large ginger cat she'd seen yesterday was now joined by a small dog. They lay on the terrace of the house below. To her left a lemon tree was almost within reach. The exotic had become everyday; a fairy-tale scene from a Ladybird book about the Ionian Sea.

Here was the island of simmering and iridescent beauty that Gerry Durrell had described, already visible on her first morning on Corfu. But was this the new beginning that she was looking for?

A quick glance at her watch told her it was 9.30 a.m., Greek time, so only 7.30 in the UK. Stifling a yawn, Penny folded her arms and hugged herself in a moment of anticipation about the day ahead. Hire a car. Plan a route. But first, explore Corfu Town.

⌒

Nicolas Constantine – 'Nic' to family and friends; 'Professor' to his students – had arrived back in Corfu the day before Penny. As Penny woke and opened the shutters of her room, a few hundred yards away Nic sat on the terrace of his small villa.

The aptly named Villa Pontiki, the Mouse House, reflected the size of the dwelling that had been in the professor's family since the 1920s. The shaded terrace with its old wooden table and wicker chairs was almost as large as the space inside, which accommodated a kitchen, living room, lounge, small bedroom, study, and a small bathroom.

It had been built originally for Nic's grandfather, a keen sailor who had kept a small boat in St George's harbour, on which he had escaped during as many weekends as he could. The main family residence had always been in Corfu Town, where Nic's mother now lived.

As a professor of marine biology based in Athens, Nic spent half the year away from the island of his birth, but the summer and early autumn were all about the Mouse House, the sea, sky, reading, writing, and rambling.

There wasn't much of the island that Nic didn't carry in his heart. The memories gathered during the long, languid summers kept him warm through the winter and spring on the mainland.

To an outsider Nic appeared to be quite a self-possessed, insular man. Those in his close circle – small in number, but cherished – greeted him affectionately and with genuine warmth and respect. Now in his mid-forties, he had never married and there was much speculation, mostly amongst his colleagues at the university, about his single status. No one could remember a 'significant other' in the fourteen years he had lectured there. Attempts to pair him up with a number of colleagues, friends of friends and, on one memorable occasion, the recently divorced mother of one of his students, had failed. Nic resisted them all with quiet charm and an innate ability to move any discussion, on any topic, on to the minutiae of marine biology, or the flora and fauna of Corfu.

His ideal fantasy dinner party included Thor Heyerdahl, Jacques Cousteau, and David Attenborough, with local hero, the Durrells' friend Theo Stephanides, making up the quartet of those who had unknowingly helped to shape Nic since boyhood.

The natural world, on land, and above and below the sea, had consumed pretty much every waking moment of Nic's life since he was a small boy, with his heroes and inspiration anyone who shared similar adventures in books or on TV. A signed copy of the Kon-Tiki expedition book from 1948 was one of his most prized possessions. All his treasures from a lifetime of research and fieldwork formed part of the Mouse House. Books lined the walls of every room.

Summer days in St George had taken on even more meaning in the last three years. His oldest friend had been Tess's husband Georgios, and Nic had experienced his loss more keenly than he cared to share with anyone. From boyhood they had been inseparable, so different and yet each seeing in the other qualities they admired and perhaps even envied a little.

It was Nic who, through a chance meeting, had introduced Georgios to Tess, an English girl he had bumped into one day on the beach as he walked back to the villa. She'd cut her foot on a rock at the harbour, below the Athena, and he'd gallantly helped her up the hill to a seat in the restaurant.

There Georgios had taken over, fetching antiseptic and a bandage, pouring Tess an ouzo, and handing it to her without even looking up from the task in hand. She had thanked Nic kindly for his help, but it was Georgios her face turned to. And that had been the start for Tess and Georgios: ten years of being in love, becoming parents, falling out, and working together every day. Corfu became home for the English girl who had come on holiday to celebrate a new job – a job she never started.

Nic remembered the walk up the hill, offering his arm so that Tess could keep her balance but, careful not to make her feel uncomfortable, keeping any bodily contact to a minimum. The warm citrus smell of her perfume, combined with the coconut waves of suntan oil, had made him turn his head and take a closer look at her face.

He'd imagined her deep honey-coloured skin paled in the winter at home. Her mid-brown hair, with a few highlights across her fringe, had possibly once been longer. Even as she'd accepted his help, there'd been a sense of fierce independence about her, and an annoyance with herself for her careless climbing on the rocks to get a better photo of the harbour.

There wasn't time in one moment, was there, to fall in love? To know nothing about a person, yet feel an instant connection? To feel drawn towards them as one might towards the sun? In the days and weeks, as Tess and Georgios grew closer and made plans for Tess to move to Corfu, Nic had provided the calm, reassuring voice and sounding board that his oldest friend relied on. Tess began to feel the same way about him, warming to his natural, quiet wisdom and what she thought was an innate shyness.

The 'shyness' was in truth more about self-protection and self-preservation. He had fallen in love with Tess in a heartbeat and although the feeling had been new and vital, it had to be immediately crushed. He'd channelled it all, then and now, into a slightly detached, but nonetheless caring demeanour, outwardly courteous and solicitous, but ready in a heartbeat to protect the two people he cared for most in the world.

As young Theo's godfather, he had been around through the years, with the understandable lacuna of the months away in Athens. His support for his late friend's little family continued, but he never acknowledged what it had cost him. The colleagues who found gentle sport in trying to fix him up with a date had no idea that his reticence was rooted in something so complex and real.

This morning had dawned as every other in summer, with the almost blasé expectation of a cloudless sky and whitewashed brightness. Nic was meeting Tess for lunch and then taking Theo to the lake to birdwatch. Before that, though, he had to drive into Corfu Town.

Chapter 8

The hire car smelt of pine air freshener and warm upholstery and was immaculately clean, something Penny had noticed in the airport and on the bus that had brought her to St George – a visible sense of pride in the way everything was presented, the food served, the tables cleaned, the polite and warm greetings.

Taking the winding road out of the village, where the tavernas became more infrequent and the small, single-storey villas petered out, Penny soon found herself on the main road to Corfu Town.

The bright light of noon made her squint a little, even with her sunglasses on. Dark, cloistered shadows under intertwining trees were sought out by the donkeys, chickens, and cats: veterans of how to escape the heat in the haphazard, obstacle course of a landscape. Supermarkets, some with sophisticated neon signs, others with boxes of golden fruit and vegetables behind a handwritten sign, jostled with small balconied flats and dancing washing.

A wooden arrow-shaped sign nailed to an old fence bore the legend 'To the Beach', the once-navy lettering faded to the palest azure. Everywhere glorious blooms climbed up walls or tangled prettily around an ugly, rusting iron window grille; pink, deep red, dazzling white, their vibrancy unabashed even in the heavy heat of a Corfu summer.

With Corfu Town only a few kilometres away, the roundabouts and traffic lights of the world of home began to make an appearance, feeling odd and out of place in this place of four million olive trees and monasteries teetering on mountainsides.

The pine and cypress aromas of the interior were replaced with a heady mix of sea air, petrol fumes, and the smell of fresh bread and cooking.

Soon she passed the New Port with the Venetian fortress that dominated the old town ahead. Finding a parking space near the harbour involved considerable luck – Spiro at the car-hire place had told her that. As she slowed down to look for somewhere to park, a small Fiat pulled out. Penny indicated quickly and parked in a breathless and triumphant hurry. She sat for a second or two to enjoy the moment. She had found her way, parked; all was good.

Garitsa Bay lay like something out of a fantasy film set in a mysterious, foreign land. Turquoise and lilac waters lapped gently at the foot of the great fortress, as millionaires' yachts lay like sharks in its shadow.

The old town created a backdrop of Venetian elegance and fading grandeur to the entrance to the bay. From afar it looked fresh, smooth, serene; close up the stucco peeled gently on some buildings; their shutters sealed. The impact was overwhelmingly beautiful. The life and heart of Corfu Town oozed from every street, meandering through picture-perfect archways, its maze of streets and lanes evoking a bazaar-like atmosphere.

Penny walked slowly, in an almost dreamlike state. Shop canopies protected her from the direct glare of the sun, while beneath them handbags, icons, perfume, and herbs vied for her attention, filling the air with their heady smells of leather, dust, almond blossom, and thyme.

Climbing up towards the heart of the Old Town, the intoxicating bustle of bars and the inviting shade of the restaurants and tavernas tempted Penny. The menus, colourful, elegant, or garish, displaying laminated practicality or vellum and tassel-embossed grandeur – it was all there. The palette and textures of each street complemented each other with a miraculous and happy accident of long-forgotten design, necessity, and heritage.

She glanced at her Greektime map. First, she needed to find St Spyridon's church and then the Liston, the cosmopolitan hub of the town. The Durrells had taken tea there and watched the world go by, just across from the famous cricket ground – the legacy of a period of British rule.

The terracotta pinnacle of St Spyridon's caught her eye and she walked towards it. She'd picked a slightly old-fashioned-looking, mid-length tea dress to wear that morning. It seemed the right fit in every sense; a nod of respect to the place and not a million miles away from what Margo Durrell, Gerry's sister, might have worn all those years before. She wanted to sit for a moment, the smell of incense all-encompassing, and think.

⌒

Sitting in an old carved wooden seat, head bowed, Penny closed her eyes and listened. Gentle hushed voices, footsteps, even the cool interior of the church . . . all had a sound of their own.

Fifteen minutes later she stepped out into the bright, watercolour world of the street and felt a sudden urge to sit in a gorgeously located café, drink coffee, and eat cake.

On the way back to the car Nic decided to stop for a coffee at the Liston. He'd just picked up his mother's African Grey parrot, Ulysses. Nic had promised to look after him when she went to the mainland to visit his brother. The parrot in its ornate travelling cage sat in the shade at his feet. He ordered an espresso, sat on a cushioned double seat on the elegant stone-floored terrace, and placed his Panama hat on the table.

To his left he saw a small dark-haired young woman at the next table, wearing a delicately patterned floral dress that would probably have been knee-length if she hadn't been so petite, but which almost reached her feet.

The sound of a squeaky voice calling out 'Behave!' focused both Nic and the girl's attention on the covered cage at his feet. She smiled and Nic felt he ought to explain. 'My apologies. I am taking my small but very loud friend home as a guest. He has to be covered in this heat and can't bear to be left out.'

She laughed, then looked down at her coffee.

Nic smiled and looked down at his feet, but before he could think of anything else to say, she asked him if he lived on the island. Was he local?

Nic explained that his mother lived in the town and that most of the year he was based in Athens.

'Are you here on holiday?' he asked, picking his questions carefully, so he didn't appear intrusive, just interested and courteous.

'Yes, I suppose I am. I've wanted to come here for a very long time and I now have a chance to make up for all the years I could have been here. It didn't feel like the right moment before. I only arrived yesterday.'

'What drew you here?'

'Well, it's a number of things, but I think I'd have to say the Durrells; that is, their books and their time here on the island. They've fascinated me since I was a teenager.'

'You're not alone. People come from all over the world to see if Corfu really is the Garden of the Gods. I was inspired by Theo Stephanides as a child: Gerry's mentor and friend, as you know. I hope you find what you're looking for. There's certainly a lot to explore.'

'Well, I have a month, but I'm already sensing that a lifetime might not be long enough.' Penny picked up her hat and handbag and held out her hand.

'Have a lovely day and a safe journey home with your friend.' She smiled again as she stood up and walked away to pay her bill.

As he said goodbye Nic looked down again at his feet and the first thing that came into his mind was that if ever someone had a story to tell it was this delicate but charming English girl who was, he felt, quite alone.

Wandering away from the Liston, Penny, map in hand, travelled back in time, to the moment when the Durrells had first set eyes on Spiro Halikiopoulos and his Dodge motor car at the taxi rank which once stood by the Liston. The natural crossroads still existed all these years later. Penny paused for a moment and closed her eyes, imagining that the noise and bustle around her were echoes of 1935. As her mind travelled further down the time tunnel, she heard the slightly raised English voices of the Durrell family as they stumbled their way, blinking against the light, into a new life: their mother with her now quite squashed hat and sensible mac; Gerry, just

10 years old, looking as lost as Roger the dog, who was always seeking out the next lamp post; Margo with a mischievous curiosity, ready to embrace new things; and Leslie sizing up the opportunities this new place and people might bring.

A motorbike roared past and interrupted the impressive voice of Spiro about to offer his services as a taxi driver and make his debut in the Durrells' story. Penny clutched the map, her rucksack resting comfortably on her back, and looked over to where she thought the noise from the bike had come from. 'They are here,' she muttered under her breath. 'They might be just a shimmer of a past life in the corner of my eye, colouring the air, but they're here.'

A familiar-looking figure stood by a motorbike. It looked like Dimitris, the man she'd seen in the Athena the night before – the restless one. Could it be him? Her eyes went straight to the back of his neck to search for the same curl of the hair. It looked the same and he moved in the same way, but before she had the chance to see him in profile, he raised his hand and began to walk. A tall, tanned, blonde woman, wearing sunglasses, shorts, and a loose linen shirt, returned the greeting and when they met, they kissed on both cheeks.

Penny turned away, distracted by the sound and feel of her phone vibrating in the pocket of her bag. She turned back as she began to check her mobile to see the person, who she was now convinced *was* Dimitris, put his arm around the woman. Both of them were laughing.

As she watched them, she tried to work out if the woman was local or a tourist, a summer conquest or a partner. It was impossible to tell, but Penny surprised herself with how much she wanted to know the answer.

Her phone pinged to tell her that a voicemail had arrived and, moving the screen out of the glare of the sun, she saw that she'd missed a call from Bruce.

Driving south back along the coast road, Penny still, in spite of the blistering sun, felt the goosebumps on her skin. The air conditioning was fierce, but it was more than the chill inside the car.

Her first footsteps into Corfu Town had been exactly as she hoped. The place had vibrancy, heart, and history. Writer, poet, or painter, who could fail to be inspired? She had not, however, expected the trip to include a sighting of the intriguing Dimitris, chatting to a man with a parrot, or a message from Bruce. Meeting the man with the parrot had been a slightly eccentric encounter, in line with the image of the Corfu she had created in her head.

On her left, the sea rose and fell in glinting peaks and troughs. Above, another plane edged towards the runway that stretched out into the sea to catch the incoming aircraft. The signs for Gastouri and Perama reappeared, but they were for another day.

The day had already delivered riches and surprises enough and the month felt as though it was slipping away before it had really started.

Before she'd listened to the message from Bruce when she got back to the car, she'd wound the windows down and felt a small but welcome breeze. In her rear-view mirror, the reassuring bulk of a blue and white ferry passed by, almost plodding through the channel. The holiday scene in all its clichéd glory made Bruce's words feel all the more disembodied.

'Hi, Penny, or should I say *salve*! What can I say? I hope you're well. I'm guessing from your dial tone that you're abroad. Good for you! Getting away to the sun is something

I can heartily recommend, all year round. I know it's been a while, but well, you were always a good listener, Penny, and I'd love to share some of what's been happening over the last six months. Has it been that long? We must remedy that. Give me a call when you can, when you're back. It'd be good to catch up. *Ciao!*'

Now, as she turned off the main road onto the narrower and cosier lanes into St George, she realized that she'd dissected Bruce's message a hundred times. Why get in touch now, after all these months? Her heart was curious, but her head was suspicious.

Chapter 9

The Mediterranean Bar was in two halves, one on each side of the main road in St George: a traditional bar with a large-screen TV and chatter; and across the dusty quiet road, a small enclosed garden, with unrivalled views of the harbour and sunset.

As well as the usual lagers and spirits, the owner was proud to serve a particular red wine sourced every year from the same local vintner, forming one of life's real pleasures – to sit and sip a glass, when contemplating dinner and dancing, chatting, or enjoying a companionable silence.

Penny chose a table at the farthest end of the garden, where she could see the Athena and the harbour, and sat with a glass of the much-heralded red wine – a departure from her usual rosé, but a nod to her promise to herself to experience the new, whether a glass of wine or a Greek island.

She had tied her hair up for the evening, to allow the gentle cooling effect of the sea air to reach the back of her neck, and wore her favourite dress in pale sage cotton, reminiscent of the 1920s with its simple split short sleeves. Flat tan leather sandals, well-worn and loved, completed the outfit. She mused whether Margo Durrell would have liked her dress; perhaps held it up against herself if she'd found it in a friend's wardrobe, and dreamed of romance and adventure, as she paraded in front of the mirror, just 18 years old, at the beginning of an extraordinary life.

Penny no longer bore the spots that had plagued her through her teens and twenties, but at 13, when *My Family and Other Animals* had first become a part of her world, it was one of the things that had drawn her to Margo – her never-ending, optimistic crusade against acne, just like her own.

The main road suddenly bustled with visitors emerging from their afternoon naps, their holiday outfits showing off newly tanned legs or reddening shoulders and upper arms. Waves of relaxation glowed from every pore as families, couples, and excited groups wandered up and down, glancing at menus, and chatting with the owners of each taverna.

Penny glanced back towards the sea and saw the small blue and white boat she had noticed the evening before, now entering the harbour. The same two figures were on deck, the ease of their familiarity and companionship as they worked relaxing to watch. It looked like a well-honed, regular routine: a day's fishing, then mooring for the night.

Only a day into her month-long odyssey and she was already intrigued by the people she had met, seen, or heard about. She had always been fascinated by other people, their lives and stories, whether at home or when people-watching on holiday. She began to wonder about the wider stories of the Corfiots she'd already met and the 'Athena family', as she'd already named them in her head.

Tess had already shared a snapshot of her life. Guy and Rich were amusing and full of exuberance. The man she had met that morning at the Liston possessed a quiet charm and quaintness about him, his conversation easy and perfectly natural.

Then there was Dimitris: what was his story? She had

only seen him from a distance, or in profile. Would he be the captain she'd trust to take her along the coast to Kalami? Was charisma a listed requirement for good captains? If so, he passed the test. She smiled wryly at this, mocking her own pretended indifference to his presence. She'd only seen him four times after all, every encounter from some distance away.

Tess seemed, even on short acquaintance, to be a woman of sense, who surely wouldn't recommend anyone untrustworthy or irresponsible. There'd be others on the boat too, she imagined. She stopped herself catastrophizing, realizing in a moment of clarity that she was – as her grandmother might have put it – giving up the race before she'd even got her gym shoes on. This was part of her Bruce legacy: a tendency to always look for a catch; expecting to be let down, to be disappointed.

She made up her mind not to respond to the voicemail. What could he do? What could he say that would make her want to speak or even see him? She was naturally curious about why he'd called, but not enough to risk all the good work and determined aloneness of the previous few months, as she'd tried to make the world normal without him – without, it sometimes seemed, anyone.

Penny stood up and almost as though she was seeking sanctuary, walked swiftly up the hill to the Athena. The gentle hum of chatter and the occasional greeting of '*Yasou*' or '*Kalispera*' formed the background music that greeted Penny as she stepped from the footpath into the Athena's bar.

A small boy, Tess's son she assumed, sat on the steps with the kitten she'd seen him with the day before, drawing a lizard with a bright green crayon in a sketchbook, concentrating so hard he barely noticed Penny.

Tess saw her first and was by her side in a heartbeat, asking her about her day.

Before Penny could answer, another voice broke the silence: 'Hello again.'

Penny and Tess turned together to see a smiling Nic. Penny at once recognized the man with the parrot at the Liston.

'Hello. Where's your feathered friend?' Penny grinned at the tall, bespectacled man.

Nic explained to Tess that they had met briefly at the Liston when he'd been to fetch Ulysses from his mother's house.

'Nic, this is Penny. Penny, this is my dear friend Nic.'

'It's a small world,' said Penny.

'It's a small island!' said Tess. 'Drink?'

'A glass of rosé, please. Does it matter where I sit?' Penny looked towards the far tables that sat above the sea.

'Sit wherever you like. You've got here just at the right time. Things will start to get busy now. Lily will bring your drink over.'

A welcome breeze flowed through the Athena, a gift from the sea. In the distance, Paxos began its nightly disappearing trick, as the darkness pushed the last patches of light from the sky. There was a touch of velvet about summer evenings in Corfu, a soft edge to a world warmed by a sun that had no intention of curbing its warmth until late autumn, when it still glowed valiantly on.

'Hi. Rosé for you?' Penny looked up at a tanned, strawberry blonde, freckle-faced girl, who radiated energy. She rolled from toe to heel as she spoke, as though the ground was hot and she didn't want to stand still for long.

'Thank you . . . Lily? I'm Penny.'

'Yes, you're here for a while, aren't you? How's it going so far?'

'I think it's wonderful. I was in town this morning and loved it. What an incredible place. How about you? Are you here for the whole season?'

'Oh yes, until October, although for the last two weeks, I'm staying here for a break of my own, before I go home.'

'Great idea. You'll have the chance to enjoy a little spoil yourself after looking after so many people.'

'Yes, I suppose so. Still a long way to go yet though, a lot of Mythos to pour, and mosquitoes to fight. They love me for some reason.' Lily smiled resignedly and started to gather some dirty glasses from a nearby table, with her barely suppressed buoyancy.

She's Tigger, thought Penny, but she sensed Eeyore in there too.

'Can I get you something to eat?' Lily glanced up as she finished filling the tray.

Penny was already familiar with the Athena menu, having read it a number of times when she'd wanted to appear relaxed in these surroundings on her own.

'I'd love the tuna, please. Thanks, Lily.'

As Lily hopped off to the kitchen, Penny turned back to look at the now amethyst-tinged sea – the *wine-dark sea* her dad used to talk about, alongside a list of books she ought to read.

'Hi.'

She looked up. The sculpted fisherman stood in front of her.

'Hello.'

'Dimitris. Tess says you're wanting to sail up to Kalami from town.'

'I'm Penny. Yes, but I haven't set a date yet; that is, I have a schedule and Kalami is sort of the last place I want to visit.'

She was aware that everything had gushed out, when maybe a 'yes' would have sufficed.

He looked down at her and shrugged slightly, almost as if to say, *I have a boat. I also fish. Some days I'm free, others not. It's no big deal.*

'You're here for a month?' His voice was calm, with a slight English intonation woven into the distinctive Corfiot rhythm. He had her attention, even though their conversation so far had felt more like being questioned.

'Yes, I arrived yesterday. I've wanted to come here for a long time.'

'A month is a longer stay than usual, unless you're planning on buying a house. People sometimes stay here for a week, go home, and come back looking for their dream home.'

'I'm making up for lost time. I should have visited years ago, with my dad.'

Penny looked down then and picked up her wine. 'Can I charter your boat just for myself, or do you prefer a collection of passengers to make it economical?'

As she asked the question she could visualize, as clearly as if it had already happened, sitting on a smart boat, hair tied up, the coastline of Corfu to her left. Everything sparkling, the water, the sky, her, from an exuberance in the air, like fizzing lemonade. At the helm stood a figure with his back to her. It was all a little hazy. The moment was exhilarating, but fleeting.

She heard Dimitris's voice in the real world. The Athena's Greek music CD played subtly in the background.

'It depends,' he replied. 'If more people want to go to Kalami on the day you do, and I'm able to take the *Antiopi* out, I can take up to five people with me. If we do go, it will mean a start from the Old Port at, say, 9 a.m. It takes less than an hour. I'm guessing you want to go to Kalami because of the Lawrence Durrell connection.'

'Yes, the White House is the last Durrell house I want to see, because it's the one that I can still get closest to on this trip. I'm not a Durrells expert. I just love their books. In a strange way, they feel like family to me.'

Her last few words seemed to hang in the air, sticking around long enough to make her feel a little embarrassed. *They feel like family to me.* Why did she have to say that? He was a stranger she was arranging transport with, not a dinner companion or a friend. She felt the heat in her face as she flushed to the roots of her hair.

He looked as though he was going to ask her something else, but thought better of it and turned away. 'Just let me know when you want to go,' he called back over his shoulder.

'Thank you. Thanks very much. I will.'

Penny watched him walk back over to the bar, sit down, rejoin his father, and pick up his Mythos, before Lily appeared with her food and momentarily blocked her view.

'Here we are. And Anna has sent you some flatbread and tzatziki. She's always doing that. She thinks everyone needs to eat more than they've ordered. It's on the house, as they say in old films. Enjoy. Can I get you another glass?'

Penny nodded, watching Lily bob back to the bar past Dimitris. Penny saw him turn to look towards her table and then, just as quickly, look away.

Tess leaned forward to hear something Dimitris was saying. She smiled and touched his arm before taking his glass and refilling it.

It was no surprise, she decided, as she felt her face return to its normal hue, that she was just as gauche and uncool on Corfu as she was at home.

I bet the sophisticated woman he was with this morning doesn't waffle on and then embarrass herself, she thought, as she turned her attention to her food, which was delicious, beautifully presented, and delicately seasoned. The wine made her feel mellow and drowsy, creating a warmth that seeped into her bones. She couldn't help looking back towards the bar, where Nic had now joined the conversation with Tess and Dimitris. Guy and

Rich then appeared and Tess passed them a bottle of Mythos each. A family got up to pay for their meal, the children rushing confidently to the edge of the restaurant to look at the sea.

Penny glanced down at the rocks and grasses below and saw a glimmer of light, then another. Fireflies. She'd never seen them before. As they darted about, she understood why people sometimes mistook them for fairies.

And now she had seen him close up . . . the interesting one. What a face. As an artist, she'd quickly noticed the texture and tone of his skin, the bone structure underneath, and the colour of his eyes – a bluey Payne's grey. The woman saw and felt the impact of the combination of all these things, in that curious first assessment that people made, both consciously and unconsciously.

The artist thought it was a strong face; the woman was instantly intrigued. She smiled, laughing at herself, at her self-deception; her carefully focused concentration on the cool and considered response to the knotty, deep-oak, sinewed arms that the rolled-up sleeves of his shirt revealed, and the dark hair with the rogue fringe he casually pushed back as he was talking. She imagined her friend Lizzie nudging her elbow behind Dimitris's back, and raising an eyebrow as if to say, *Blimey, look who just walked in! Which Greek god bagged Helen of Troy?*

He looked about 40, but could have been younger, she thought, the brightness of his eyes and the lack of grey in his hair contrasting with his powerfully reassuring presence. He looked like someone she'd want, funnily enough, in her lifeboat if the ship sank.

All of these thoughts were interrupted abruptly by the small but still persistent voice in her own head that still believed she was someone's fiancée rather than an ex one.

She suddenly felt tired, sleepy; a pleasant, sea-air-induced lethargy that she was more than happy to give in to.

As she approached the bar Guy turned to face her and welcome her into the group. 'Hi, how are you?'

'Fine, thank you. I've just had the loveliest meal.' She turned to Tess. 'Please, tell Anna the fish was delicious.'

'I will,' said Tess. 'Can I get you something else? A dessert or another drink?'

'I'm fine, just ready for a read and a sleep.' Although it was true, she sounded about 100 years old. The vision of the cool room and a chance to stretch out on the yellow bedspread felt like sanctuary. Tess stepped in and saved her from her own thoughts.

'It's the sea air. In a day or two you'll have adjusted and be dancing till dawn, if that's what you fancy.'

Penny remembered the last time she'd danced at one of Bruce's university formal events, a few months before they'd parted. As she'd felt his arm around her back and his hand in hers, she'd closed her eyes and tried to conjure up the feelings she'd had on the first night they met. She'd looked up at his beautiful face to see what she could read there, but he'd been looking across the room, acknowledging a colleague.

Guy broke the silence, repeating his offer of taking her out on a night out in Corfu Town.

'Perhaps when I've got my sleeping and waking hours back in order,' she said.

'Lily, do you fancy a night out with us in town?' Rich shouted across to Lily as she left the kitchen with another tray of food.

'Depends. Days off might not match yours, but let me know when you're planning to go.'

Lily's response kept alive Rich's dream of one day supplanting Ryan Gosling in her affections and he took a celebratory sip of his drink.

As Penny walked back to her villa, more fireflies danced in the darkness, illuminating her way, but the warmth she felt was at her back. Dimitris had not looked at her directly when she'd stood at the bar, but she'd felt his gaze nonetheless. She felt it now.

She was probably imagining it.

None of that foolishness, Penny, she chided herself. *He's probably already put you into the slightly weird woman-on-holiday category anyway. There's no room in your head for a fling right now. Keep things simple.*

Chapter 10

The shared pool at Penny's apartments was already surrounded by occupied sun loungers when she passed on her way to a late breakfast at the Athena. She'd begun to settle into her new *home* and had slept well, although woken briefly by a vivid dream of her dad's illness –proof, if proof were needed, that wherever anyone went in the world they took their baggage, their hopes, fears, and story with them. Eventually, she'd fallen into a second, deep, early-morning sleep.

Today Penny planned to stay in St George and had packed her rucksack with watercolour paints and sketchbook. On every holiday she'd ever been on she had captured little vignettes of the world around her as she sat at a café table, or in a bar: a wine bottle, vase of flowers, coffee cup, cake, or chair . . . whatever looked interesting, or caught the light in a particular way.

She had first begun to draw when not much more than a toddler. When it became clear she loved it, and her talent grew with every drawing, her dad had bought her some proper drawing pencils and a watercolour box. The natural and happy progression had then been art college, a degree in Fine Art, and a slowly building career in book illustration. Now, ten years on from her graduation, she was a freelancer, whose work had been described variously as 'charming', 'exquisite', 'otherworldly', and 'enchanting'.

She was not famous, her life was comfortable rather than opulent, but most importantly, she loved her work. Creativity was in her heart and hands.

As she walked down the now-familiar lane to the sea, Penny hoped that Tess wouldn't mind her painting if she tucked herself into a corner and kept buying coffee and water.

Greek yogurt and honey, fresh fruit, and a Nescafé felt like the food of the gods. The only other people having breakfast were the two older ladies who'd arrived the same day as Penny, and a ponytailed man in his fifties, who was enjoying a full English breakfast and pastries.

The sea sent waves of sound and scent over the low white-painted wall of the Athena. Tess delivered two generous omelettes to the ladies, who twittered their thanks, and smiled at each other in anticipation of working their way through the enormous and appetizing breakfast.

Her customers sorted, Tess wandered over to Penny. 'Another coffee?'

'That would be lovely, thanks. Would it be okay if I sat here for a while and painted? I can move if the table is needed when you're busy.'

'That's fine,' said Tess, picking up Penny's empty plate, 'as long as you can cope with the thousand questions and curious eyes from just about everyone here. You'll soon find out everyone eventually knows pretty much everything about everyone here.'

Spiro, Tess's father-in-law, who was always sitting by the entrance, rose to take payment from the man with the ponytail.

Tess turned back to Penny conspiratorially and whispered, 'Simon, who's just left, for example – expat, been here for years, writing a book on Corfiot cookery. But I've only ever seen him eat. He *never* asks about the food and loves an English breakfast. There's a mystery right there.' She smiled.

'Do you miss England?' The words were out before Penny had time to check herself.

Tess leaned against the table and looked across at a yacht making its way across the bay. At first, Penny worried that the question had been too personal and Tess was going to be polite, but elusive and vague in her answer. Then she spoke. 'I've been back a few times over the years, and my parents and other relatives have come here and Theo, my son, has stayed with his grandparents a couple of times. I miss old friends, but they've come to visit. For me though, places are about people – if you're with the people you love, or in the place they loved you, that's all that matters. So, I miss people, especially my husband, but not England, or the life I had there before I met him.'

Looking at Penny's intense face as she listened, Tess felt empathy flow from the younger woman and quickly explained, as she had done so many times before, how she had lost Georgios. Penny was touched by the sharing and the strength of this serene and strong woman. Tess suddenly stepped back from the table. 'How about you? I have a feeling you're here for more than a holiday, given the painting, your itinerary, and Kalami?'

As she shared with Tess the details of her Durrell quest, the loss of her dad, and her broken engagement, Penny felt a lightness she hadn't felt for a long time. Telling someone about the last few months felt like catharsis rather than a painful retelling of a tragic tale. It lessened its power.

She was encouraged and uplifted by Tess, and the Athena that morning felt like a safe place, a place of healing.

'So,' Penny concluded, 'being an illustrator is my job, but also my life. I'm so glad I'm here. My dad would have loved this place. I've only been here two days, but it feels like somewhere I should be just now.'

'Well, you chose a good spot on the island, even if I'm a little biased,' Tess said. 'I'll get you another coffee, but stay as long as you like.'

A large family group was being shown to a table by Spiro, so Tess turned to leave, then remembered something. 'My father-in-law met Gerald Durrell and his brother in Corfu Town in the 1960s, I think. They were here on a visit. He's mentioned it a few times. I'm sure he'd tell you about it. I'll explain to him why you're interested.'

'Thank you so much. That would be amazing.'

Penny felt a surge in her stomach, and for once in a very long time it wasn't anxiety.

The rest of the morning flew by. Coffee and iced water from Tess and a little dish of strawberries and cream, a gift from Spiro, punctuated Penny's sketching and painting.

From her table, she could see the harbour, a series of beautiful coloured pots overflowing with flowers along the sea wall, and to her right, the Athena's restaurant and bar, with the road beyond. A series of small drawings captured the changing light, comings and goings, and small objects and people in Penny's eyeline – her coffee cup, the strawberries, a large urn filled with bougainvillea, and a wooden chair.

Nic popped in to see Tess and waved to Penny from the bar. Theo sat in his favourite spot, with his kitten and a book. His grandfather called him to the table for a plate of fruit and some water. Anna popped out of the kitchen now and again, chatting for a moment to Spiro and Theo, until Lily arrived for the start of a shift that would end around midnight.

At the far side of the Athena, Guy and Rich began to pull together some tables for their afternoon welcome meeting. They weren't on airport duty today, but twelve new holidaymakers had arrived early that morning.

'Lunch?' Penny looked up to see Tess. 'It's not compulsory, but it might be an idea to eat a little something.'

'I'm going to pack up the paints, but you're right, it would be a good idea to eat something. I feel like a walk, then a read by the pool. I haven't been in the pool yet.'

'How about a salad? Feta, olives, glass of rosé?'

Everything Tess suggested sounded like a dream; a meal to be savoured, remembered and lingered over. Its simplicity and fresh ingredients, a taste of paradise.

Ten minutes later she had a Greek salad and a glass of her now favourite rosé. Why did a simple collection of cucumber, cheese, green peppers, tomatoes, olives, and onions, drizzled with a light olive-oil dressing, taste so delicious? There was alchemy in everything on this island.

As she ate, she looked over at the harbour, half-expecting to see the little blue and white boat. It surprised her how often she found herself thinking of it, anticipating its return as part of the rhythm of the new life she was living.

'So, what's next on the Durrell agenda?' Tess asked.

'Perama, the first Durrell house, otherwise known as the Strawberry Villa. It's a privately owned home now and has been remodelled, although I think you can rent it as a holiday home. I hope I can get a sense of the place just by being in the area. Without sounding pretentious, this is as much about doing something for my dad as for me. He always wanted to come here. If he'd had a bucket list this would have been at the top, so in a way this feels like the last thing I can do for him. And perhaps selfishly, the best thing I can do for myself right now.'

As she said it out loud Penny realized for the first time why this trip had become less of a spontaneous, random act and more an essential part of her healing process.

Tess nodded, but didn't speak. Penny continued: 'There is another house, near Kontokali, that featured in the TV series, but the real Durrells didn't live there at all. They actually lived in three villas, but with all of them, it will be more about being in the area than actually visiting them. I've heard they're a little hard to find and I don't want to intrude, as they're private properties.'

'Why not ask Guy and Rich to help? They haven't been here long, but they've been asked about the Durrells many times. Guy spent some time around Perama at one of the hotels when he first arrived. Failing that, Dimitris is asked to go up to Kalami quite often, so there's every chance he knows more about the Durrells. Have you asked him about taking the boat up the coast?'

'Yes. I explained that Kalami is going to be the last on the list. It's where Larry Durrell lived and wrote, at the White House. I love his work and I'd like to eat at the White House too. Before I came here, I thought it would be the best place to toast the Durrells at the end of my trip. But then, what you imagine and what happens isn't always the same, is it? I have a feeling already that Corfu can easily distract someone from an agenda.'

'True, but I think the trick is not minding and going with the flow. When I can manage it, it's always better for my sanity and peace of mind.'

Penny hesitated for a moment and then said, 'Dimitris seems to have a bit of an English accent. Has he picked that up from visitors here?'

'Dimitris? No, he lived in England for a while. He was a solicitor, in London . . . something to do with finance and the markets, I think. I'm not sure what happened, why he came back, but he's been back for nearly two years now. There were stories of course, about a woman – a fiancée, I think – Sarah, yes, that was her name. So, a big change for him, fishing and taking people around the coast. He lives here in St George some nights with his father, but also has a flat in town. It just depends whether he's fishing or sailing.'

'Well, that's quite a change of direction.' Penny said, wondering who Sarah was and if she might have been the catalyst for his return to Corfu. There was an aura of solitude about him, a gravitas that made him feel detached. The 'statue' was coming to life though, with a history, a story.

'Whatever it was that brought him back has taken away any desire of his to travel,' Tess added. 'I don't think he's been off the island for more than a day or two since he returned.'

Tess noticed a collection of new customers at the entrance and rose. 'Duty calls. If you're up to it tonight, or don't have any other plans, it's our legendary – so I'm told, although I may have read it on a leaflet – Greek Night. Seriously, it's great fun. The musicians start at 8 p.m.'

Penny watched Tess as she walked away, wishing they'd had a moment more so that she could have asked about the woman she'd seen Dimitris with in Corfu Town – the woman she'd already built a backstory for, and endowed with every enviable quality she felt she, Penny, didn't have. The mystery woman was beautiful, confident and at ease with herself. No wonder – in her imagination – that Dimitris was besotted with her.

Chapter 11

The Athena was packed. The elegant, open-sided interior and the terrace beyond were a jumble of musicians, dancers, amps, mics, and musical instruments. Like a reception in the foyer before a performance, the air thronged with palpable expectation and the hum of excited chatter.

Parents warned children away from the trailing wires that lay like sleeping snakes on the stone floor. Traditionally costumed dancers – a flurry of white flowing shirts and beribboned dresses – stood in small groups, talking, gesturing, laughing. The last rays of the sun gilded the scene, any movement subtly lit and underlined by the glowing embers of the day.

Guests at the Greek Night pinched themselves and glanced at each other as if to say, 'This evening is going to be something we'll always remember. Aren't we lucky?'

Arriving just after 8.30 p.m., Penny saw that the Greek Night had already gathered pace, as the wine flowed, the night cooled, and guests veered towards that happy place where food balanced well with the wine, and they started to feel the pull of the dance floor.

Penny swiftly claimed her favourite little table overlooking the sea and harbour. The Athena felt like a slightly chaotic but jolly school outing. Parents, children, random groups, and couples settled in for a night of food and fun. The air smelt of perfume, aftersun, and herbs; a heady mix, the signature scent of a holiday in warmer climes.

With an artist's eye Penny took in the shapes, lights, and colours; and then in a heartbeat she was the girl again, who'd just lost her father, washed over with sadness because he would never again experience and feel the joy of a night like this.

As Vassilis and his band began the evening with a gentle folk ballad Penny looked up to see Simon, the would-be Jamie Oliver of Corfiot cookery, alone in a corner, a large carafe of red wine already in place. He looked like a man who would have struggled to work a microwave, so why invent a food-writer persona, she mused? Perhaps he'd needed a character to feel part of the island, boost his confidence . . . a hat to wear, to give him courage to start afresh, create a new life.

Nic walked towards her with a glass of rosé. 'Compliments of the management.' He gestured towards Tess at the bar, who waved and smiled. He hovered for a moment before being whisked away to help at the bar by a bouncier-than-usual Lily, followed closely by Rich carrying a laden tray of dirty plates.

Then like a chaotic tide of exuberance carried in on a wave from the Ionian Sea, the local dancers began. The moon, now risen, silvered the sea and the benevolent but impressive mountains became a sounding board, absorbing and then sharing the music from the Athena. Beat after beat, a persistent throb that couldn't be ignored, mirrored by the delicate but deliberate footwork of the dancers as their arms made elegant arcs in the air, their faces intense and absorbed in their craft.

Leaning back against the sea wall, Penny let the sound and the scene flow over her, acknowledging as she did so that, had she still been with Bruce, she would never have been able to enjoy this moment. Bruce wouldn't have chosen Corfu, St George, or the Athena. He would have discouraged any interaction with strangers, criticized the wine, and found the apartment too small. *Thank goodness it's over*, she thought to herself.

The music stopped and as applause and whooping filled the air, her eye was drawn to the harbour. There, at the end of the moon's watery pathway, cradled in the natural curve of the curved harbour wall, the little blue and white boat gently bobbed in the shallow water. She wondered if Dimitris and his father had gone home, tired after a day out at sea. Perhaps Greek Night was too lively and they'd gone to another bar for a quiet drink.

Guy appeared suddenly at Penny's side and interrupted her train of thought. 'Tess tells me you are interested in Perama and the Durrell houses nearby. There are two quite close to each other. Rich and I are off there on Sunday and available for hire as human satnavs, for a small fee. Maybe a Mythos or two?' He grinned.

'I'll be honest though,' he continued, sipping his lager, 'there isn't much to see house-wise. You have to use your imagination; you can't wander in the gardens or anything like that. There's also a small beach and Mouse Island. Durrell fans tend to go there too.'

Penny considered the unexpected kindness of relative strangers. 'What an offer. How could I refuse?' She accepted gracefully. Already her itinerary was coming to life in a way she had not anticipated.

'Great,' he said. 'Gotta dash . . . unless you're tempted to join in the next dance?'

'Maybe later.'

She watched him, with all his 20-year-old exuberance and confidence, plunge back into the mêlée of dancers, musicians, and small children, and reflected on how much nicer it felt to make a plan with real people.

A chaotic line of dancers, made up of children, adults, and a terrifyingly energetic Guy, paraded and passed her table, all arms and discordant feet, trying to catch up with each other and control their own limbs.

Before she could protest, Guy's hand was in hers, gently but firmly pulling her to her feet, while one of the women she'd seen at the welcome party grabbed the other. Breathless because she'd been caught off-guard, and swept at full speed into the mêlée, Penny found herself trying to move in sync with the troupe.

The music vibrated through the air, pulsing and catchy, loud enough, she felt, to be heard across the water in Italy, where she was sure Bruce would not be mirroring her movements. He was no doubt sitting elegantly in a piazza, sipping a delicately chilled glass of wine, and nodding sagely as the sommelier revealed its provenance. There'd be a woman at his side, she thought, perhaps impressed by his confidence and pulled in by his monumental handsomeness.

As she tried to imagine what this fantasy woman looked like, the music suddenly began to slow down, and the line of dancers broke up. She reached up and pushed her hair back from her forehead, half-laughing at herself as she made her way back to the table, nodding at Guy and making a mock curtsey.

⟨⁓⟩

It was just after midnight when Penny stepped into the street. Tess shouted goodnight from behind the bar and Nic waved from the terrace.

'*Kalinichta*,' she responded and let a coach pass on its way to deliver guests to the hotel at the end of the beach. Penny remembered that she needed to buy another bottle of water and wandered into the neon-lit cool space of the Achilles supermarket, which catered for the traveller who liked familiar things, even on holiday: chocolate digestives, Typhoo teabags, Mars bars, and other such exotica.

Passing row after row of olive oil, gift soap, herb mixes for Greek dishes, and novelty bottles of ouzo, Penny found the water, then grabbed a packet of crisps just in case hunger hit before breakfast. She'd already bought biscuits the day before, as sitting on her little balcony in the morning with a small coffee and a biscuit or two was becoming the curtain raiser to each day.

As she stepped back out into the balmy and velvety night she glanced back over at the Athena. The music, though slower and softer now, drifted towards her on the fragrant air; the soundtrack to the living painting of pearly white fairy lights and illuminated lemon trees that framed the Athena.

Turning down into the little lane that pulled her back to the apartments, she felt the urge to look around and there he was, at the bar, his back resting against the counter as he watched the dancing. His dark eyes scoured the restaurant, as if searching for someone, then stared into the surrounding darkness. Penny instinctively moved back into the shadows, away from the little lamp that lit the pathway. She wanted to watch him unobserved. *Who or what was he looking for?*

She wasn't sure why he caused her to react so strangely. He seemed so aloof, alone. He wasn't exactly rude, but he didn't feel easy to talk to. What was his story? Why had he given up a presumably lucrative career in England, to return to Corfu? Would someone so brusque be deeply wounded by a failed relationship? Could you judge a book by – she conceded – its very attractive cover?

Then she saw the woman – the one she'd seen Dimitris with in Corfu Town.

Penny watched as the blonde sat on the bar stool next to him, crossing her elegant, tanned legs with ease. She saw the woman nod, then casually raise her arm and place a hand on Dimitris's shoulder, as she leaned in towards him. For a moment Penny wondered if they would kiss, but then Tess appeared behind the bar and they turned to talk to her.

Feeling her heart sink, she wondered why she'd spent part of her evening thinking about two men she had no claim on, or real connection to, and the women they might be with. Bruce, Dimitris . . . what were they to her now, or ever likely to be? Why did they matter to her?

She looked up at the moon, directly above her apartment now, and carried on walking towards it.

Chapter 12

Time on Corfu operated according to different rules that started as soon as a visitor left the French Alps behind and approached Italy and then the island from the north. The hours, like the heat, seemed languid and unhurried, and yet the days passed swiftly on the calendar. Days melted into each other and phone calls and appointments became a hazy and happily discarded memory.

Tess marvelled how the days could feel interminably long and yet the time between greeting visitors and saying goodbye passed in a heartbeat. Nic looked back in September every year and asked himself where the weeks had gone. The summer always left him with a sense of ennui, regret – of something not quite finished, or perhaps not started.

Small but significant pieces of individual stories carried secret inner battles and hopes. Older people possessed the same inner dialogue, but regret and hopes were often handled in a more pragmatic way – more bucket list now than baggage. Spiro, after forty years of running the Athena, woke each morning knowing in his heart that he and the restaurant were two halves that made a whole.

Tess used to joke that the Athena was built on a ley line as so many people came there to find a kind of peace or respite, or closure, or to begin a new chapter.

For some the island of their birth would always be home, pulling them back by an invisible umbilical cord, even when other shores and opportunities beckoned. Some moved away to study then came back, having tasted the world beyond the Old Port and decided the comforting embrace of familiar shores equalled a better life.

Others left the island full of hope, waved off by tearful but proud families. Whether Athens or Australia, the separation was keenly felt by their mothers, fathers, brothers, and sisters. A few sons and daughters of Corfu had a more complex relationship with the island so many regarded as paradise.

Dimitris Koulouris was one of these.

Now approaching his 38th birthday, he felt he'd not had quite enough time back on the island to have exorcized the ghosts from his past. Each summer's day brought new hope, new visitors, new passengers for his yacht, the *Antiopi*, but also a restlessness, a gnawing discontent. Studying Law at the University of Turin had been a joy, an adventure. Staying on in Italy, the next few years had brought freedom and fun, and, he often thought, had been the last time he'd been truly happy. A few years later, taking up an offer to join his legal practice, from an uncle who had lived in London for some years, had felt like a natural next step.

Arriving in a colder than usual October, he'd stayed with Uncle Theo, his mother's brother, and Theo's loud, large, and lovable family. He worked happily alongside Theo, his social life was pleasant, and he had made some friends whose company he enjoyed.

In the spring and autumn of each year, Corfu called him back. He flew home for a week, to update his parents on the progress of his career and a life that seemed to him so very different, and far better, than their quiet, predictable one. His father responded to the stories of high-value clients and cases won with a genial pat on the back, but Dimitris sensed no real understanding of what he did. His mother smiled and stroked his face lovingly, always asking the question: had he met a nice girl?

He met a girl when out celebrating with colleagues from the practice. One evening he spotted a tall, elegant woman sitting at the bar with another woman, who he knew. Sally, also a lawyer, was smart, independent, and already making an impact in the profession. She specialized in Family Law, and although not yet a partner, was heading for greater things. The attraction had been instant and mutual. They made a handsome couple: the dark-haired, handsome Greek and the statuesque strawberry blonde.

The months that followed were filled mostly with work, but the rest of the time they spent with each other. Dimitris stayed over at Sally's and Sally helped him find and buy his first flat. His autumn visit home to Corfu was postponed as London life with Sally pulled him further away from the island and the people he had grown up with. The weeks and months flew by, and spring and another visit home was postponed. There was no time for anything beyond the world of work, Sally, and an increasing collection of friends, acquaintances, and business contacts. Phone calls, the occasional text, and Skype calls formed the delicate thread that held the Koulouris family together.

His mother and father weren't of a generation that found new tech easy to manage and so conversations were a little stilted and disconnected. Dimitris was always upbeat and full of news, but apart from asking his parents how they were, the traffic was pretty much one-way. He didn't know that when the calls were finished his mother would kiss the screen where his face had so magically appeared, knowing that her husband understood the gesture and missed their son as deeply as she did.

The faces that stared back at him from their bright, clean, and slightly chaotic kitchen in St George were tanned, familiar, comforting. The family dog barked at small lizards in the garden beyond. Not for a moment did he imagine that the world he had left behind, perfectly preserved in the folds of his memory, might change, nor that his new life might deviate from the path of Sally, work, and a charmed future.

Then Sally was offered the opportunity to become a partner at a large law firm in the north of England. The firm hinted that she might be transferred back to London in a year or two, but in the meantime, Dimitris knew he had to stay behind at his uncle's practice.

There was no question at all that she wouldn't go, but her almost dismissive and seemingly casual response, when he tried to discuss how they would keep their relationship going when apart, unsettled him.

Sally moved to Leeds and her family helped her to settle in. The threads that bound them together slowly unwound day by day, text by text, call by call. By the autumn, Dimitris looked towards home and realized he needed to sit in the sun with friends and family, on the terrace of his parents' house, and press the pause button on his life for a moment. A few days before he was due to fly home, his uncle stepped into the office, closed the door and, ashen-faced, told him that his sister, Dimitris's mother, had died.

He didn't remember packing and leaving, his heart heavy with grief and guilt.

A different Dimitris arrived back at Corfu airport and threw his arms around his father, who waited there for him.

Two years on, the visceral effect of his mother's loss, and

that of the woman he'd imagined he'd spend the rest of his life with, had mostly healed, but the experience had left him wary. Love was the thing that hurt. If he could avoid it for now, he would. Even if that meant hiding in plain sight on his island.

Chapter 13

Sunday awoke with the scent of lemons, as Penny absorbed the first heat of the day from her balcony. From below came the muted but bright sounds of chatter from the villa next door, as the neighbouring family readied themselves for a trip to the water park in the middle of the island.

Penny had planned to meet the 'Three Musketeers', as she'd dubbed Guy, Rich, and Lily, outside the Athena. Guy had been a bit vague in a text he'd sent about the route and the Durrell locations: *Sort of know where we're going. We'll head towards Benitses and Perama first, then have a think. Some great places to stop before Corfu Town. We may have time for Mouse Island too.*

Finding traces of the Durrells' life on the island was clearly not an exact science for Guy, but as he'd said, it was more about being roughly in the right area and using your imagination.

She wondered, as she dressed, what the Durrell family would have thought of all the fuss if they'd still been here. They could never have dreamed that decades later their own steps on the island would be followed as a kind of homage.

When she looked at the titles of each chapter in *My Family and Other Animals* they were, she thought, really a shorthand for the jewels that made up the treasure chest of the island: the family villas – Strawberry, Daffodil Yellow, Snow White; then the seasons, captured in every chapter, but most poignantly in 'The Sweet Spring Conversation' and 'The Woodcock Winter Conversation'; and last but not least, as you'd expect in the memoir of a budding 10-year-old naturalist, the episodes featuring the animals and insects with whom he shared this Eden – 'A Treasure of Spiders', 'The Pageant of Fireflies', and 'The Tortoise Hills'.

Each chapter was woven seamlessly and delightfully into tales, some perhaps tall, but all with a grain of warmth and truth that only such joy, lovingly remembered twenty years later, deserved. It was difficult not to fall in love with them all, each member of the family – animal or human – unique, flawed, and unforgettable.

When Penny read the book, she'd envisaged the moonlight guiding them down to the beach for a swim, had smelt the rotting turtle being merrily dissected by Gerry on the veranda, and heard the screams of anger from Leslie as he discovered the snakes cooling down in the bath, where his young brother had left them.

As she walked towards the restaurant, the luminosity of the lemons against their emerald leaves and the crushed-blue-silk sky beyond, all shimmering in the heat, caught her illustrator's eye. She captured these jewels on her phone, sometimes a rose in all its stages, from tightly closed green and red-tinged bud, through to its tentative blossoming, and then at its full-blown blousiest. She curated the things rarely noticed, regularly missed, yet always beautiful, to be used at some point in the future to depict a story that had probably not even been written yet.

It was one of the features of her work, her trademark, to include details of flora and fauna, drawn with fineness and compelling accuracy, wherever she could fit them in. They weren't just clever copies of nature, but realistic and textured, reacting to light as though they were real on the page. They brought the narrative to life with an honesty and heart that lifted the story and helped the reader live in the moment as they read the book.

Someone had once asked her why, particularly in fairy tales, she didn't just invent the flowers and landscapes. Her answer was simple: there was nothing she could create that was as beautiful as what already existed.

'Hi!' Guy waved at her from the end of the lane.

'On my way,' she called back, popping her phone back into her rucksack, next to the obligatory sketchbook and small watercolour palette.

It was a morning to bottle, she thought, as she spotted Lily and Rich standing outside the Athena. As Penny unlocked the car, Rich opened the back door for Lily, and Guy claimed the front passenger seat and calling out, 'I know where we're going. Guide's perks.'

Rich didn't look remotely disappointed as he sat in the back, smiling at Lily as she waved at Tess. Penny lowered the car window and shouted across: 'Guy's our official tour guide today. So if we're not back before sundown, send out a search party.'

Theo looked up from his book and waved, Guy calling out that they'd bring him something back as a treat.

'I haven't got a snake yet,' he suggested.

Tess smiled down at Theo and mouthed, 'No snakes', behind her son's back.

⁓

Benitses and Perama clung to the ribbon of road that hugged the coastline south of Corfu Town. Each had a unique charm, moulded by geography, the sea, the seasons, and the thousands of people who visited each year. Benitses, huddling cosily between the towering hills and mountains rising up into the ether behind her and the sea that lapped at her feet, had begun life as a traditional village and been one of the first resorts on Corfu.

They passed scattered roadside houses, some hidden from view, only their roofs visible, built on the hillsides to be closer to the sea, where some enjoyed private access to the shingled beach below.

Guy sat back in the passenger seat, looking like an extra from a Noel Coward play set on the French Riviera, dressed in crisp linen shirt and shorts. There was an elegance about him, Penny thought, even when casually dressed, that she guessed was probably carefully created. She glanced in the rear-view mirror at Lily and Rich. Lily fiddled with her phone, while Rich looked at her, then abstractedly out of the window, as though desperately searching for something to say.

Penny decided to step in and end his agony. 'Lily, I know Rich and Guy are at the same university, but did you know each other before you came out here?'

Lily took an earbud out. 'No, we met here a few weeks ago, at the start of the season. I didn't know anyone when I came.'

'Didn't you know Tess? I thought that's how you ended up working at the Athena,' Rich said.

'No, not really. My aunt knows Tess and heard she was looking for someone for the season, as she was let down at the last minute. So, she put me in touch. Tess interviewed me online and I arrived two weeks later.'

'She seems lovely,' Penny said, her eye caught for a second by a new signpost.

Guy whispered, 'Straight on.'

'She is. I can't believe I have my own little room, a tiny kitchen, and a balcony, all so close to my work. I just walk down the track and I'm there. I've almost perfected getting up, showering, having breakfast, and getting to the Athena within twenty-five minutes. Extra sleep time.'

Lily paused for a minute, looking out of the window deep in thought, then said, 'I don't know how Tess does it. She runs the Athena and the holiday apartments, orders all the food, keeps all the accounts, and looks after Theo.'

'But she has her father-in-law and Nic to help out,' Penny said.

'I think there's a bit more to Nic's support than meets the eye though,' Lily said. 'Have you noticed the way he looks at Tess when she's chatting to customers at the bar? I don't think he realizes he's doing it, but Anna's noticed it too.'

Lily looked out of the window again, leaving her fellow passengers to muse in their own different ways on the news that Nic might be in love with Tess.

They were brought sharply back into the moment as Lily pointed to the sea and exclaimed, 'Oh, I love the way that little wooden pier goes out across the bay.'

They glanced to the right and saw a rustic pier, along which tables with fluttering cloths caught the cooling breeze, under a long white canopy. Smiling diners relaxed with cold drinks or nursed their coffees after a late breakfast.

'It reminds me of the pier scene in *La La Land*,' Lily said, her face suffused with a grin.

Rich stared out of the window, wondering how Ryan Gosling had managed to quickly become, in spirit, the fifth member of the party on a day for which he had entertained such high hopes.

Chapter 14

As they approached Benitses, Guy told Penny to pull over and park next to the marina. 'Is this where the Strawberry Villa is? I thought we needed to be in Perama,' she asked as she steered into a parking space.

'Not quite yet,' Guy said mysteriously. 'Trust me, you'll want to make this stop, and we have plenty of time.'

They crossed the road, following Guy's lead and watching out for cars and coaches. Within a couple of minutes, they strolled among charming open-air tavernas and cafés, looking up at buildings that had been part of a thriving fishing hub.

The mountains towered on the horizon, behind the bustling market which offered everything from painted, ceramic vases to jars of honey that caught the sun and reflected it back in a liquid, amber glow.

'Here we are.' said Guy, with a flourish of his hand directing them towards a table in one of the outdoor cafés. 'You won't regret this detour,' he declared and went off to order.

He soon returned and, a few minutes later, a young man arrived at the table with their drinks order and large, lustrous slices of baklava.

'This is my friend Philip, who's here on the good ship *Corfu* for a summer stint, the same as us – Penny excepted, of course, who seems to be here of her own free will. He normally resides in Athens.'

Philip smiled in greeting. 'I thought you might like to try the baklava and tell everyone how good it is. My aunt made it. This is her and my uncle's business.'

The pastry oozed honey and promise. Nuts and cinnamon wrapped in filo pastry gave off a heavenly aroma of the freshly baked and homemade. It had been eaten by their senses before they even took a bite.

Lily watched Philip with enough interest to give Penny a pang of sympathy for Rich, who, his focus on the baklava, had not noticed her glance at Philip's retreating back.

The baklava lived up to its promise: syrupy honey, intermingled with flaky, crisp pastry and toasted nuts, all melted together in a cinnamon-infused taste sensation that necessitated an appreciative, companionable silence.

As she washed it down with coffee, Penny considered how random everything was. Here she was sitting with people who only days ago had been strangers, living on an island more than 1,500 miles away from home. Every day had endless possibilities.

She realized that one of the first casualties of her grief had been the optimism she'd always naturally exuded and relied upon, which had carried her through so many days of uncertainty. At this moment, the sun was a gift, the baklava a bonus, and courage was dropping gently back into her soul.

The Durrells had been here. They had looked at the same jagged peaks and turquoise sea, perhaps from this very spot, and gazed over the same ancient olive groves. Larry and his wife Nancy had left a trail of lighted torches in their wake for the family to follow.

Penny's dream, a pleasing diversion as she'd stared out of the window at school, then college, home – or more recently, the hospice – had merged into reality. The narrative in her head, the adventure of transforming the places from a novel into somewhere she had actually visited, had already begun.

'Ready?' Guy looked across at Penny, who smiled and stood up.

'Absolutely,' she replied. The trio meandered back to the car, with Lily turning to wave a casual goodbye to Philip.

They had only been back in the car for two minutes when Guy pointed across Penny and said, 'There they are: Mouse Island and, just across the water, closer to us, the old monastery.'

The two islets, like siblings that had turned away from each other, arms folded after an argument, were jewel-like in their azure setting. One reached by boat, the other by a causeway, Mouse Island had a bleached white church and the other had the Vlacherna Monastery, the latter resplendent with a bell tower and a rustic red-tiled roof.

'I can't believe Margo and Gerry Durrell used to swim across from Perama to Mouse Island.' Penny glanced at the watery blue expanse between the island and Perama. Please, tell me there's a boat!'

'Oh yes, there's a boat, which I'm reliably informed is the fun bit. Now take this road here.' Guy pointed and Penny pulled off the main road. Just as the road began to rise Guy told her to stop the car.

'This is as close as we can get without looking like we're tourists or voyeurs,' Guy said as he stepped out of the car. 'Bear in mind that the house has been rebuilt. So although it's still lovely, if you know what it looked like in the 1930s you'll have to adjust your expectations.'

They were on a small road, lined with established, lush green trees, set against a picture-book blue sky, with no sense of the remoteness of the landscape of the 1930s, described so richly in Penny's beloved book. No braying donkeys to annoy aspiring writers or overwhelming flora and fauna tumbling in a cultivated and wild mixture down the hillside. But the air still exuded the rich scent of flowers and closer to the houses, the aroma of lemon and garlic might easily have stolen out of the kitchen window – the hallmark of any house on Corfu – with mother, Louisa Durrell, in residence, cooking with her favourite aromatic herbs and spices.

Lily and Rich followed, but weren't really sure what they were looking at, or looking for. 'I've seen a few episodes of *The Durrells* on TV. Is this the house where they actually lived?' Lily asked. 'It looks different from the one I remember, which was right next to the sea. The sea was part of the front garden and there was a terrace.'

Before Penny began to speak, she checked herself, trying to balance her enthusiasm for *her* Durrell family with an understanding that once she began, there was a danger that she might have to retell their whole story.

'The main family lived in three different houses on Corfu – the Strawberry Villa, the Daffodil Yellow and finally the Snow White. The fourth house associated with the Durrells is the White House in Kalami Bay, where Larry and his wife Nancy lived.'

They walked towards the terracotta roof of the villa beyond the trees. Penny continued: 'This is the Strawberry Villa. Guy, you were right . . . it has changed since the Durrells' day; a lot if you compare it to the drawing Gerry made of it in childhood, which shows the house all on one level with two windows either side of the central front door and the gardens full of ornate flower beds. But I suppose, it's now wearing its new clothes.'

The villa, although walled and private, no longer lay in splendid isolation as it shared the hillside with more houses. The rebuilt, two-storey, russet-pink house embodied the Venetian style, complete with a white-columned entrance. The garden boasted a swimming pool overlooked by beautifully proportioned, white-shuttered windows, and the villa was without doubt now a smart, sparkling holiday destination; no longer small and faded, with bubbling, cracking paint on ageing shutters, as described so lovingly in *My Family and Other Animals*.

After a while, Penny said, 'This was where the Durrells lived when they first arrived in 1935, followed by two other houses. The Venetian villa they used in the TV series is quite close to their second house, the Daffodil Yellow Villa, near Kontokali, but all the houses are now privately owned, so not open to the public. Except of course this one, which anyone can book for a holiday.'

As silence settled on the little group the soundtrack and aroma of the pine trees filled the air: the humming chorus of flying insects, alongside the chirping of cicadas and occasional birdsong. The natural songscape still captivated the onlooker, but lacked the chorus of a peasant song rising above it all, taught to the young Gerry on his many wanderings by an elderly Corfiot woman, who had become one of the small English boy's many friends. A cavalcade of characters crowded into Penny's mind: the eccentric and transient Rose-Beetle Man; Agathi, the singer and teacher of songs; Theo Stephanides, oracle and inspiration; even Achilles the tortoise pushed his way in.

She suddenly wanted to sit down, make contact with the

earth, close her eyes, and try to conjure up those who had gone before but were now as elusive as the wind. And she realized abruptly that, along with the Durrells, her dad no longer inhabited the earth she lived on, and existed only in her mind and memory. How sad and strange that felt.

Penny wondered if it was possible to hear the echoes of the past if she concentrated and remained motionless for a moment. She closed her eyes and imagined running, sandalled feet; the sharp crack of gunshots from a bored Leslie's gun, as he practised hitting tins cans across the garden; Lugaretzia, the maid, sharing the story of her latest ailment in mournful tones; or the rumble of an old Dodge motor car, which signalled the arrival of the Durrells' dear friend and Mr Fixit, Spiro.

This, after all, was the place where their great adventure had begun; the location that had launched a thousand days of discovery, that had shaped a life – Gerald Durrell's lifetime's mission and labour of love in the natural world. A man who David Attenborough had described as 'magic'.

Penny reopened her eyes, weaving into her memory the picture before her that she felt must still resemble the scene from 1935. She sensed the pure, undiluted joy of being 10 years old and landing on this island; an island so rich in wildlife, with many worlds to explore, and seasons to astonish and enchant – the Garden of the Gods, which the grown-up Gerry had written about so vividly, with such warmth, humour, and poignancy.

Green dominated the surroundings, and the sea reflected the azure heart of the sky. Despite the modern world and the demands of tourism, these untouched natural treasures stayed the same, even if the lives of the people here had changed. In her heart, Penny knew that progress involved gaining and losing. It was now possible to drive up north to Kalami from

Corfu Town on established roads all year round, instead of navigating rough tracks that used to wash away in winter storms, making it easier to get there by boat.

'It's getting hot now. Are we ready to move on?' Guy interrupted her thoughts.

Penny nodded. She had seen enough and for the first time felt a little foolish in her quest. Was she chasing something that existed most potently and perfectly in the pages of a book? Lily and Rich looked distinctly underwhelmed. The connections meant nothing to them; the power of the place, she thought, prevailed in the words, in a book they hadn't read. The world turned and changed, people arrived and left – only a book stayed the same.

But even that wasn't quite true, because every time she'd reread *My Family and Other Animals* over the previous twenty years, the text had yielded something different: comedy when she needed to be lifted; escape when she had a moment to relax; and the beauty of the world it encompassed when she needed to refocus on the things that mattered – the eternally important . . . family, love, nature, and the importance of small things.

As they turned their backs on the villa, what remained of the 'Chessboard Fields' lay to the left, the old Venetian salt pans, intersected with tiny waterways, full of mini beasts, and explored so tenaciously by Gerry. Mouse Island loomed straight ahead, amid the blue, white-tipped waters of the sea fringed by the far outline of the Greek mainland on the horizon, like an image from a pop-up children's book.

Penny wandered a few steps down the hill and then, taking a long, deep breath in, she turned back to the car.

Chapter 15

'If we're all up to it, I thought we'd walk across the causeway and have lunch in Kanoni, at a café there that has a great view of Mouse Island and the church,' Guy suggested. 'Then we can visit the monastery and the island when it's a little cooler, later in the afternoon.'

'You've gone to a lot of trouble thinking things through, Guy. I really appreciate it,' Penny said.

'No problem. It's a pretty well-worn route these days, but much more fun when you've made up your own itinerary, can stop when you like, and choose some great places to eat.'

The walkway across the sea linking Perama and Kanoni formed the boundary among the old salt flats and lagoons, the start of the airport runway, and the open sea. It was a spectacular place to watch the planes swoop in and out, before contemplating the surrounding view.

At first Penny didn't know which way to look. To her right, coming closer and revealing more of its beauty with every step, stood the Vlacherna Monastery and just behind it, looking deceptively close, Pontikonisi – Mouse Island.

They walked slowly along, the heat and light drawing energy from their bodies, as thoughts of a shaded terrace and a cool drink urged them towards the far shore. A collection of small boats was moored near the pathway that veered off at right angles to the monastery islet. People in a boat headed to Mouse Island.

Penny automatically began to deconstruct the scene into lines and light, horizons and shapes. The boats were a breeze-blown jumble of objects, all angles and discordant lines, criss-crossing in their movement and complexity. Her pencil would have laid down the first marks on the paper, as she worked out how to mix the colours in her head; colours that, spread so carefully, layer after opaque layer, recreated the light that brought the scene to life.

With her phone she could capture the image in front of her, but her heart and mind filled in the emotional memory gaps as she stood and absorbed it for a moment: the salty, fishy smell of the sea; the uneven path beneath her feet; and the timpani of the boats as they bumped gently against their moorings. Already nostalgia for these things emerged, even before the moment passed.

Hands in pockets as was her way, she watched the far shore as it came into focus. More distinct and animated, populated with chattering shoals of people.

'Is that where we're going?' Penny asked Guy, as she shielded her eyes against the sun and pointed to a terraced café-restaurant with groups of people sitting at the tables.

Lily and Rich looked up, relief in their faces as Guy nodded and said, 'Yup. The view is amazing and the food even more so.'

A few minutes later they were seated, elevated above the causeway, watching the scene below and above, the boats, sea, fellow diners, and planes centre-stage. Lunch came in wave after wave of freshly prepared loveliness: fish; salad; crusty, warm bread; green and golden olive oil for dipping that smelt like a herb bed; creamy, garlicky tzatziki; and ridiculously pink taramasalata . . . all presented on white, rustically made dishes. The table resembled a still life with its rough-hewn surface of knotted olive wood, its colour rich and varied, decades of growth now polished and exposed to the sun. The food revealed smooth and inviting textures, all arranged without artifice, impacting the eyes, the nose, and then, in appreciative silence, the sense of taste.

'*Yamas!*' Guy raised his glass and they all toasted each other.

'So,' Guy said to Penny, 'tell us why you're here for more than the usual week or two, and why the Durrell thing.'

The question caught Penny off-guard, as the answer – the truth – was not, she imagined, the usual traveller's tale of needing a break, switching off from the office, or wanting to lie on a beach all day and party all night. Looking up at the faces now turned towards her, she took off her sunglasses, crossed her now browner legs, and turned the questioning back towards her newfound friends.

'After you, if that's okay. I know you're all at university and just here for the summer, but where do you live in the UK? Why did you choose Corfu? What are you studying? Do you have brothers or sisters? What do you want to do when you leave uni? I'd really like to know.'

They all looked a little surprised and then glanced at each other to see who would go first. Rich took the plunge.

'Guy and I are at the same uni. We're sharing a small flat for our final year from September. I'm studying film, but I'm not really sure what I want to do, although I've always wanted to know how things work. I suppose I'm more on the techy side than the arty stuff. I have a younger sister, Kate, and my home town is near Chelmsford, in Essex.'

As Rich spoke, a plane coming into land fought for

attention with his words, but Lily and Guy focused on their friend's face. Neither of them remembered Rich saying so much in one go.

'So, why here, Rich? Why Corfu?'

'My dad's friend worked for Greektime a few years ago and said it had been fun and a great summer job. So, I told Guy, we applied together, had an interview in London, and here we are.'

Guy stretched back in his chair and smiled at two girls who had just taken a seat at the next table. 'So, Guy, what about you?'

'Well, I'm studying English, but sometimes it feels like I'm actually in suspended animation or Groundhog Day, doomed forever to listen to the droning on of lecturers who should have left the lectern long ago. Actually,' Guy paused, 'there is one who's not too bad, but she has a fixation on Sylvia Plath, who she somehow manages to insert into every single writer we study. I think she even had a connection with Shakespeare – perhaps time travel was involved.'

He diverted attention away from himself by telling Lily, 'Your turn.'

She put down her phone on the table. 'Well, as the lads know, I'm from Devon. I have a baby brother – my mum has remarried – my dad lives in Scotland and I was studying . . .'

'Was?' Rich interrupted her.

'I *was* studying music,' she continued, 'but I'm not going back. I've left. That's one of the reasons I'm not leaving here until the end of October.'

'We thought you were just going back a little later than us,' Rich said, his confusion obvious. 'It's your final year.'

Penny studied Lily from behind her glasses, noting her body language. She leaned forward, filled instinctively with the strange feeling that she might have to catch her.

'I didn't really want to be there any more,' she said quietly and simply. 'I lost a friend. That wasn't the whole reason, but it was enough to make my mind up. I don't think university life really suited me.'

Lily stood and mumbled something about being back in a minute. Penny waited a few seconds then followed her. 'I'm paying for lunch,' she called back over her shoulder to Guy and Rich as she waved to the waitress, pointed at their table, and made the internationally recognized handwriting action to indicate she wanted to pay the bill.

As Penny stood in the cool interior of the café, she watched the door that led to the Ladies, where Lily had disappeared. She wanted to catch her before she rejoined the boys.

Suddenly Lily was there, holding open the door for an older woman. She spotted Penny by the bar and walked over slowly.

'Sorry, I had to stop for a minute. I still find it hard to say out loud what happened to Sophie.' She paused, looked around, as if to check if anyone else was listening.

'Sophie killed herself, took an overdose. I found her in our bathroom, in the flat we all shared. I haven't told anyone here. I don't want people – the boys – to know. Even Tess doesn't know.'

Penny took a step towards her and put an arm around her shoulders. 'I won't say a word. If you change your mind and want to share, that's fine, but you can always come and talk to me in the meantime. I can't imagine how hard that must have been, Lily.'

'We didn't know she was depressed. She was quiet sometimes, but then she'd suggest we all went out, or sang along to a film, or just did something a little bit daft.'

Lily stared at the floor and Penny felt her begin to tremble. She walked her gently out of the bar, to the far end of the terrace, away from the diners. 'Do you want to go back?' she asked. 'We can come back here another time. Guy and Rich won't mind and they don't have to know why.'

Lily shook her head and rested her hands on the stone wall that held back the sea. The cool sensation on her palms calmed and settled her. 'I think Guy is looking forward to showing off in a boat and you've only two or three weeks left here. Anyway, I want to visit the island too. I'm all right, really. But thanks.'

Lily turned to Penny, hugged her, then stood back as though surprised by her own response and walked back towards the terrace, where Guy and Rich were enjoying the last of their drinks.

Chapter 16

The atmosphere surrounding the quartet was quite different as they walked down the steps of the café and strolled towards the monastery islet.

Lily walked alongside Penny and the lads trailed behind, as if there had been an unspoken promise to be quiet for a moment; a sense that something significant had happened, but it wasn't the moment to ask more, particularly the what or the why.

Rich noticed that Lily's usual bounciness had been quashed, which bothered him. He knew he shouldn't and wouldn't pry, but he wanted to be a quiet presence close by, just in case.

'Guy,' Penny looked back, 'are we walking to the monastery? Is that where we'll pick up a boat?'

'Yes, just keep walking. They're every few minutes.'

Some places in the world were so well known, their outline or location, height or design made them instantly recognizable: an architectural or geographic ambassador for whichever country they happened to grace. The Eiffel Tower, the Taj Mahal, Sydney Opera House were potent and often-reproduced symbols of their countries – a whole culture packaged into one landmark; a short cut that sidestepped the real complexities of place and people.

The Vlacherna Monastery was one such place. Featured on everything from mouse mats to tea towels, it could be folded or carefully wedged into a suitcase and transported home.

A white-walled monastic world greeted them, complete with open bell tower and sun-bleached, red-tiled roof, enhanced by the vibrant green of a tree that hugged its landward side.

Penny and Lily entered the small chapel. After Lily's revelation and distress just twenty minutes earlier, the cool and calm descended on them both. Penny knew that having no one to share the fears and joys of everyday life with – let alone an extraordinary, shocking event – was hard enough at 33, but at 20, so far from home, it must have felt overwhelming at times.

They sat in the chapel, as the boys stayed outside checking on the time of the next boat to the island. The stillness exuded vulnerability as well as sanctuary; a baring and acknowledgement of pain. Lily closed her eyes and after a few moments the images that tormented her – Sophie, panic, the tears, and horror – were pushed away by the silence, as it made itself more present than anything else. They both lit a candle before they left.

The hot, sea-scented air hit them as the door released them into the waiting world. Lily took refuge on her phone again, a convenient barrier against any questions she didn't want to answer.

Rich called them over to a boat that was filling up, ready to set off for Mouse Island.

'This is us,' said Guy, helping Penny into the boat.

Rich held his hand out to Lily, who looked bemused momentarily but took it anyway to steady herself as she stepped into the swaying vessel.

'Thanks,' she said. Her hand trembled slightly. A thoughtful Rich watched as she seated herself on the wooden benches that followed the line of the boat and listened to her music.

The hop across to Mouse Island took a few minutes, but was a perfect opportunity to enjoy the breeze and the brilliance of the view from the water. Other boats passed them, smudges of rising and falling colour, with their happy holiday passengers. Music drifted from somewhere, and the pilot of their boat sang the last word of every line and hummed along to the rest of an old song. Penny saw where they'd been earlier, up in the hills at the Strawberry Villa. The sea, sky, and land that ran down and through the villas and hotels all met at the now-distant causeway.

Suddenly Guy stood up and waved, attracting more attention than the scenery or the fast-approaching island.

'It's Dimitris, in his boat. He must have taken a group cruising down the coast.'

Penny looked across to where Guy was pointing, but didn't see the familiar blue-and-white boat. 'Where? I can't see the boat,' she said, before realizing that Guy was looking at a beautiful, perfectly proportioned, elegant yacht in full sail that resembled both a child's drawing brought to life and a glossy photo from a lifestyle magazine.

'It's the *Antiopi*. What a great day to be out. I expect he picked people up in Messonghi and they're on their way to Corfu Town.'

Guy sat down in the boat. Penny found she couldn't break her gaze from the gliding craft as it moved away, soon passing Kanoni to be hidden from view.

'What a beautiful boat. I'm definitely going to ask Dimitris if he can sail up to Kalami, during the last week I'm here.'

Penny looked across at Guy, who was staring at her, as were Lily and Rich, and she realized with a tinge of embarrassment and surprise that she sounded overexcited, breathless, and juvenile.

Then she saw Guy smile and laughed at herself, at the joy of being on the water, and the unrelenting heat of the day. For a few seconds, she'd felt the touch of real life, a possibility and promise beyond the darkness that still crept up on her some days.

The vision she'd experienced when she'd spoken so briefly to Dimitris, the frisson of imagining herself on such a boat as the *Antiopi*, now cemented itself into potential reality. How could something so dreamlike lift and sustain? In the past months she'd tried so hard, so many times, to go somewhere else in her head, but so often her imagination and heart had failed her.

The little boat swayed as it stopped and they stepped onto Mouse Island. Guy led the way once more and Rich, ever hopeful but now also concerned, hung back to see if Lily needed his hand to steady her exit from the boat.

The boats returned every twenty minutes to ferry visitors back to the monastery islet, and Lily sloped off towards the gift shop. Rich followed.

'I'm just going to wander over to this side where I can look back at Perama,' Penny said.

Guy raised his hand and with a casual 'fine' sat down on the nearest wall and began to look at his phone.

⌣⌒

Penny walked towards the water and looked back at the monastery, the beginning of the runway, Kanoni beyond, and then Perama on the mainland to her left. She retraced where they'd walked from the car, then across the causeway, and on to the café with the miraculous view and the fabulous food. This, Penny was suddenly acutely aware, was one of those long-awaited and anticipated moments she had hoped for before arriving in Corfu.

Mouse Island had been a beacon in the Durrells' universe. In legend, the island itself had been created from Odysseus's boat, turned to stone by an angry Poseidon. In Penny's memory, it was the place where the young Gerry and his sister Margo, in the heady and ever-shortening days before the clouds of war gathered, had waded ashore after swimming across from Perama. Gerry had later described the island church as the size of a matchbox, with a monk of questionable sartorial habits. Larry mentioned it too in his love letter to Corfu, *Prospero's Cell* – a place that impacted the heart and was difficult to capture by conventional means, whether in paint or words.

Mouse Island was also where some of Gerry's ashes had been scattered.

It was strange to think of the boy he had been, here for just a few short years, but drawn back time and again. She imagined him never losing the sense of the joy that being here had brought him, wishing in later years that if he'd had one gift to give the children of the world, he would have given them his childhood.

My childhood shaped my whole world too, Penny thought, as she looked at the sea and, not for the first or last time, thought of her dad. How could she measure her grief? How did a person's ability to carry on compare with how someone else coped with loss? There was no handbook . . . no 'how to' . . . no one-size-fits-all . . . no map.

Chapter 17

For Tess, the ebb and flow of visitors arriving on the island defined the days of the week through the summer. Looking after the Athena and the apartments returned to their annual, well-worn, and mostly smooth routine.

Occasionally, a small drama became an epic production. This particular Sunday had been no exception and by noon, yet another kitten with an infected eye had found its way to the front steps of the Athena, two large bottles of olive oil from the kitchen store had slid to their doom after a shelf collapsed, and Tess had missed Lily's quick hands and feet, and quirkiness, as she usually provided comfort in the chaos, with a mutual roll of the eyes and a share in the madness. Ina from the village had come to help, but it wasn't the same.

The boys and Lily's away-day had been a catalyst for, or coincided with – she wasn't sure – a *down* day. A day when Georgios had been at her side, in her mind, and yet painfully absent. He would have exclaimed loudly about shattered bottles of olive oil, cursed a little, then kissed her on the head, poured a beer, and mended the shelf. The cursing would have been more about the loss of the golden nectar bought from local olive growers, whose trees were hundreds of years old.

The kitten was easier to mend. There were still some eye drops left in the bottle the vet had given them for Theo's kitten, Dora, who had now recovered.

Tess moved briskly from table to table, chatting, clearing, asking the diners if they were okay, and listening to stories of buses missed, dolphins seen on boat trips, fabulous ice cream discovered in Corfu Town, a new silver ring bought for a partner, and irritating mosquito bites. There was never – or rarely – anything new that she hadn't heard as a complaint or praise.

Everything good, bad, and all points in between was exaggerated on holiday by the heat and heightened emotions. Even a small lizard minding its own business, nestling in a cool corner of a bedroom, became an international incident in one visitor's eyes.

As she worked, with Spiro and Theo in support, she tried to pull herself back into the present, grateful for all that she had: for the full tables that meant a financially stress-free winter ahead and the friends who helped her carry on.

The only empty table was the small one by the sea wall, and she wondered what sort of day Penny was having. She smiled to herself as she imagined Guy, narrowly resisting carrying a flag or umbrella, leading the group and where he didn't know stuff, making it up.

She'd heard him tell two older ladies that Roger Moore had dined regularly at the Athena when making a Bond film on the island years before. He'd built on stories from Spiro, about how he'd met the actor when he'd been making a Bond film – 'Charming and wonderful man. We didn't want him to leave Corfu.' – and Guy had then invented the Athena tale around that. Tess guessed that Penny knew her Durrell history and a little part of her hoped that Guy would be kindly but firmly corrected if he went off on too many flights of fancy.

By mid-afternoon and the pull of a nap in cooler rooms, a lull interrupted the flow of diners and drinkers. Only Simon, the cookery doyen, sat with a day-old newspaper and a carafe of red wine, and a young couple contemplated food for the first time that day, after an early-morning return from Corfu Town.

Nic walked into this peaceful moment to receive a high-five from Theo and a warm hug from Spiro.

'Have you eaten?' Spiro was already heading in the direction of the kitchen, worried as always that people weren't eating enough food to sustain them.

'I'm fine. Good day?'

Spiro shrugged his shoulders to indicate it was normal for a Sunday and sat back down to admire Theo's new drawing.

Nic looked across and saw Tess laughing at something a diner was saying; clearly a tall tale, as she appeared attentive and engaged.

He'd seen that face so many times over the last few years, knew what that smile that didn't quite reach the eyes meant. She was having one of those days where the past was painfully present, when memories of Georgios turned on her, and reminded her of her loss.

Tess looked up, saw Nic, and gave him a smile that confirmed her low ebb. 'Busy day?' Nic took Tess's tray as she nodded. He followed her back to the bar. Theo ran up and grabbed his mother around the waist, the new kitten in his other hand.

'Mama, I think the drops are working already. Look, her eye has opened.'

Nic knew that Tess wouldn't want him to take the drinks order, or suggest she sat down and had a five-minute break. Tess knew he knew; understood that he had seen the truth behind her eyes, but knew he would never acknowledge it. It never helped her if she stopped. The hand that rested briefly on her arm as she stepped behind the bar to make up the order sufficed.

'Theo, you're doing a fantastic job with that kitten.' Tess took her son's small face between her hands and kissed him on the forehead.

'Theo, shall we take a walk down to the harbour?' Nic smiled at his godson.

'We will go,' said Spiro, taking his grandson by the hand. 'There's a new yacht on the horizon and I have some excellent binoculars. Perhaps the captain will wave to us. Before we go, ask Anna if she has some fruit, Theo. We need food for our journey.'

Spiro winked at Tess and walked away to wait for Theo on the steps.

'I can do the welcome if it helps,' Nic offered, taking his hat off and placing it carefully behind the bar.

Tess accepted gratefully, even though Nic wasn't really needed at this quiet hour. He never made things more difficult, never asked anything of her, nor questioned her moods or decisions. That meant so much more than any email from an old friend in England, or the well-intentioned but casual 'How are you?' delivered with a concerned face by many others.

Tess knew, or at least felt, that they didn't really want to hear how it really felt to be a widow. Even after only a few weeks had passed, it had seemed, understandably perhaps, that others had already moved on with their lives and expected her to do the same.

Slowly, she had adjusted and learned to live with a differently shaped family – part of which was Nic. And in the summer, when his Panama hat lay behind the bar and he sat with Theo and Spiro just enjoying the silence between good friends, or talking animatedly about the beauty of Corfu's ancient ruined city of Paleopolis, all seemed well.

Nic was a unique and, at times, bafflingly vague man, but she realized he embodied a key part of the armour she wore to face the world.

Even when he wasn't here.

Chapter 18

The journey home from Mouse Island was quiet. The afternoon sun had crept stealthily upon the group and sapped their energy, even before they returned to the car.

Penny glanced at a dozing Lily on the back seat, earbuds in place as she half-listened to her music, no doubt tired by the heat and her earlier revelations. Rich stared out of the window, thoughtful, reminiscent of a tired child after a day at the seaside. Guy glanced at his phone as the scenery flew by, then turned to Penny.

'You didn't tell us the reason you're here and all the Durrells stuff. Why are you so interested in them?'

Penny sighed. 'It started twenty years or so ago, when my dad gave me Gerald Durrell's book *My Family and Other Animals*. I was 13, covered in spots, and it was a miserable February Sunday afternoon. Can you imagine turning the pages to find all this?' Penny gestured at the sea in its best watercolour blue and the deep green cypress trees swaying rhythmically in the breeze. 'I loved it so much that I promised myself I'd come here one day. I always assumed it might be with my dad or a friend. But I broke up with my fiancé at the end of last year, at the same time as my dad died. So, that's why I'm here now, on my own, enjoying the first chance I've had to make it happen – a dream come true, if you like, but not quite the way I imagined.'

Guy shifted in the passenger seat and adjusted his seatbelt. He hadn't expected the answer she'd given and wanted to be reassured she wasn't about to cry.

'So, how's it been so far? Why is it *not* quite the way you imagined?' he asked.

'It's everything I thought it would be, but still nothing like I imagined. Does that make sense?' Penny said eventually. 'The original Strawberry Villa isn't there any more, but it sort of is, as the view, the smells, the hillside, the trees, the sea haven't moved. I looked out at one of the olive trees clinging to the hillside behind and wondered if Gerry had ever climbed it, or dozed under it, with Roger the dog lying by his side.'

Guy thought about all the things he'd tried to be positive about in life. So far, his approach had yielded nothing other than disappointment. Things had been everything he'd hoped they *wouldn't* be, and just how he'd imagined. His family had never been the same after the day his mother announced she was going to live with someone else.

'Yes, I see what you mean. At least, I think you mean you're glad you're here.'

'Yes, I am,' Penny responded and smiled, conscious that Guy had leapfrogged over the break-up and her dad's death.

'Great!' Guy replied.

For the last few miles of the pleasant, winding road back to St George South, Penny drove in companionable silence.

On Corfu at a certain point in the day, the heat sometimes overpowered visitors and residents alike, and the cool of an air-conditioned room beckoned. For some, if out on the water, the sea air took the tiredness out of the humidity and a contemplative doze, or behatted sunbathe, replaced the full-on nap. After a day out, all four travellers were ready for time apart and a change of pace.

As they parted outside the Athena, Guy and Rich went into the bar, and Penny and Lily walked home, down the small lane.

Penny began to climb the marbled steps to her apartment as Lily wandered on to her staff accommodation. 'I'm in Apartment 10 if you need anything,' Penny called after her.

Lily waved her thanks and kept walking.

Penny mused how a place could be so exhilarating and energizing and yet leave her, at times, with a lethargy that almost felt like being drunk. Sensory overload? Too many new sights and experiences to process? Perhaps. But the less time there was to brood on recent months, the better. Today she'd seen someone else trapped in a similar way, but starting, she hoped, to share and acknowledge her pain.

She passed a couple in their thirties and noticed they were holding hands and carrying their beach towels, probably on their way to the pool. There was nothing like seeing an affectionate couple to bring home the stark reality of being on her own; to remember how it felt to have a partner, make plans, feel secure.

And Penny saw them everywhere – or at least noticed them more. She remembered a friend telling her that after she'd had a miscarriage, she'd seen a pregnant woman every time she turned a corner.

In the cool refuge of her room, her shoulders drooped and exhaustion hit her as she sat down on the bed, then flopped backwards with a sigh onto the soft cotton covers.

Flashbacks of Bruce when they'd first met appeared,

causing her forehead to crease in a mixture of sadness and annoyance. Why did he keep making unwelcome visits, pushing his way into her head? The voicemail she'd decided to ignore was still not forgotten.

The remembered morsels and memories of happiness were just that – snapshots, rare moments and from long ago. In reality, now Penny had a chance to look back from a safe distance, their relationship had felt more like a habit than a happy union.

In moments of solitude, when the walls didn't so much close in as host shadow-puppet vignettes of the good bits of her life with Bruce, she found herself raking back over the ashes of what had gone wrong and why.

Splitting up had been a relief, but even so, *right* wasn't always easy and the dark room intensified her desolation and sadness. The fact that the only person she might have shared all of these thoughts with – her dad – had gone, completed the circle of grief.

With these thoughts running unbidden around her head, she fell into a dream-infused and sketchy sleep.

Chapter 19

That Sunday night the Athena evoked a quiet, mellow feeling that was unusual in the middle of a busy season, despite the natural lull between departing guests and those about to arrive.

Nic sat by the entrance with Spiro and Theo. The yacht Spiro and Theo had gone to look at more closely twinkled on the horizon, lit up like a small precious jewel, blinking from its anchorage.

A large coach pulled up outside and two reps from another tour company hopped off, as the driver started to unload the suitcases and holdalls. Tess looked across at Nic with a wry smile, as if to say, 'Here we go. Give them twenty minutes to settle into their rooms and they'll be back for food.'

There were of course many excellent options when it came to dining in St George, but as the coaches quite often dropped off new holidaymakers near the Athena, and as it looked so inviting, on guests' first night the restaurant was invariably a popular choice, for which Tess felt eternally grateful.

With the foaming edges of the sea below and the beautifully arranged tables, the restaurant's setting conveyed the impression it had been staged by a theatrical set designer – a homage to technicolour dreams and the undiluted charisma of Grace Kelly and Cary Grant.

Tess recollected sitting at a table by the sea with Georgios, on their first date. She had never smiled so much or felt so relaxed and happy. No doubt the passage of time, accompanied by hindsight and reflection, added an extra glow to the powerful memory.

Back at the bar, as Nic placed some clean glasses back on the shelves, Tess paused to whisper, 'I think we'd better check that there's a bottle of champagne or prosecco on ice.' She nodded discreetly in the direction of a table she'd just guided a young couple to.

'Ah, so you think you've detected an imminent proposal?' Nic raised his eyebrows in mock excitement.

'Maybe,' said Tess. 'Care for a bet?'

'I would be foolish to accept, as I'm clearly in the presence of a gifted psychic and relationship expert,' Nic replied and laughed.

'Something funny?' Lily asked, stepping behind the bar and picking up her apron and order pad.

'Tess thinks the couple over at the far table may be engaged by the end of the evening.' Nic tapped the side of his nose.

'Well, she's usually right about that sort of thing,' Lily responded, tying back her hair as she spoke.

'On to other matters – why are you here?' Tess asked. 'It's your day off.'

'I had a day off and then a good sleep, and thought you might need some help with the new-arrivals rush. I hadn't got anything planned for the rest of the night.'

'I can see I'm not needed here,' Nic said. 'My godson has disappeared with his grandfather, and I have a parrot that needs company,' he joked. 'Seriously though,' Nic continued,

'I do have some papers I need to look at. As you know, even in the holidays, Athens and the one or two students who don't know how to stop, keep me on my toes.'

'I absolutely understand the "being kept on your toes" bit.' Tess smoothed the front of her dress and added, 'I'm going to check on that champagne and prosecco . . . just in case.'

'I've promised Theo I'll be back on Wednesday to take him out to the olive mill. I've arranged with Kostas for him to see the whole process. The mill isn't running, but all the machinery, the groves, the donkeys, and the shop can be visited.'

'He'll love that, Nic, and so I will let you go. I can't bear to think of Ulysses with no one to talk to all evening.'

Nic grabbed his Panama and waved goodnight.

Chapter 20

Penny woke from a sleep in which she'd emptied the overfilled filing cabinet of her head into a series of disconnected, anxious, and frighteningly real dreams. The atmosphere they'd created remained with her as she opened the shutters to let in the warmth and the dying rays of mellow light.

One of the many scenes that had played out featured the hospice that had become like a second home in the last weeks of her dad's life. In her dream, through an open window, she could hear a car horn every few seconds, and knew it was Bruce, sitting in his old sports car, angry and impatient, expecting her to run out and leave with him.

Even the Durrells had made an appearance, joining her for a brief moment in Corfu Town as she sat with a coffee and cake, and they reassured her that they'd never left and were so glad she'd come to visit.

Still feeling odd and disorientated, although glad to be awake, Penny showered and found comfort in the simple routine of washing, dressing, and drying her hair.

As she walked along the now-familiar lane, the small lamps lit up as she passed them, and she knew that she'd head straight for the Athena for dinner. Her more adventurous friends might have said, 'Why not try somewhere new? This is your chance to do whatever you like.'

But I am doing whatever I like, thought Penny as she walked across the small road to the Athena. *This is what I like.*

As her mobile buzzed unheard in her bag, she couldn't help wondering if Dimitris would be there. There was no reason why he should be, he had his own place in Corfu Town, but then again if he was fishing tomorrow . . .

Located at her favourite table, Penny relaxed into her chair and took a few deep breaths of the evening air. The tang of dusty earth and wild mint wafted from the surrounding mountains.

From the safety of her quiet corner and cradling her glass of rosé, she looked around at her fellow diners. As she'd adapted to the ebb and flow of the life and landscape of Corfu and begun to know some of the people a little better, Penny found herself becoming fiercely protective of them and their island.

A couple of days before, a man had sent back a plate of food because, he said, the sausages weren't 'proper English sausages' and the beans tasted funny. It wasn't, he added in a loud voice, clearly enjoying having an audience, as good as anything he'd get at home.

Anna had added her own version of a traditional English breakfast to the menu because so many people asked for it, and it was beautifully cooked, with the best ingredients she could find, to match the British staples most closely.

Penny hated the man's rudeness and hubris. There were those who visited the island, fell in love with it, and never wanted to go anywhere else. Others enjoyed the weather and the beaches, but found the village they were in too quiet, or too loud, or − as one tourist had once bizarrely declared to Tess − 'too Greek'. Last but not least, there were those who fitted the category of the loud man: the ones who come on holiday to find fault, to compare whatever they were presented with, with everything they had experienced on previous holidays.

Penny had watched Tess's smooth and calm handling of the man's self-righteous indignation, as she removed his breakfast from his bill, and offered an alternative second breakfast.

Tess had deflated him with kindness and concern; more, if she was honest, for the sake of his slightly nervous and pale-faced wife, their two small children, and everyone else enjoying their food. It was, of course, although rare, all part of the day-to-day experience of running a restaurant and apartments.

Thankfully, the smiling faces and the usual vibrant atmosphere of the Athena were all present and correct this evening. Nic was at home, Spiro with Theo, and there was no sign of Dimitris or his father. Penny imagined Dimitris sailing on the *Antiopi*. If he was still on board there was little chance, she concluded, that he'd be in the Athena tonight. After seeing the yacht that day, having a sudden sense of the weeks passing too quickly, she had made up her mind to book her place for a trip up to Kalami when she saw him next.

That particular place was beginning to acquire more significance than a personal pilgrimage, more resonance because he would now be taking her there.

She'd played the film of her Corfu adventure in her head on a loop for weeks after she'd booked it in the dark, brackish days of winter, imagining scenes of breathtaking beauty, colourful tavernas, and unforgettable encounters. The details of people and places had been sketchy in her head, but all had the Durrells and their story woven delicately into every scene she placed herself in.

Now, here she was in a new story; a story of her own. The previous books and chapters of her life were still part of who she was, but this time, here in Corfu felt different – a newly drafted text and an opportunity to live and move forward.

The music and murmuring across the restaurant suddenly stopped. A tall man with a beard had stood up and was now getting down on one knee. Everyone seemed to be holding their breath, sharing surprised or knowing looks, and putting a finger to their lips, signalling children to be quiet.

From where she was sitting Penny didn't hear the words the man said, but suddenly a small fair-haired woman jumped up and was kissing the man, who lifted her up and hugged her tightly. Penny realized it was the couple she'd passed earlier.

There was applause all around and then the popping of a champagne cork. Tess caught Penny's eye and for both women a second of unspoken sisterhood passed between them: from one who had broken off an engagement; and the other who'd been broken by the loss of a husband.

Lily appeared next to Penny's table. 'Tess guessed this was going to happen as soon as they walked in earlier.' She refilled Penny's glass from the little carafe on her table as she spoke.

'Did she?' Penny responded. 'Perhaps she could read the body language, or maybe she had one of those feelings you get sometimes, when you know things . . . things that are yet to happen.'

'Do you ever get that feeling?' Lily looked at Penny.

'Sometimes. Usually when I least expect it. I think most of us do, even if we don't acknowledge it.'

Lily looked thoughtful and then spoke. 'I don't get those feelings. But I wish I did.'

Before Penny had time to say anything else, Lily walked

back to the bar, picking up empty glasses from tables as she went, stopping briefly with practised ease to take more orders.

The music returned; the background chatter resumed. The frisson of recent events filled the air. The sea below leapt up towards the wall and fell back onto the rocks with a hiss and a sigh. Penny's eye fixed on the yacht across the bay, imagining sophisticated folk at an elegant party on board, and recalled an awkward, smart university dinner she'd attended with Bruce. Gauche, a little anxious, and wanting to be somewhere else, she'd felt like a fish out of water.

'Bright chatting', as her dad had once described slightly vacuous, semi-formal conversations, was not her forte. She had smiled throughout the dinner, which Bruce thoroughly enjoyed, but her mind had lingered in her studio, painting.

At the time it hadn't really mattered that she didn't have fun, but after other differences in temperament and character had become too numerous to ignore, she now looked back and observed the relationship with all its cracks and fault lines.

A hand on her shoulder brought her back into the present. 'A nightcap on the house?' Tess asked. 'Would you like to sit with me at the bar?'

Penny nodded and followed. Once at the bar with a brandy – a relatively new experience for Penny – she felt a little self-conscious. She'd always been more of a glass-of-wine-at-home girl, curled up with a book.

She straightened her back as she adjusted her weight on the high bar stool and checked her balance. She had to concede that this elevated position provided a panoramic view. Messages, cards, and photos from loyal customers of the Athena, who returned year after year, created a collage of happiness and good times along the bar: summer stories revisited on colder, harsher winter days.

Tess saw her looking. 'We're very lucky. We have people who come back every year, to stay in the apartments, or just to eat.'

'I can see why they do,' said Penny, taking another sip of her brandy and beginning to enjoy the warming sensation in her stomach. 'What do you do in the winter?' she asked. 'Do you stay here?'

'No, we move closer to town. We have a villa near Gouvia, which is ideal for Theo's school and his friends there. We close here at the end of October and everyone huddles together, gathering around the town if you like. I love that, particularly as we get a chance to see friends who have their own seasonal businesses, as we don't really get a chance to catch up from May to October.' She stopped to take an order from Lily, reached for two bottles of beer, and handed them over.

Penny imagined how lovely it would be to sit down with Tess away from her work, in a quiet time, with the luxury of space and calm. She instinctively felt a kinship with this woman who carried, with seeming ease, the randomness and sometimes swift cruelties that life could bring. She was also quirky and kind.

Staring for a moment at the golden-brown liquid, viscous and inviting at the bottom of her glass, Penny noticed her hands, usually pale and almost translucent in hue, were turning brown, warm in tone, like copper.

How odd that her body reflected the changes she felt in her heart and mind. Her own sense of self was being rewritten in real time, partly by herself, but there were other forces at work, benign but unseen.

'Dimitris, I didn't think we'd see you this evening. Fishing tomorrow?'

Tess was already opening a bottle of lager to hand to the new arrival.

'Hi,' he responded, taking a seat next to Penny. 'Yes, we'll be sailing early, so it's easier to ride over now and stay here.'

Watching him take his first drink, Penny wondered if he'd acknowledge her presence with more than a nod, as they'd only spoken briefly and he'd been direct and not overly friendly. Why did she want him to look at her? Where did she think that might go? Why did she want to have a conversation with him? She'd seen him with the same woman twice. Even if it was a holiday fling, he was clearly engaged elsewhere. She could pick him out in a crowd from a distance, she realized. What was that all about? It had to be more than the sheer physicality of him, the way he looked and moved.

Suddenly she heard her voice from far away. 'We saw you today, sailing near Mouse Island.'

He looked straight at her and it seemed like an eternity before he answered. So long in fact, she wondered if he'd heard her. She noticed he was dressed more smartly than she'd seen him before, in chinos and a blue and white striped shirt. She could not read him as he met her gaze, but she had to hold her nerve and resist the temptation to smile inanely or look away. Did he always look so directly at people, even when – and she could feel the resistance, almost petulance from him – he was bored or feigning disinterest? Was he humouring her by noticing her at all?

'I took some people up to Kalami, but they wanted to go south first. How did you know it was the *Antiopi*?'

Penny felt as though she was being cross-examined. 'Guy spotted you. He stood and waved, but you couldn't have seen him. Your boat is beautiful,' she added, because it was true – the yacht was a sleek craft, like a sea creature with elegant lines and an inherent smoothness through the water. It was suddenly important to her for him to know that.

He looked at her again and she had her first real

opportunity to study his face, at the same time fighting the impulse to look down again and away from his gaze. He was fascinating, with a sculpted head, she'd noted before, but up close she discovered grey eyes, dark hair wanting to curl, a shadow of stubble, and a nose that would have looked out of place, had it been smaller, in the midst of so many strong features fighting for her attention.

The overall impression was one of solidity, but there was also something otherworldly and illusory, something hidden too. It reminded her of what her dad used to say about what mattered about a person: the flame behind the face. The impassive face that Dimitris presented to the world masked a flame behind it, but for some reason it didn't reach his eyes.

Then, to her surprise, she felt he knew what she was thinking and finally, she glanced down. If she'd raised her eyes, she would perhaps have been comforted by the fact that he appeared as discomfited as she.

'Thank you. She is very beautiful. I'm lucky to have her.' His voice was quiet, but deserved her attention and eye contact.

Tess poured Penny another brandy. 'Thank you again for taking Spiro and Theo out last week,' she said. 'I now have a son who's as obsessed with what's in the water as on the land. If the apartment was bigger, I'd probably have given in to his constant nagging for an aquarium by now.'

'Perhaps you'll be able to enjoy a day off and come for a sail, when things are a little quieter here. Nic too if he's still here,' Dimitris suggested.

'Now that would be great. I'll have to find my old deck shoes, not to mention my sense of adventure and capacity for fun.' Tess winked and walked off into the kitchen.

'So, are you still wanting to sail up to Kalami?' Dimitris asked.

'Yes, I'd like to go up there towards the end of my stay, in a week or so, but now I've seen your boat, I don't think I can afford to charter it just for myself. So perhaps I could be part of a group?'

'Okay. I'll give you some dates. Do you have any plans? Days when you're not free before you fly home?'

When Penny heard 'when you fly home' the idea felt like a threat rather than a fact of life.

'Yes, a few, but at the moment there are no set days for anything. I had a feeling before I came here that Kalami would be a highlight, so I can always change other things to suit your sailing schedule, if you give me enough notice.'

'That's fine,' he said, his face closed, giving nothing away.

The ensuing silence caused Penny to wish she possessed the 'bright-chatting' gene, but before she had the chance to think of anything to say Tess returned and Penny took the opportunity to slide off the high bar stool.

As she did so, she caught her sandal on the side of the stool. Penny put her hand out to steady herself on the bar and felt a sudden shock along her arm as a strong, callused hand steadied her. Dimitris held her firmly. Her heart raced at his sudden touch.

'Thank you.' She met his gaze as she managed to plant two feet back on the ground.

'You okay?' he asked, his expression unchanged.

'Yes. I think I'm too short to get down from a bar stool without injury or incident.'

'You're just fine,' he replied, his face still impassive.

Tess came to the front of the bar and put her arm on Penny's as Dimitris released his hand. 'I haven't even had a chance to ask you what sort of a day you had with Lily and the boys,' she said.

'It was great. Guy planned it all out and we went to all

the places I wanted to see. The only thing missing was the Durrells themselves, although I think they were probably there. At least, it felt as though they were to me. Imagination can be a powerful thing, can't it?'

Penny stopped herself, conscious that when she started talking about the Durrells she had a tendency to go off into another world.

'The Durrells? Hence Kalami.' Dimitris nodded, as though a penny had dropped.

Penny moved towards the entrance and then turned back to Dimitris. 'I hope we can work something out for the trip.'

'I hope so too,' His tone was formal, but a little warmer. 'Call me. Tess has my number.'

Penny couldn't work out if this was the yacht-owner's response, or the man's. He exuded an air of reserved politeness – words weighed in his head, but were not always spoken, which in some ways, she guessed, was a move forward from brusque indifference.

As she stepped out of the Athena, Penny noticed a motorbike she hadn't seen before. *It probably belongs to Dimitris*, she thought. He'd said he'd *ridden* over.

She'd never ridden a motorbike, or been a passenger. There were so many things she wanted to do. This was a revelatory moment. She wanted to do things, try things, experience the world. She was a woman travelling alone. It may not have been extraordinary for some, but this was something she'd never done before, had never really thought of doing. She was here now and had been drinking brandy in a bar with new people she didn't know last week, within touching, kissing, distance of someone who interested her. Attracted her. The last two words sounded in her head like a fanfare – or was it a wake-up call?

Footsteps sounded behind her. 'Penny?'

Dimitris caught her up and handed her a small plaited leather bracelet.

'Tess thinks this might be yours. It was on the floor.'

Penny took the friendship band she'd bought in the local market and felt her wrist, realizing it must have come loose when his hand had steadied her. She felt her face colour and was glad it was dark.

'Thank you. I'm glad it's not lost.'

She smiled up at him, realizing for the first time how tall he was, as they stood toe to toe.

'You're welcome. *Kalinichta.*'

'*Kalinichta.*'

Penny felt a sudden impulse to call him back and make an arrangement there and then to sail up to Kalami, to make him stay a moment longer, to hear him say her name again. Then her mobile rang.

Surprised and vaguely panicked at the same time, she dived into her rucksack trying to find her phone, aware as she did so of Dimitris heading back to the Athena.

As she pulled the phone out of the bag the ring became louder, almost deafening.

She glanced down at the caller ID.

Bruce.

Chapter 21

The following day, the sun rose in the mountains behind the harbour at St George, warming the air with its reassuring promise. For a few minutes a golden-grey, almost tentative light defined the shapes on shore and glanced across the top of the waves.

Dimitris squinted as he stared up at the distant hills and sky. Another day in the small boat – the *Dora*, named after his late mother – would give him a chance to think. He and his father had mastered the art of comfortable silence.

Yesterday's trip along the coast had gone smoothly. The people he'd taken had been thrilled. The *Antiopi* was always spotless and meticulously maintained. Dimitris knew the coastline of Corfu well, had mapped almost every rock and shallow in his head, having sailed there all his life.

He'd practised his seamanship almost daily since he'd returned home, and didn't underestimate the power of the sea. No fishing trip or excursion trumped being safe. The world was already overflowing with random acts of hurt and loss, and to add to these would be reckless.

Even his motorbike was a convenience, combined with the joy of smelling the air and feeling the breeze, rather than being about a need for speed. Life had taught him one thing: keep your loved ones close. Right now, he treasured his father, and recognized the responsibility and privilege of watching over him. His mother had slipped away when he wasn't looking. It never occurred to Dimitris that his father might have wished for his son to find his own life again, on or off the island.

Today several things occupied space in his head without invitation. Two women to be precise.

The Sunday cruise had gone smoothly. Once he'd greeted and settled his guests, he'd pointed out sites of interest onshore as they passed, but he had been aware as they left Garitsa Bay that one of the party, a young woman in her late twenties, had planted herself very firmly in his eyeline. Throughout the day whenever he looked up, he met her gaze. From behind her sunglasses, he sensed her scrutiny or, if he'd been a vain man – which he was not –her admiration.

His passengers disembarked for lunch at a bay where one of the most celebrated tavernas in Corfu nestled on an idyllic beach. Alicia, for that was the attentive woman's name, insisted that he join them rather than stay on the yacht.

He would have preferred to stay on the boat, as small talk wasn't his forte, but something about this Englishwoman's confidence reminded him of Sally, and for the first time in ages that felt like something he could deal with.

Alicia's friends seemed like a nice bunch of people, all old school friends, and their holiday was a kind of reunion. As they'd left *Antiopi* that evening Dimitris had been sorry to see them go, and then Alicia had turned back and handed him a piece of paper on which she'd hastily written her mobile number.

'We're having dinner tomorrow night at the Rex in town. Come along. As you know, we don't bite, even when we've had a few glasses of wine.' She'd kissed him very lightly on the cheek, touched his hand as she turned, then left.

A few hours later on the harbourside in the first light of a Monday morning, he remained undecided about whether to join Alicia and her friends. She was a very attractive girl, full of fun, and her friends were pleasant and good company, but he'd avoided socializing, staying away from gatherings, even within his wider group of childhood friends, and had forgotten how it felt to be with people. In a conscious attempt to remove himself in every possible way from any connection with the lifestyle he'd had in London, Dimitris had turned keeping himself to himself into an art form.

Apart from his father, Nic, Tess, Theo, Spiro and an old school friend, Niko, and his family in Corfu Town, Dimitris inhabited a very small circle, expanded only by casual acquaintances, who knew him by sight or had known him since he was a boy.

It was almost as though he considered any deeper connections, let alone relationships, an unwelcome intrusion. In some ways it came down to simple maths: the fewer people he knew or welcomed into his world, the less chance there was of being hurt, or hurting others – or being distracted, unless it was clear from the start that the connection was only temporary, had no chance of developing into something deeper.

Old friends from Italy and London appeared for the occasional holiday, the most recent being Pamela, the woman Penny had seen him with in Corfu Town and the Athena. Catching up with her had been an easy and pleasurable encounter, but had also convinced him that although he was pleased to keep in touch, he didn't miss his previous life.

The second woman occupying his attention was the English girl, Penny, who always seemed to be in the Athena, painting or chatting to Tess. He found it unusual for someone of her age to be on her own: women her age often came in pairs, as part of a group, or with a boyfriend.

Surely, he thought, she hadn't chosen to be on her own for this trip? For someone who was en route to perfecting the art of solitude, Dimitris ironically couldn't understand why someone else would choose to be alone.

He paused, deep in thought. There was something about her that was . . . He stepped onto the boat, holding the heavy oil-stained rope that secured the boat to the harbourside ironwork, and struggled to think of the word. Then it came: *different*. She was unusual. Not alluring or sexy in a way that hit you when she walked into a room, but he had still noticed her the moment he saw her. She was a pretty girl – prettier than she probably acknowledged herself – and she dressed in an interesting way. Tess had said she was an artist, which maybe explained the floaty dresses and quirky hat. Whatever it was, he felt drawn towards her.

He'd already begun to notice that he looked for her when he arrived at the Athena, which had surprised him. Where had that come from? Why was he even thinking about her? Giving anyone space in his head, allowing himself to let life in all its glorious, random messiness back in, was not part of his plan.

⌒⌒

The *Dora* wasn't in the harbour when Penny wandered past. Shielding her eyes, she looked across at the horizon towards the island of Paxos, shimmering, elusive, inviting. The sea looked calm, set fair for another day of uninterrupted sunshine.

Removing her sandals as she reached the beach, she carried on walking towards the sea, lifting her face towards the sun, her skin glowing and the gentlest of breezes lifting strands of hair from her forehead.

'If you're out there, dear gods, and you're not feeling vengeful or mardy today, give me a sign,' she muttered to herself. 'Tell me what I should do about Bruce. Why is he calling me? If I ignore him, will it make it worse? What do you think?'

Her gut instinct the night before had been to let the mobile ring until silence was restored, with the reassuring chirp of the cicadas dominating the soundscape. Then as she'd reached the apartment the buzz from her phone told her she had another voicemail.

She had listened to the message sitting quietly on the balcony, staring up at the stars. 'You have one new message.' She put the phone on the table as though it was too hot to hold, as Bruce's message filled the air:

'Penny, it's me. I hope you got my last message.' There was a moment's pause. 'I really wanted to talk to you. How are you? I'm coming back to the UK next week and I wondered if we could meet up. It'd be good to see you, but call me, please. Take care, Penny.'

The tone of his voice as he said 'Take care, Penny' was soft and, for Bruce, usually so confident and assured, a little uncertain.

As she relived the call, weighing each word, and reading many meanings into each sentence, she felt her natural curiosity kick in. Why had he rung? Why now? Why did he want to see her? Why call from Italy . . . again? Couldn't it have waited? He could have rung her once he got back to the UK. If he was talking about them meeting in England next week then he clearly expected her to be at home by then.

The elephant in the room was whether or not she responded to the message – and how.

As she sat on the sands, elbows resting on her knees, her head naturally fell into her hands. Whether it was in her own head or from beyond, a voice told her, 'This can wait. You don't have to do anything right now. The answer will come. All is well.'

Chapter 22

Guy and Rich had arrived early that morning at the airport, ready to greet passengers from two flights that had landed five minutes apart. They were both a little weary, having stretched their day into the early hours in Corfu Town. Once the new arrivals found their way onto the coaches, Rich and Guy separated: one headed to Kavos; the other to St George South.

Rich grinned to himself. They'd tossed a coin to see which bus each would take, and he'd *won* St George South. He wanted to see Lily, catch a glimpse of her as he helped the passengers disembark and settled them into their accommodation.

He realized that Lily hadn't shared something with them the day before — namely, why she wasn't going back to university — and he wanted to know. Lily had clearly shared something with Penny, and it was fine if she didn't want to say anything else; but genuine concern filled his mind. He didn't like to think that she was unhappy. It unsettled him more than he would have expected.

As the passengers adjusted to the heat, with the usual post-flight relief of landing and excitement about their holiday beginning to start, Rich handed out the Greektime maps and leaflets. After the welcome chat, including the itinerary for hotel stops, he nodded to Aeneas, the driver, and they set off along the southbound coastal road.

⟨⟩

Guy couldn't wait to get to Kavos. The bus was full and the chatter loud. Most of those on their way to the southern tip of the island were Guy's age or a few years older.

They had a week – or if lucky, two – to eat, drink, sunbathe, swim, read, sleep . . . or not . . . and repeat each day. Feeling fragile after a late night, Guy couldn't shake off his tiredness that morning. The banter and bustle of the new arrivals normally energized him as the life and soul of the party, the rep with all the answers, who knew where everything was, including where to go and where not to go.

If he thought about it – he didn't want to, but it kept coming back like an ear worm – the trip to Kanoni and Penny's story about why she was here had strangely disturbed him.

The fact that there was also something up with Lily had made him think: she seemed so bright and upbeat, but everything wasn't as it seemed. She wasn't going back to uni for her final year and that was a big decision to make. Concern, as well as curiosity, made him want to know why she'd made that choice.

Yesterday's trip had also reminded him in some ways of what family felt like: a day out with people you liked and wanted to be with; a day when he'd had the chance to be the organizer, to share his local knowledge, such as the baklava at Benitses.

That sharing, collective enjoyment of a moment was something he realized he missed at home, or at least with his father and Lucy. The word 'home' had so many connotations and attachments.

He missed the time *before*, when his parents had been together. The *after* formed a void, and those few hours – an excursion in a car, a shared meal, the baklava, the boat trip to Mouse Island – had brought back a wave of what had been.

There was no point in reminding himself. He needed to grow up and crack on.

Finally, at Kavos, he helped the driver pull the luggage from the side of the coach. Guy grabbed hold of a large cream-coloured holdall with a bright yellow ribbon tied around the handle.

A girl came forward, and held out her right hand tentatively. 'That's mine. Thank you.' As he handed her the bag Guy felt the weight of it and was conscious of the small hands and stature of the red-haired girl. It was almost as big as her, he thought.

She swung it stoically to one side, her small frame lopsided now, her hair like a golden red curtain falling on one shoulder. She looked strong and determined, even in the execution of this mundane task. She rejoined her friend, who was as tall as she was short. The tall girl bent down to her short Titian-haired pal and whispered something. The red girl shook her head, then looked back at Guy.

Suddenly she reappeared. 'Are all the details about the excursions and buses and places to visit in the leaflets?' She looked up at him and before he could answer, asked, 'Will you be at the welcome meeting this afternoon? Is that part of what you do?'

She sounded earnest and a little gauche, as though she'd never been abroad before. Maybe it was her first time abroad without her parents.

'Yes, for my sins, it's part of what I do,' Guy responded,

disarmed by the sincerity and tone of her question, so different from the self-confident and frequently cheeky, flirtatious approach he was used to.

'Thank you.' The grey eyes that met his had an almost melancholy look that was offset by a wide and generous smile.

'You're welcome. What did you say your name was?'

'I didn't, but I'm Faith.'

She extended her hand for Guy to shake.

Chapter 23

In times of doubt, anxiety or sadness there were two things that Penny had always turned to: books and painting. Never in her thirty-three years had they let her down, even during the heaviest of days when she couldn't focus on the words or the work in front of her, when tears had dropped onto the pages, blurring her vision or the paint.

So, as she left the beach, her mind quietened by the answer she felt she'd just had from the gods, as well as her paints, she also had her copy of Gerry Durrell's *Corfu Trilogy*, well-thumbed and slightly grubby now. She hoped the powerful combination of these items would lift her today and give her some perspective on Bruce's voicemail.

She almost felt sorry for him. Even his faults, unkindness, and inherent selfishness did not exclude him from her instinctive goodwill to all things.

First things first though. Breakfast.

⌣

Greek yogurt in all its creamy glory was never more glorious than when accompanied by dark, Greek pine honey, not as rare as the lighter-coloured thyme variety, but a deep amber colour with a taste that delighted time and time again. Penny was resisting the temptation to lift the bowl and lick the sticky residue from the glass bowl, when Spiro appeared at her side with a small dish of strawberries.

'For you, from me and Anna.' He placed the bowl on the table and then to Penny's surprise and delight, sat down. 'It's good, isn't it? The honey?'

Penny smiled, wondering for just a microsecond if he'd guessed she was thinking about licking the bowl. 'Everything's good.'

'Tess tells me you're here because of the Durrell family and their story on Corfu.'

'Yes. They sort of pulled me here. I've wanted to come for a long time.'

'So, was it the book? The family and animals' book? Did you read it and think, *that island sounds amazing, I must go there?*' he teased her kindly.

'I did.' She smiled back.

'My home, the Corfu I know, lives in those pages,' Spiro said. 'It's changed in some places, but Corfu is still here, still beautiful.'

'It is very beautiful,' Penny agreed. 'I thought I knew what it would be like before I came here, but I couldn't have imagined this.' Penny looked at Paxos on the far horizon across the sea.

'Tess said that you met Gerald Durrell.' Penny hoped Spiro wouldn't mind her bringing it up.

'I did, a long time ago. I was very young, about 18, I think, and I saw the two brothers, Gerald and Lawrence in the 1960s.'

Penny couldn't conceal her excitement. This was a connection, however small, she hadn't expected – meeting someone who had seen and met members of the family.

'I was working in a small bar in town, in the old town just around the corner from Arseniou. I think they were staying in a house there. I'm not sure.'

'Which bar?' Penny asked as Lily placed two coffees on the table.

'The bar? It was just around the corner from the Liston, but it's not there any more. I think there's a jewellery shop in the building now. It was small, a little dark inside, and so better to sit outside.

'They came on a few nights. I didn't know at first who they were, but Nico, my boss, did. He asked them to sign a piece of paper, which I think he framed. They didn't look like brothers. The younger, Gerald, was very tall. Lawrence was small.'

'Were they nice?' Penny knew this was probably the blandest and most insipid question to ask, but it just came out. She needed to hear good things about the people she'd grown so fond of over two decades, while also acknowledging their likely human failings, faults, and frailties – the essence of their humanity. When people spoke about the Durrells, it felt as though they were speaking about her own family.

Spiro continued. 'I didn't have much conversation with them. I was serving drinks. But one thing I did notice was that Gerald Durrell looked at his brother with affection and respect . . . looked up to him, I think. I observed this before I knew who they were. My friend Stavros told me they were famous writers. I learned later that both of them had written about Corfu and lived here before the war. They were here for a holiday, staying in a house on Arseniou that belonged to a relative of Mr Stephanides.'

'Theo Stephanides?'

'Yes, the famous Theo.' Spiro smiled. 'Please don't tell him, but our Nic – you've met Nic, haven't you?' Penny

149

nodded. 'He reminds me of Mr Stephanides: his interest in the land, the plants, the sea, and all the creatures. It's what he teaches in Athens too, at the university . . . marine biology.

'There's no more I can really tell you, Penny. There are still others here who knew them well, who might have bigger stories to tell.' Spiro drained his coffee cup.

'It's enough to be sitting here listening to someone who met them,' Penny said. 'Believe me, this is a highlight of my stay so far, Spiro. I love hearing about them being here. It makes it all real somehow.' Penny wasn't sure why she felt so emotional. Perhaps because Spiro was older and reminded her of her father.

'You are very welcome. One note of caution: if you come across a rogue called Yannis while you're here, don't believe a word he says. I've heard him tell everyone so many untrue tales about the Durrells, Roger Moore, the old king, even Empress Sisi. He means no harm, but gets carried away because his grandmother knew someone, who knew someone, who knew Spiro Halikiopoulos . . . you know, the great friend of the Durrells, Spiro Americano. His family still lives here by the way. When they filmed the TV series here last year, Yannis was a menace.'

Spiro stood up and patted Penny's hand. 'Tess tells me you're planning a trip up the coast with Dimitris. Now, he knows many true stories. I know he seems quiet, distant sometimes, and that wasn't always so, but when you're on the boat to Kalami, ask him what he knows.'

'I will,' said Penny, wishing that she could ask him more about Dimitris and what he had been like before the distance and detachment.

Chapter 24

Spiro was wise, warm, full of careworn empathy. For a few minutes Penny stepped wholly and willingly into a new world that waited on the other side of her grief, her focus on what Spiro had related. Her stomach felt heavy, as thoughts of Bruce hovered once again, waiting to land, as the time they had discussed having children forced its way to the front of the queue.

He had said, 'Yes, at some point,' rather than being enthusiastic, and had quickly changed the subject. At the time, she'd thought he was caught up in the moment of being newly engaged and their plans for living together, rather than it being any indicator of his feelings about parenthood.

She couldn't pin down the exact moment she'd stopped feeling warm or confident about the idea of Bruce being a dad, but there must have been one. His impatience had been a key factor, followed by the realization that his impatience was primarily with anything or anyone that stood between Bruce and what Bruce wanted to do.

He could be charming and there had been friends who'd been bemused when she'd shared the news about their separation. 'Bruce? The tall, Heathcliff-clone Bruce? The handsome one?' She'd heard someone say once, 'Handsome is as handsome does', but she'd never really known what that meant.

Even if the relationship had become a habit, even if she wasn't sure she liked him any more, there was still history between them. She couldn't just forget the last few years of her life – yet. The memories of so many moments and shared experiences, time invested and friendships made as a couple, hadn't disappeared just because he was no longer in her life.

Penny wondered if, without the job offer in Italy, she and Bruce might have muddled along for longer. She admitted to herself that there had been times, even after they'd separated, when she might have been tempted to call him, in those shadowy, stark days after her dad had died. But what now? Even at a distance it felt like he'd reopened a closed book with his messages.

'You okay?' Lily was at her side with the coffee Spiro had promised her.

'I think so. I was miles away.' Penny smiled. Lily's arrival brought her back into the new reality of Corfu. 'How are you today?' Penny asked.

'I'm all right, thanks. Feel a bit better now actually, about Guy and Rich knowing that I'm not going back to uni . . . less pressure in my head somehow. I wasn't intending to keep it a secret. It just sort of became one,' she continued. 'I've told Tess now as well. She was great . . . like you. So, thanks.'

Tess wandered over. 'What's the plan for today?' She stood with one hand resting on her hip, cloth in hand.

'I'm wandering down to the harbour to paint, take photos, and probably just watch the sea for a while.' Penny almost added – *wanted* to add – *Bruce left me a message last night. He wants to see me. I'm not sure what to say or do*. But she didn't.

'That sounds good to me. We will be super busy today:

more arrivals expected at lunchtime and a welcome meeting. Ah, the heady excitement of it all.' She laughed at herself, as Theo ran up.

'Mama, it's Nic on the phone.' He handed her the unit. When she hung up Tess looked down at her son and pulled a disappointed face.

'Nic can't make it today. Something has come up with the university. He says he's sorry and will make it up to you later on this week.' She gave Theo a quick hug and he shrugged, looking up at his mama.

'It must be important,' he said simply.

Penny looked at the little boy and wondered at his calm acceptance of not being able to spend time with Nic. He was clearly disappointed.

'What was the plan?' Penny found herself saying.

'Monday is one of our busiest days, so Nic usually tries to take Theo to another beach, harbour, somewhere as a treat. But today he can't and that's unusual, so something very important must have come up with the university.'

'Would Theo like to come with me down to the harbour, to paint?' Penny heard herself say the words before she'd had time to think them through.

Theo nodded enthusiastically.

'I'll keep a close eye on him, I promise.'

'Are you sure? I mean, you've already got a vote of confidence from Theo, as you can see. If you're planning on painting for an hour or two, then lunch is on me, for both of you.' She laughed at Theo, who had rushed off to fetch his crayons and sketchpad.

'There's no need for the free lunch. It'll be fun and we'll be back for something to eat later.' Penny stood up and grabbed her rucksack.

Chapter 25

Nic sat on his terrace with his laptop and a pot of strong coffee on the table in front of him, checking his emails – a daily ritual through the summer.

In the villa behind him Ulysses chatted away to himself soothingly, Nic decided, with only a few words here and there that needed censoring. He skimmed casually through the collection of messages, half a mind on his plans to take Theo out for the day, to give the boy a change of scene and Tess a chance to cope with one of her busiest days.

Clicking on an email from Melina, his departmental colleague – a friend and someone Nic respected – the first few lines immediately grabbed his attention.

It was a message he had been half-expecting for a while, but somehow that didn't lessen his sadness or shock. She had decided to resign from her post for health reasons. Nic immediately wanted to help her, give her the support and space that would hopefully mean she didn't have to make such a drastic decision. He picked up his mobile, searched for a flight to Athens, and booked a ticket for that evening. Then he rang Tess.

He felt a pull in his stomach as he heard her voice, hating

the thought that he was letting her, and Theo, down. He apologized for not being able to take Theo out, as her usual kindness and understanding made light of it.

He knew she'd be fine: busy days were not a new phenomenon to Tess and she balanced many things. She'd told him once that losing Georgios had felt like looking over a cliff edge. It tripped him up too, especially when he passed old haunts that he and his best friend had made their own, a lifetime before Tess had even arrived on the island.

He looked at his watch. He had a few things to organize before the flight, but planned to pop into the Athena for something to eat after one o'clock.

As he walked into the house, he saw Annabelle, his neighbour, heading for her car. He raised his hand and called out to her. He needed to ask a favour . . . he hoped she liked parrots.

~~~

Penny and Theo walked slowly down the street, towards a spot by the rocks at the harbour entrance that provided some shelter if there was a breeze, and several views to choose from.

'I've got my best sketchbook with me and my new pencils from Nic. He brought them from Athens, from a special shop for artists like me. Although I'm not an artist all the time. Sometimes I'm a writer. Sometimes I help Mrs Papadopoulos with animals that need help, in St George. I have a badge at home, but I can show you later.'

Theo hardly paused for breath, as though he'd made a bet with someone to share his entire history, likes, dislikes, list of friends, and favourite foods with Penny before they reached the harbour.

She responded with the odd 'Really?' 'That's good', and 'I didn't know that', as she listened to his seamless monologue.

They turned left to follow the short dusty track down to the sea. Settling themselves at the edge of the water with the sun behind them, they started to unpack their pencils and sketchbooks. Penny noticed Theo's self-possession and quiet confidence as he set out his crayons and a bottle of orange juice in front of him.

A wave of compassion and tenderness towards him almost overwhelmed Penny as she watched. To lose a father at just 4 years old was beyond her comprehension. All the years of paternal love she had received felt more miraculous than ever. Gratitude blocked out her grief as its healing warmth embraced her. It was a blissful moment, her feet touching the water, the coolness of the gentle waves flowing over her skin.

'I'm going to draw the boats.' said Theo, his face a picture of concentration.

'Good plan. I think I'm going to look around for a minute or two and have a think about what I'd like to draw – see what catches my eye.'

As she said this, she saw a familiar little blue and white boat edge towards the harbour. Already she could make out the distinctive figure of Dimitris at the front gathering up some rope. Theo hadn't spotted it yet and Penny prepared herself for his inevitable reaction when he did. She decided to sit back, try and focus on the sketchpad in front of her, and go with the flow.

A few seconds later came the cry: 'It's the *Dora*!' Theo jumped to his feet and waved excitedly as the boat pulled into harbour.

'Dimitris!' Theo hailed his friend, who waved back and jumped ashore as the *Dora* bumped into her usual spot. Penny swung her legs back onto the side of the harbour and stood up.

Theo reached Dimitris in a few paces and threw himself at him. Dimitris responded with a smile and hugged his young friend as he looked over Theo's head at Penny. It was the first time she'd seen him smile. The effect was heart-stopping.

'So, you're painting today?' As he asked the question, he looked over at Penny again. The smile was still there.

'Yes, Nic couldn't come over, so Penny is my new friend. We're going to have lunch later, when I've drawn the boats.'

'Can I see?' Dimitris started to walk over to where they'd settled to draw. As he came closer Penny felt as though she wanted to move closer and step back at the same time. His closeness made her aware of every part of her body. The way she was standing – hands in pockets, her bare, damp feet planted on the stone path – felt defensive. What was she afraid of?

'We haven't really started yet,' she said.

'Perhaps you can show me your drawings when they're finished,' Dimitris said to Theo, then looked at Penny. 'I have to help my father with the catch. I'll see you both at the Athena later, I hope. Perhaps I can buy the artists a drink?'

As Dimitris turned and walked back to the boat, Theo slipped his hand into Penny's and pulled her back to sit down and draw.

Sitting cross-legged on the stone paving, reaching for her sketchbook, and feigning interest in the far horizon, her eyes darted back to the figures on the boat unloading the fish.

'I like Dimitris.' said Theo, matter of factly, tracing the outline of a boat with a blue crayon. 'Do you?'

'Yes,' said Penny. 'He seems nice.'

'I'm glad,' said Theo. 'I like my friends to like each other.'

Chapter 26

Tess had seen the *Dora* return, as she watched Penny and Theo choose their spot and hoped that Dimitris and Aris had caught some sea bass as Anna wanted to make it the 'Special' that evening.

Glancing around and seeing that all was well and no one was waiting for service, Tess popped into the kitchen and cut a slice of bread, drizzling some honey onto the soft white surface. She closed her eyes and savoured the moment. Anna, busy chopping onions, smiled across at her.

'Don't forget to have a coffee.' Anna sounded like a benevolent aunt. A sprightly 65-year-old, her energy had not diminished with the years. She loved to cook all day and considered the kitchen at the Athena her own space and sanctuary.

'Aris and Dimitris are back with the catch. Let's hope they have some sea bass.'

At the mention of sea bass, Anna's eyes looked over to the large basket of fresh lemons and the garlic hanging above her head.

Tess pushed the last piece of honeyed bread into her mouth, aware that Anna would already be creating the fish dish in her head, checking she had everything she needed to make it.

Minutes later Aris and Dimitris appeared carrying boxes of fish. They set them down on the counter at the far end of the kitchen and washed their hands. Dimitris leaned back and watched Anna as she examined the glistening sea bass and red snapper.

'Coffee?' Tess addressed both men and as they nodded their thanks, she headed back into the bar.

She heard Anna chattering animatedly about the plans for the fish, Aris enjoying her appreciation. Dimitris had followed her back into the restaurant and sat at the bar.

As he sat waiting for his coffee, he heard a large coach, the first of the day, pull up outside the Athena.

'Here we go,' said Tess, passing him an espresso. Dimitris raised the cup to catch the aroma, transported momentarily back to his favourite coffee shop off Chancery Lane – very different days.

'I've just seen Theo down at the harbour with Penny, the small girl who draws . . . the Durrells fan.'

Dimitris looked intently at Tess, trying to read her face as she spoke about Penny. 'Yes, bless her. When Nic couldn't make it today, she asked if Theo would like to join her while she sketched. He jumped at the chance, but I won't share with Nic how quickly he got over the disappointment of him not being here.'

'Well, they seemed like old friends when I spoke to them. Theo seemed happy and excited. He said they're coming back here for lunch.'

'That's the plan. She didn't have to offer to take Theo with her.'

'Maybe she wanted company. She's here on her own, isn't she?'

'She is, but I think she's okay with being on her own when she has to. She's always drawing, reading, or planning trips.'

'Do you know why she's here on her own?' Dimitris tried to look nonchalant as he drained the last of his espresso.

Tess paused, turning away to clean the coffee machine steam pipe, trying to decide what to say and how much.

'Well, I know she's a book illustrator from Yorkshire,' Tess began.

Dimitris immediately thought of Leeds and wondered if Sally was still there.

'She lost her father last year and the Durrells thing is tied up with her dad and a promise to him to come here, I think.' Tess looked across at him, as he listened intently to every word she said.

She didn't know why, but she suddenly didn't feel comfortable telling him the rest, about Penny's break-up with her fiancé. It was Penny's story to tell in her own time, if she wanted to share it.

⟵⟶

After an hour or so, Penny and Theo sat with their sketchbooks in front of them. They'd chatted with a few visitors who had stopped to look at their drawings, something Penny had always been uncomfortable with, although Theo handled comments about his work with thanks and ease. It was now so hot that dangling their legs in the cool sea was a necessity. A familiar voice rang out. 'The artists are having a rest, I see.'

Nic crouched down beside Theo and picked up his sketchbook. 'Very good. I love the colour of the boats.'

Theo scrambled to his feet and nearly knocked Nic over as he tried to hug him.

'Hello,' Nic said.

'Hi,' Penny returned, laughing at Theo's enthusiastic greeting. 'I think someone has missed you. We were just having five minutes off before our next drawing, but I think we may have to retreat inside. It feels extra hot today.' As Theo's face dropped, Penny added quickly. 'We can carry on painting at the Athena, in the shade by the sea wall.'

Theo bent down to hug Penny, who had her legs in the water. His spontaneity was disarming and touching, and the simple gesture brought home to her how long it had been since she had hugged or been hugged.

Penny and Theo gathered up their things and the three of them began a slow, hot walk back to the Athena.

'What did you paint?' Nic asked her as they strolled side by side.

'That's a secret, for now.' Penny answered. Nic looked intrigued.

'A secret, eh? Well, I shall have to be patient then.'

'Don't expect too much. It's just something for Tess, to say thank you.'

'Thank you?' Nic asked.

'Yes. Sometimes people help you just by being who they are, listening, acknowledging you're there, understanding without having to know the whole story. Am I making sense?'

Nic looked thoughtful. 'Yes, you're making sense,' he said finally, 'especially with regard to Tess.'

The tone in his voice made Penny look at Nic more closely, as she remembered Lily saying, 'Have you seen the way Nic looks at Tess?'

'Mama, Nic's here.' Theo ran into the restaurant and behind the bar where Tess stood.

'So he is. Cold drinks everyone?'

Penny and Theo settled themselves at a table at the far

end of the restaurant under an awning, where the freshness of the sea delivered the rich fragrance of wild herbs. A ginger cat waited expectantly on a wall, wondering whether to join them.

Nic sat at the bar, waiting for a moment when he could update Tess on his trip to Athens.

'Don't give it a thought, Nic. Nothing serious I hope?' Tess put down the cloth she was wiping the bar with.

Nic waved his arm dismissively. 'I'm sure it will be fine. I'm just a little concerned about a colleague.'

'You must be more than a little concerned if you're flying to Athens.'

'It's something that I need to do in person. I'm sure all will be well. A friend is having some health problems and she thinks she should resign. I need to talk to her, to reassure her that if she wants to stay, she can, and that she'll get all the support she needs to do that. It's not the sort of thing you can express in an email.'

'No, I imagine it isn't. When will you be back?'

'Tomorrow evening, I hope. Earlier if I can make the lunchtime flight.'

'What about Ulysses?'

'Don't worry. Annabelle, my neighbour, has him. I don't think I'll be missed. I just hope he watches his language.' Nic sighed.

'Have you got time for something to eat?'

'Coffee first would be great. Is there anything I can do as I'm here?'

'No, Nic. All's well, thank you. And thanks to Aris and Dimitris, I have a very happy Anna, who's planning all sorts of specials with the fish they've just brought in.'

'Have they gone or are they still in the kitchen?' Nic asked, looking through the doorway.

'They went a while ago. Dimitris saw Theo and Penny at the harbour this morning. He was asking about Penny when he came to deliver the fish.'

Tess looked at Nic. He knew that face. It seemed to say, *I could say more, but I'm not sure I should, but on the other hand, I trust you.*

'Penny seems lovely. I'm not surprised he was asking about her.' Nic nudged the conversation. 'But that's not normal for him, is it? I can't remember him asking about or being interested in anyone, particularly a visitor. There was an old girlfriend from his university days that turned up a couple of years ago, but that didn't go well.'

'No,' said Tess. 'I don't think any of us will forget that.'

They looked at each other and then across at Penny.

'I know one thing,' added Tess. 'She's someone who doesn't need any more heartache right now.'

Nic nodded, as if to say, 'I see', and Tess knew that, in his quiet and thoughtful way, he always did see. He was a kind and considerate colleague and mentor too. Whoever he was flying off to see, she was a lucky woman.

Tess paused for a moment, her own thoughts stopping her in her tracks: yes, whoever she was, she was a lucky woman. This was a normal reaction to a crisis for Nic; he'd want to be there, to help. So, why did this trip make her uneasy?

As she lifted a glass from the bar, Nic turned away, distracted by something Theo was shouting. How many times had she looked up to find him there for her? Tess wondered. He was never intrusive, just always quietly there. She knew his presence wasn't just for her – Theo, Spiro, anyone who needed a listening ear would always find it in Nic – but his flying to Athens to see a woman . . . that felt like new territory.

If Nic had turned around at that moment, he would have seen Tess frowning and preoccupied.

Chapter 27

Penny sat contentedly, as Theo, lost in deep concentration, carefully coloured in the stripes of a 'tiger' that bore a more than passing resemblance to the ginger cat at their feet.

Now they were out of the glare of the sun, her body had cooled down and her mind had followed. Bruce's voicemails had retreated in importance to mimic white noise, like the whining hum of a night-time mosquito.

Someone had once said to her that emails weren't a 'to-do' list and so, she reasoned, nor were voicemails.

'I did the right thing,' she muttered to herself under her breath.

'What did you say?' Theo asked.

'Nothing, Theo. I was just thinking out loud.'

'Mama does that too,' he said.

'Does she? I'm glad it's not just me then,' Penny replied. 'I love your tiger.'

Theo stopped and looked intently at his work. 'I'm hungry now. Are you hungry?' he said.

'A little bit. We can eat anytime you like.' Penny finished her glass of water.

'I'll tell Mama.'

He ran off and Penny sat back in her chair, looking around and realizing the restaurant had quietly filled up. Theo was soon back with Tess in tow.

'Apparently the artists are hungry.' She sat down at the table, and picked up Theo's work as he snuggled into her side. 'This is smashing.'

'And can I see what you've been drawing, Penny?' Tess raised her eyebrows, looking directly at Penny and then pointedly at her sketchbook.

'Well, there's not much to see yet. It's a work in progress.' She winked at Theo.

Penny turned her sketchbook so that Tess could see her work, holding the page down so she was unable to turn onto the next page.

'The *Dora*,' Tess exclaimed. 'That's lovely. Does Dimitris know you've painted this?' Tess asked, genuinely impressed by the simple lines and jewel-like colours of the painting. Penny's style was loose and free, but the way she captured the essence of her subject was charming and subtle.

'No. I didn't start painting until after he and his father had left.'

'You should show them. It's really good. Aris loves the *Dora*. It's more than a boat to him. He would love this.' Tess knew if he saw it, Aris would be moved and touched that someone had drawn his boat.

'Perhaps I will when I see them.'

Penny covered the painting up. There was something about Tess's response that had made her feel as though she'd intruded somehow, that she should have asked permission to paint the *Dora* – that the boat was like a person.

Don't be silly, Penny, she scolded herself. *It's a boat in a harbour, not the scene of an accident. The only sensitivity here is yours and as usual you've gone into overdrive with the empathy and imagined sensibilities.*

'So, any idea what you'd like to eat?' Tess asked, with Theo immediately responding with 'Pasta!'

'You'd think he was half-Italian, not half-Greek,' Tess sighed. 'Penny?'

'Just a little bread, olives, and hummus would be lovely. I'm going into town later, so I'm going to read by the pool for a bit before I go.'

'Lunch is on its way.' Tess walked off and Theo ran to see Spiro, who'd just emerged from the kitchen.

Penny poured herself another glass of water and began to pack away her paints to make space on the table.

Nic, finishing his coffee at the bar, managed to look as though he couldn't stay but very much wanted to, as he glanced at his watch and tapped the top of the bar absentmindedly. Penny watched as his concern at missing the plane won the day and he stood up and made his farewells, which included a light kiss on the cheek for Tess, a handshake for Spiro, and a tousle of the hair for Theo. To her surprise Nic turned, found Penny, and waved.

Waving back, she felt glad and touched that she'd been singled out for this salute. It felt good to be part of something, to be thought of, included.

She pulled *The Corfu Trilogy* out of her rucksack, planning to read for a few minutes until her food arrived.

The sun was now working its way around the restaurant, long fingers of light stretching across tables, illuminating wine glasses, faces, and cutlery. It shone directly onto the page of Penny's book, bleaching the paper, and making the words leap out like random, dancing shapes. There was a comfort in rereading familiar and much-loved words. Almost like a mantra, they soothed and transported her away.

A wave of homesickness swept over Penny as she thought of the bookshelves she had at home, containing volume after volume of well-thumbed, often-reached-for books. Each one a part of the jigsaw of her personality and history. Each treasured.

At the heart of these were the books written by the Durrells, particularly Gerry and Larry, but also a jewel of a book by Margo that chronicled her adventures as the landlady of a boarding house. What richness existed in their writing: lived experience, lyrical reflection and, at times, visceral poignancy.

'Hello.' Penny knew the voice before she looked up. It was Dimitris.

'Hi,' she responded, pleased but a little surprised to see him, even though he'd said he would see both her and Theo.

'Can I get you a drink?'

How different he seems; not ready to walk away like he was when we first met, Penny thought. Then, he'd thrown a casual remark back at her over his shoulder, as though dismissing her as just another tourist, a woman on her own to be humoured – or perhaps to flirt with.

This offer of a drink now, the way he was standing almost tentatively, perhaps half-expecting a 'no', felt like a new page being turned.

'Thank you. Water would be great.'

She watched him walk to the bar, taking in every inch of his form, and knew in that instant that if Dimitris had been dancing with her and she'd looked up, he wouldn't have been looking away.

She still knew so very little about him, as they'd exchanged very few words. As she waited for him to return, she felt a shiver of uncertainty and asked herself once again if she was right to ignore Bruce's voicemail. Bruce had never liked being ignored – he had to be the centre and catalyst, the hub of anything that mattered to him. Everything else he just ignored.

Penny looked across the sea for an answer, but it wasn't giving anything away.

When he returned, Dimitris was followed by Theo who, now Nic had gone, seemed to need the reassurance of another male presence. Dimitris's face gave nothing away, as he placed the drinks on the table and the boy settled himself at their feet with the ginger cat that had appeared from nowhere.

'What do you call him?' Penny asked Theo.

'Tom,' said Theo, stroking the animal, who purred quietly.

'He's very handsome,' Penny said, bending down to stroke the relaxed cat, which now stretched languorously like a Greek god.

'He needs to rest,' said Dimitris *sotto voce*. 'He's fathered more children than we can count. Also, he doesn't know it yet, but he's off to the vet next week, so that the feline population doesn't go up any more.'

She nodded conspiratorially at Dimitris, caught for a moment in his gaze, which she noticed rarely left her face.

He was about to say something else when their attention was diverted by a couple approaching their table, asking if Dimitris was the person they needed to speak to about a boat trip.

Penny sat back patiently, enjoying the breeze from the sea and listening to Theo's background chatter, as she reminded herself that Dimitris was working, whereas she was on holiday. She had time to watch Dimitris as he spoke, clearly anxious to finish the conversation, but not wanting to lose a customer.

She noticed for the first time how he used his hands to speak, how expressive his face was, the meaning and weight of his words passing through and over it. She could have watched him for hours.

Chapter 28

By the beginning of July, the Corfu sun approached its zenith, settled into a routine of seeming ever-present, and kept its part of the centuries-old agreement to greet every traveller to its shores with warmth and light.

For Penny, as the sun glided elegantly towards the sea, locked as she was at that moment into the Corfu of 1930s, it matched her languid, relaxed senses and her mood. It was the perfect day to explore Corfu Town and experience its evening colours.

She had set aside this evening to wander, think, and read. And dine.

Unlocking the hire-car door, she felt the escape of hot air as a tingling sensation across her slightly sunburned face. She looked across at the Athena before she got into the car and saw Spiro at the entrance, with Theo sitting by his side. Human connection, however brief – with Tess, Guy, Rich, Lily, Nic, Theo, Spiro, now even the enigmatic Dimitris – was, she acknowledged, the glue that held her together. She needed people.

As she drove out of the village, the road twisting and turning as it led her out onto the main route to Corfu Town,

Penny switched on the radio.

Sitting with Dimitris earlier she had realized that hearing from Bruce again was a double blow. The last time they'd spoken, her dad had been alive and she had never been more sure at that moment that breaking away was the right thing to do. Now, it felt as though he was forcing her to turn back time, reopen a chapter that had been closed. She didn't really want to think about why, but knowing Bruce, there had to be an angle.

Although there was no harm in being a healthy sceptic, she had never been a cynic, although Bruce brought out in her an uncharacteristic and unwelcome cynicism.

It had even coloured her time with Dimitris, such as it had been so far. The drink they'd shared earlier in the Athena had been interrupted by Theo showing Dimitris his drawing of the *Dora*. Then the English couple had asked about the next *Antiopi* chartered trip up the coast.

He had been pleasant, but she'd sensed something in him; almost as though he was trying too hard to be relaxed and friendly; asking her questions about her trip so far in a staccato way. The conversation hadn't flowed.

She didn't know whether this was because she didn't want to encourage Dimitris, or was afraid of whatever it was she might be feeling for him. Perhaps it was just simply too soon. This holiday was about healing, space, and connecting with the Durrells and the beauty of Corfu. Exploring their world.

As she approached town she began to think about where to park. The Old Port would be perfect for her walk around the esplanade and Arseniou, the two locations she wanted to visit. But would the god of parking be with her for a second time? Penny remembered that Mother Cabrini was the saint to pray to for a space – something an American friend had told her.

Half-closing her eyes for a second in silent prayer, she slowed down as the glory of Garitsa Bay revealed itself on her left, hoping that this might help the request along. And suddenly there was a space.

'Thank you, Mother Cabrini,' said Penny, wondering if there was a patron saint of ex-fiancés she could have a quick word with about the voicemails and what she felt – or didn't feel – for Dimitris . . . and he for her.

⌒

Arseniou was part of the miraculous road that wound from Garitsa Bay along the coastline into the heart of Corfu Town. The pale biscuit-coloured Venetian buildings led graciously to the cricket ground and the Liston.

Having listened to Spiro's story of Gerry and Larry Durrell visiting in the 1960s, Penny wanted to try and guess which house might have been the place where they had stayed. The view from any of these houses captured a portal to paradise.

Now as the light mellowed, the Greek mainland loomed in the distance. A large ferry chugged through the channel like a child's toy, pulled by an invisible chord to Igoumenitsa.

Penny leaned on the weathered iron railings that were the only barrier between her and the pink-and-turquoise-tinged sea below. She wore one of her favourite vintage-style cotton dresses. With its dropped waist, partnered with little flat shoes and floppy sun hat, she looked like an extra from a 1930s tableau. Only the rucksack brought her outfit back into the twenty-first century.

How the world turned. She thought back to her and Bruce's early days together when she'd watched her mobile like a hawk, almost tripping over her own feet one day as she'd scrambled to grab the phone from her bag. Every call had felt like another building block in their relationship, a new discovery about each other revealed with every conversation.

Every classic romantic novel she'd read in her teenage years had had at its heart a Byronic hero: Rochester, Heathcliff, Maxim de Winter. When they'd first met, Bruce had seemed like a marvellous conflation of all the fascinating and complicated men she'd ever read about. The fact that Heathcliff or others of his ilk would have been impossible to live with had, at the time, barely touched her consciousness.

Once again, with a little shudder of embarrassment at her slightly younger but naive and impressionable self, Penny replayed in her head the edited highlights of her time with Bruce and saw clearly the downward trajectory of their relationship. Was it distance, of geography or time, that gave her this new clarity? She didn't know.

Had he always been so self-centred, so manipulative? Why had it taken her dad's illness to give her enough courage and insight to walk away? Why did she still wonder if she could have changed him . . . that some of the blame for the way he was lay at her door?

Bruce knew she was abroad somewhere, was clearly keen to speak to her; and right now she had no one to share that information with. It helped to think of the bigger picture when faced with personal problems.

She looked behind her at the crescent of sea-facing houses. What had they seen over the years, across the bay, or in the heart of the old town? The bustle and trauma of life across the centuries was written on the features she could see. The old Venetian fortress formed a craggy, stone-carved lookout post, watching, waiting, guarding. The Venetians who had triggered the cultivation of olive trees on an industrial scale across the island, shaping its contours and character, had brought their craftsmen with them. The curves, triangles, and elegance of the pastel-hued houses offered a sense of permanence and solidity. They remained the same, despite a little softening and ageing of their edges, observing centuries of comings and goings. Trade, bombardment, and invasion were imprinted on every building and vista that had been worn smooth by feet, carts, hooves, and now cars. All the while olive trees had kept growing, many for over 500 years, with some approaching their 1,000th birthday.

She also walked in the footsteps of her favourite family, who had packed into Spiro's large American car and been driven along this airy promenade on their way to town.

Rucksack firmly back on her shoulders, she strolled on as the softening sun caught her hair and the swirl of her dress; a serene meeting of movement and light.

Chapter 29

Arseniou soon ran into Kapodistriou and then the cricket field, around which was some optimistically arranged parking. Penny smiled at the thought of a ball flying through the air, accompanied by the shout of 'Six!' followed by the comedically timed sound of breaking glass.

On the right was the Liston, lamps lit in anticipation of the twilight. As inviting as it looked, with golden pools of light and cosy seating, she turned right before she reached the covered walkway that echoed its Parisian counterpart.

She looked for a restaurant she knew must have been there when the Durrells visited. She'd read about it online. Established in the 1930s, it was called the Rex, and located two minutes' walk from the Liston.

The sun was now very low as she turned right again into a smaller street, part of which lay in shade, and there on the left, in mellow antique-gold colours, stood the Rex.

White-clothed tables were arranged outside in two rows and were almost full. Glancing over Penny noticed one free table, against a warm wall that carried a plaque with the legend, 'Established 1932'.

She was greeted warmly as she stopped by the lectern that

held the menus.

'*Kalispera*. A table for one, *parakalo*,' said Penny, carrying her rucksack close to the floor as she wove her way through the tables behind the restaurant manager.

'Is this okay for you?' said the restaurant manager.

It was the small table snuggled against the wall that she'd spotted. 'Perfect. *Efcharistó*.' With her bag on the spare chair and facing the other diners, Penny studied the menu.

As she looked across the ancient street and up at the high windows, some open to catch the last rays of the sun, the vibrant scene boasted an eclectic crowd: glamorous couples, wearing casual clothes with the confidence of being catwalk-ready; families and children with ice creams; the middle-aged cruise fraternity in port for a day; and younger individuals, looking forward to a night exploring the bars and tavernas.

As they passed, she heard many different accents and languages, which made the people-watching more exciting and entrancing.

What a place. What a gift to be here. I shall never forget this moment, she thought to herself. A woman framed in a small attic window across the street called down to a girl below. The two exchanged a few words, the woman in the clouds laughing and signalling she would come down to the street. The air smelled of garlic and lemons as the heat of the day receded, and herbs and the fragrance of a thousand flowers released their scent.

Penny recalled the thousands of words that Gerry Durrell had committed to the page, capturing the essence of this miraculous island, as well as the exquisite jewel of a book, *Prospero's Cell* – Corfu as remembered and captured by Larry Durrell.

The trip to Kalami and the White House, Larry's home, would be a special moment. Of all the villas, perhaps partly because it was now the most accessible, that was where she could see herself. It would also most likely feature Dimitris, when she booked her place on the *Antiopi*.

Before that, though, she would visit the Daffodil Yellow Villa near Kontokali. The pilgrimage had become, without her really noticing, as much – if not more – about people than places. The people who had lived there before and the people she was spending time with now. Times past influencing times yet to come.

Her food arrived, the shrimp delicately arranged, its aroma intoxicating. Delicious.

She noticed the waiters pull some tables together as though expecting a large party, and settled back in her chair to see who arrived.

She heard them before she saw them. A man's voice, loud and confident, rose above the chatter of the group. 'Alicia, I have never seen you lose. I, for one, will never place a bet against you, whether it's the outcome of a tennis match or whether or not your Greek Adonis turns up for dinner.'

'David, behave! You all liked him. If he does turn up, it's to see all of you . . . though why he'd want to, I can't imagine.' Alicia walked ahead of her group of friends and gave her name to the restaurant manager. Penny watched as the group of five sat down.

The two men and three women were tanned and smartly dressed, their overall impression casual, but a look created with practised and confident elegance. An attractive bunch, who wouldn't have looked out of place on a film set or a yacht, she thought; who embodied everything she felt she wasn't.

Her own prettiness eluded her. She thought her features small, like her stature. Her hair was dark, but hovered indecisively between inky blackness and chestnut. Her hazel eyes were, she conceded, her best feature, but she barely bothered with make-up at home and lived in her dungarees – the wearing of the latter being a sign, according to her friend Lizzie, that she had given up on life.

In a moment of inspiration, Penny decided she might ring Lizzie about Bruce. Despite being busy with her business and two young children, she was invariably kind and wise. Even when her dad had been around, she'd always had a small but perfectly formed group of friends to share confidences and the minutiae of life with. Now different lives and commitments kept them apart.

The failing sunlight was silver now. The lights on the tables burned a little brighter and the shadows softened everything around her. The street was no less busy and the Rex tables were full, inside and out. Laughter rose in welcome waves.

The five at the neighbouring table decided what to eat, their drinks already ordered. One of the women looked around and behind her every minute or so, as though expecting someone. She stood up, placed her hand on the shoulders of the man sitting next to her, and whispered something into his ear. He responded with a laugh, before she walked into the restaurant. They seemed to know each other well, an easy camaraderie visible between them.

'Can I get you anything else?' The host was at her side, lifting her empty plate and waiting for her answer.

'Espresso, *parakalo*,' Penny said, happy to stay a while longer and watch the stories playing out at each table. It was easy, when she didn't know anyone, to imagine their history, why they were here, what their lives were like.

Then suddenly there was someone she did know.

She instinctively pressed herself back against the cool stone on the wall behind her.

Dimitris.

She recognized him as soon as his walk and outline caught her eye. He stopped at the table with the five friends, the lights from the table illuminating their faces. There was much animation and David, the loud man, stood and shook Dimitris by the hand. Alicia, the blonde, returned, appearing from inside the Rex holding a champagne glass.

'Good to see you. I'm glad you decided to join us.' She reached out for Dimitris's hand and as she did so, she bent forward and kissed him on both cheeks.

Alicia sat down and Dimitris took the empty seat next to her. She poured some wine into a glass in front of him and the chatter around the table resumed.

Penny's coffee arrived and as the waiter left her table she knew before she looked up that she'd been spotted.

She felt his gaze before she looked up and responded immediately with a smile, and mouthed 'hello' before she had time to think about it.

He raised his hand and nodded back at her, saying nothing but not looking away either.

Penny smiled again and then looked down at her coffee, trying to create a natural break in the greeting and the eye contact. As she took her first sip of coffee, she heard a familiar voice behind her. 'Penny, a night out in the big city?' It was Guy and behind him a small red-haired girl.

'Hi.' She was relieved and delighted to see him. In the midst of her awkwardness at Dimitris's arrival, he was a warm and welcome distraction.

'This is Faith,' Guy offered as Penny looked across at the pale, pixie-like girl who hovered behind him. 'She arrived today. Her friend Dee is somewhere around too. We lost her in one of the icon shops, I think.'

'Hello, Faith. I'm Penny – another visitor. Is it your first time on Corfu?'

'First time here, yes. I've been to Greece before, with my family, but I'm here with Dee this time.'

'Well, it's my first time here too. I hope you end up loving it as much as I do. Are you eating here?'

'Perhaps later. We have to find Dee and then we're all going to a bar. Rich might join us. You're welcome to come if you've finished here,' Guy said kindly, but Penny got the distinct impression that there was already one gooseberry too many on this outing.

'I'm fine. I'm just going to wander and have a look at the shops, I think,' Penny said. 'Good to meet you, Faith.'

She'd barely finished her sentence when Guy called out. 'Dimitris!'

He made his way over to the table. '*Kalispera.*' Dimitris shook Guy's hand, nodded at Penny, then looked at Faith.

Guy made the introductions. 'Hi.' Dimitris smiled at Faith.

'Dimitris has a beautiful yacht, and a visit to Corfu isn't complete without a trip up the coast,' Guy gushed. 'We saw you yesterday, near Mouse Island.'

'Yes, Penny told me last night,' Dimitris said and to Penny he made it sound as though they had spent quality time together, when it had been a casual encounter of minutes and small talk.

'I'm here with the people I took out on *Antiopi* yesterday,' he continued, looking behind him to the table where Alicia watched him discreetly, her head turning animatedly towards her friends whenever she felt he looked her way.

'Great,' said Guy. 'We're off to a bar with Faith's friend Dee.'

At that moment Dee arrived, breathless, carrying a large plastic bag, her now-redundant sunglasses balanced precariously on her head in the twilight.

'Here you are,' she gasped. 'I got waylaid by a shop – well, several shops if I'm honest. There are so many. It's heaven.' Dee stopped for a moment, transported by the memory of so many places to spend her parents' generous gift of holiday spending money.

Becoming aware that Faith and Guy were now part of a larger group, she introduced herself and asked where they were off to next.

'The best bar in Corfu Town,' was Guy's reply.

'I must be off too,' said Penny, 'but I have to pay the bill first. Lovely to see you all. Enjoy the rest of your evening.'

Walking past Dimitris, she brushed against his arm as she negotiated the space between the tables. Her rucksack hit her calf as she did so.

'*Kalinichta*,' Dimitris called after her as she went into the restaurant to pay. She turned back to smile, catching out of the corner of her eye a look from Alicia that managed to be simultaneously interested and dismissive.

After paying the bill she waited for a moment until she saw Dimitris diverted by the conversation at the table.

She wanted to slip away quietly, having no desire to be introduced to the people who'd been on Dimitris's boat. He'd said nothing about spending the evening in Corfu Town earlier, but then why would he? She'd been almost as dismissive of him as he had been of her when they'd first met; all monosyllabic answers and awkwardness.

It was funny, but even though he was not much more than an acquaintance she felt instinctively he wasn't particularly comfortable with his dinner companions. As she'd noticed before, he looked restless, as though looking for an escape route.

Minutes later she walked on her own through the bustling old town, veering into the smaller streets as quickly as she could, as though she needed to disappear back into her own world again, as she realized she wasn't ready to be pulled back again into the randomness of sudden introductions and an ever-widening circle of acquaintances.

Her natural instinct was to be curious and concerned about everyone she met and the holiday had brought so many new people into her world so far – people she already cared about. She knew she was fooling herself if she imagined that fewer people in her life would give her any more control about outcomes or the randomness of it at all. Nevertheless, her instinctive need for self-preservation kicked in when she felt herself pulled into the lives of others – lives with too many notes, like a complicated aria.

After a few minutes her pace slowed and her mind began to follow. The mêlée around her brought her back into the silver threads of street after street of moonlight-soaked Corfu Town. Jewellery, turquoise, and mother-of-pearl rings lay in tantalizing rows, next to matching necklaces and earrings. Pots of honey and aromatic herbs jostled for position with olive-wood bowls and carved toy donkeys.

The smells of lemons, thyme, coffee, baking, and honey tempted her as she passed tavernas, cafés, and bars crazily but magically arranged alongside each other.

Above her the high bell tower of St Spyridon's church, a beacon by night and day, glowed against the blue-black backdrop of the sky.

Ancient and modern dovetailed here with ease. Corfiots had adapted themselves to the hurly-burly of visitors for half of the year, but olive trees, bees, kumquats, and winemakers represented the eternal heart of the island's produce and purpose.

The road before her swept gently down back towards the bay.

She wondered if she'd bump into Guy and the girls, or

Rich on his way to find them. But although faces passed by in a never-ending cavalcade, she saw no one she knew or recognized, now that she was several streets away from the Rex.

Then in front of her she saw a man strolling casually, hands in pockets, blue cotton shirt and pale chinos topped off with a pale straw Panama hat.

The gait, slightly bow-legged and jaunty, was so like her dad's that for a moment she thought it was him. This had happened once before in the second-hand bookshop in her hometown, where, she'd reasoned, if her dad was going to come back in spirit form at all it would have been a likely and totally fitting location. He'd haunted the shop when he'd still been alive, and her childhood home had positively groaned on both floors with the weight of books.

The man in the hat disappeared before Penny could see his face, and she carried on wending her way slowly, but surely, back to the car.

Chapter 30

The intensive seven-month holiday season involved a whirlwind of meals, deliveries, cleaning, conversations, and crises, large and small, all absorbed with good humour and patience. The seasonal rhythm combined with an expectation and understanding that no two days were the same. At the Athena they invited life in and embraced whatever it brought.

Standing in the kitchen, checking on the stores and about to run the coffee machine through with its first espresso of the day, Tess felt grateful that morning in a way she never had before. It had been difficult to feel that since Georgios' death. Yet every time she looked at Theo there was an overwhelming sense of being blessed, as he was the link that meant Georgios remained with her; Spiro too.

They were a team.

Her mobile vibrated in her pocket. A text from Nic. He'd return from Athens that evening. So, hopefully he'd still be able to take Theo to the olive mill on Wednesday. Theo missed him when he left, and for the first time, Tess realized that so did she.

She admitted to herself, reluctantly, that when he had mentioned his colleague was a woman, she'd felt a physical reaction, a falling sensation in her stomach. Why would it have been fine if it had been a man he was going to see? Why should it matter to her? She hadn't wanted to look as though she was prying, but she wondered if he was flying off to help Melina. Melina had come up in conversation before, regarding the end-of-year ball in May. Nic usually came home before that took place and actively avoided the annual social event. But this year he'd stayed on for it, and Melina had been the name mentioned; the colleague who his other university friends had tried, once again, to pair him off with.

Visions of Nic dancing with this mystery woman now pushed their way into Tess's mind, where they stayed and simmered gently.

Yes, they were used to the months he was away in Athens, so a day away from Corfu was nothing really. But in her mind, he was theirs for the summer, another important connection to Georgios, his friend from childhood.

Thinking about his call yesterday morning to say he couldn't be with Theo that day had delivered an impact, Tess now knew, beyond the disappointment that Theo would feel.

Nic was a good man, a tad eccentric, difficult to read, and quiet to the point of introversion sometimes, but utterly consistent in his reassuring support of her, Theo, Spiro, and the Athena.

There was, she thought, no one better to rely on at a time of crisis.

No one.

As the smell of the coffee floated in the air, it brought Tess back into the room and the moment. She was surprised and not a little alarmed to feel her eyes fill up, her vision becoming blurred. She pressed her palms under each eye and then looked up.

Theo and Spiro walked up the lane from the apartments,

stopping every few yards to look in a crevasse in the wall for a lizard or two.

Gratitude overwhelmed her again, even though deep down an absence made its presence felt.

Whether inspired by seeing Dimitris in town earlier with a group that included an attractive blonde woman, or a need to complete unfinished business, Penny had finally made up her mind that she would respond to Bruce's messages when she got back to the apartment that night. Rightly or wrongly, she felt she owed him that. Things were never, she reasoned, black and white. The truth was found in shades of grey. It had been easier to think of all the darker things about their time together in order to cope with the decision to leave.

Her mind had not changed and she had no idea why he had suddenly decided to get in touch, but a reply to his message was the grown-up response.

She made it brief, but friendly.

'Hello Bruce, this is Penny. I've just received your messages. I'm away at the moment as you guessed and won't be back for a while yet, so I'm sorry, but we won't be home at the same time. I hope everything's going well in Italy. I imagine the weather, food, and wine are fabulous. Anyway, take care and I hope you have a good holiday.'

Her hand trembled as she put the mobile down and stared at the familiar and comforting view from her apartment. Starlight, interrupted by the red winking lights of a passing plane, framed the outline of the mountains. The sea gleamed like mercury. The ever-present cicadas sounded in the vivid darkness like a memory from another time, the soundtrack of a Corfu night that had played for centuries, never changing its tone or tune.

Sitting on their veranda at the Daffodil Yellow Villa more than eighty years earlier, the Durrells would have heard the same chorus, been entranced and delighted by the fireflies as Penny was now. The heat stored in the stone and ground from the day escaped into the night air and carried the fragrance of lemons, sea, and fallen rose petals.

She read quietly, the light from her bedside lamp casting a distorted shadow on the wall. From the description of faded yellow walls and green shutters, to the lemon and orange trees of a Venetian mansion, how poignantly, with the simplest of words arranged in magical order on the page, had Gerry Durrell captured his second home here. And tomorrow she would try and find it.

Yes, she'd done the right thing in her neutral response to Bruce. Hopefully that was the end of whatever it had been.

So why did she find herself wracked with uncertainty and unsettled the following morning? The source of her discomfort was, she admitted reluctantly to herself, Dimitris.

Every time they met, she felt a connection there, although she really knew no more about him than when he'd first walked over to the table to ask her about her trip to Kalami.

It was also true that for days she'd tried hard not to acknowledge the attraction, trying not to act on any feelings or impulses that might arise, whatever they were.

But when she'd seen Dimitris last night in Corfu Town being greeted by the beautiful blonde woman, she'd felt something in the pit of her stomach — a deep sadness, a dragging sensation, like the loss of something before it had even begun.

The most disconcerting and frightening thing about this development was the self-discovery that she could be reached and touched. After months of emotional isolation, nursing her grief as though it was a life raft, she'd believed herself impervious to the experiences and relationships open to everyone else. Clearly that was not the case.

Whether this was a welcome discovery remained to be seen.

For all Dimitris's air of quiet strength and strong physical presence, she sensed a sadness, a wariness not dissimilar to her own.

But today she wanted to be back on track and that meant taking the coast road north, travelling past Corfu Town and on towards Kontokali and the Daffodil Yellow Villa, which was also close to the house used for the TV series.

Perhaps a step back in time would take her mind off the present and help her refocus on the reason she had come to Corfu.

'Daffodil Yellow Villa, here I come,' she said as she grabbed her car keys and rucksack, throwing her books and phone into it, as she walked out of the apartment.

Chapter 31

North of Corfu Town the main road hugged the coastline, interrupted by smaller byways that led to shops, hotels, or beaches. To the north, Penny's car climbed as the foothills of Mount Pantokrator pulled her towards them. Olive trees by the winding roadside guided her along the sometimes narrow thoroughfare. Large coaches squeezed into the small villages, on roads that had originally been created by the passage of donkeys and their owners.

The wilder, higher, and elemental north was a place of exquisite natural beauty. Gorges and hidden streams, old villages, and remote, secret places where you could imagine you were the only person left on earth – now much-sought-after locations for buying a house on Corfu, as a permanent home or a holiday getaway.

Ironically, Penny wondered what it was about human beings that, when they saw a clean, clear, and solitary place of beauty, they immediately wanted to build on it, take ownership of it, conquer it with bricks, and glass, and gazebos.

Agni, Kalami, Kouloura, and Kassiopi – four golden enclaves along this picture-postcard coast. Each bay, without ever seeing the other, attempted to outdo its neighbour. Each succeeded in bringing a different and uniquely enchanting experience, despite the essentially same ingredients of beach, sky, olive groves, harbour, jetty, and a view of distant Albanian shores.

Penny didn't need much imagination to conjure up a vision of gods and mortals from long ago: days of myth and the heroes of legend who had never really left, with only a thin gauze-like veil between this time and theirs. Here was the landscape that had greeted Odysseus, rough-hewn but verdant, the snow-capped mountains of Albania visible from the shoreline and the shingle beaches, that once bore the tracks of boats heaved ashore, now sporting parasols and sunbeds.

Lawrence Durrell used to speak of the 'spirit of place'. *I know what he means now*, Penny thought, as she followed the deep curve of the hillside road. It involved feeling the essence of somewhere in your bones and finding that you shared the same DNA, had found your match for life. *Corfu is becoming part of me. It's opened a door and is inviting me to walk through*, she mused. The Durrells' books and stories of their life here had been the beginning; this was the next step. Being here, experiencing everything.

Day by day Corfu wove its magic around her and pulled her in, closer and closer to the heartbeat of the island.

Penny travelled on towards the second home the Durrells had lived in during their Corfu idyll. The far north would have to wait for another day. The only Durrell dwelling located there was the White House, at Kalami.

Kontokali stood less than a quarter of an hour beyond Corfu Town. Penny had trawled through many Durrell-based websites, taking notes from previous travellers and their tales. She knew that the Daffodil Yellow Villa was now a privately owned house and not open to the public, so her curiosity would be tempered by a restricted view from the gate.

A stone's throw from the real villa was the one used in the TV series, a multi-storey Venetian dolls' house, with a stone terrace that caught the sunsets and held back the Ionian Sea.

As Penny drove, familiar names on signposts drew her attention and distracted her with an overwhelming sense of déjà vu and familiarity. Her confidence in finding the spot grew. Her dad had demonstrated the same ability. This legacy, as much a part of her as the eye colour she had inherited from him, was an innate ability to make the most ordinary trip or moment extraordinary. To conjure days to bottle out of sometimes very small things – which she would have argued were really the big things: a sunset, a delicious meal, a poem, or a piece of music.

Penny had no one to share this gift with, no one who understood the importance of stories past and present, the narrative of people's lives, and the joy of elevating them to something uplifting and fine, making them live again.

As she acknowledged the uncanny sense of being at home, the prospect of living on Corfu forever suddenly appealed to Penny more than anything else had for a very long time. Nothing bound her to any particular place other than memory, and she carried that with her.

Penny basked in the warmth of the dream, as a gift to herself, surprised at her train of thought and the clarity of her vision, as endless days of light and small miracles played out in her head.

The Daffodil Yellow Villa hid at the end of a gravelled road, revealing little other than white-pillared gates and a lush, foliage-filled entrance. Penny strained to see glimpses of yellowed stucco and a corner of the villa's pantiled roof in the distance. The house, silent in its closed-off kingdom beyond a high wall, gave away no secrets.

She stood still and tried to absorb the sounds around her. The cicadas chirped loudly as always, but the footsteps and laughter, the bray of Gerry's donkey Sally, and the calls of other animals in his menagerie, had been carried away on the sea breeze long ago. Penny looked down at her feet contemplating, absorbing the atmosphere. Her eyes were drawn to the view across the road, towards the sea.

As cars passed, she imagined local drivers spotting her, knowing why she was standing by an anonymous-looking closed gate at the side of the road. Another fan. Another pilgrim. Just another Durrell sightseer.

A yearning ache for the *simple* gifts of family, home, love, community, and gratitude for the ordinary overwhelmed her in that moment. The Durrells' life on Corfu had encompassed all these things, but Penny's life at home stretched emptily ahead of her, devoid of family and love.

Minutes later, after parking at a local supermarket, buying a cold bottle of water and walking the few yards back towards the sea, Penny found herself close to the Durrells' *fictional* TV home, contemplating what a joy it must have been to recreate some of the scenes of those lives. Maiden aunts and tortoises, donkeys and drunken sea captains – the harlequin colours and shapes of lives lived richly and spontaneously.

Penny's time revolved around the gentle rhythm of walking, sitting, and drawing, all accompanied by the sun. After several languid days in the sun and out of it, her skin felt softer, kissed by a dark honey hue, so different from her pallid winter look.

She recalled Margo Durrell and her sunbathing adventures, her endless optimism. There had been something fearless, as well as naturally warm about her, that Penny had related to. As she stood close to the place connected to the drama series rather than the real family, the air still shimmered with something special. The whole island resonated with the heart and presence of those who'd been there before.

The mysteries and lyricism of the Corfu landscape had been the catalyst for Gerry Durrell's unique and powerful world of words, and that of his brother, Larry. The contrast with 'Pudding Island', as he'd called England, was palpable. The Durrells' trip from Bournemouth and Blighty in the midst of a cold winter to the warm welcome of Corfu mirrored her own journey, from grief-laden silence to the warm chatter of life.

She turned around at the top of the road and shielded her eyes to look across towards the tiny island of Lazaretto. Through the centuries it had been a place of quarantine and incarceration, now it was a greenish-blue hump on the horizon, benign and at peace with itself.

It was just after noon, the heat relentless and unyielding. Penny wanted to take photos, to capture the colour of the sand in the light for a storyboard she was creating in her head for a book. Although she'd illustrated many, Penny had never written a children's book.

As she'd sat with Theo, drawing and painting by the harbour, she'd listened to his tales, watched him draw, and fallen into his 7-year-old world of animals real and imagined, the places they lived, by the coast and in the tumbling, verdant interior, all made vivid by the wonder without walls that only a child could conjure up, as he subconsciously reassembled the jigsaw of his life, making up for the missing piece of his father.

He'd said something that had touched Penny deeply, caught her out as it mirrored her own inner turmoil. 'When

I woke up this morning, I tried to see my papa's face in my head and I couldn't.'

Penny had listened quietly and let him chatter about his dad, feeling every word he said, knowing the truth of absence. Where were they now, these departed souls? If their faces were no longer in front of those left behind, would they be remembered or forgotten?

In different ways Penny had asked herself all of these things. But with the resilience of a child, a few minutes later, Theo was drawing again and laughing at the new animal he'd created.

Walking now to the sea and beach in the sun, Penny found incongruent the idea that anything tragic, hurtful, or heartbreaking could happen on Corfu. But the sometimes deeply cruel randomness of life touched all corners of the earth.

A large ferry chugged its way to Corfu Town, among several smaller boats, including a yacht at anchor and a speedboat closer inland. One boat veered a little closer, probably to take a look at the house around the corner. The onboard guide's commentary was muffled, but sounded animated and excited in tone.

As she took some photos from the beach, a couple walked across the sand towards her, the woman struggling to walk in her espadrille sandals. Her partner held her hand, guiding her slowly, step by step. As they reached Penny, the woman acknowledged her: 'That'll teach me. I shall choose my footwear more carefully next time.'

Penny smiled.

'To be fair,' said the woman's partner, 'we didn't know we'd be wandering about today.'

She stopped and took off her shoes.

'If it's the Durrells' house you're looking for, you've nearly found it,' said Penny. 'It's just around the corner. It's a private house now, but you can see a little of it from the gate.'

'That's great, thank you,' said the woman, but looked a little quizzical.

'You'll probably get a better view of the house from the sea,' Penny added as the excited voice floated again in the air towards them from the water.

'We're taking a boat down the coast tomorrow,' the man said, taking the sandals from the woman, 'from Kassiopi to Corfu Town, and then back by the coastal road.'

'That's one of the highlights of being here, I think,' Penny replied. 'Are you staying in Kassiopi?'

'Just above in a villa in the hills. It's the first time we've been here. The villa belongs to friends, so we had no real excuse to say no.' The woman folded her arms, as if annoyed that she'd ended up on holiday in Corfu.

'They're Peter's old colleagues from the practice,' she continued. 'We'd usually be in Florida now,' she declared, as though this might explain her apparent ennui.

Peter tried to change the subject and asked Penny if she was a regular visitor. 'This is my first time here, but I've wanted to come here for years. So far, it's been everything I hoped, and more.'

Penny was on full pro-Corfu alert, surprised to find that she took personally anything implied or said about the island that wasn't wholly positive, and never one to let a slight or indifference pass without challenge.

'Who wouldn't love being here? It's paradise,' she concluded. With a jaunty wave, her heart beating just a little faster, she walked back to the road, muttering to herself under her breath: 'What does it matter to you what one person thinks about Corfu?'

Her dad had once quoted a line from *A Midsummer Night's*

Dream after she'd taken part in a school debate when she was 16: 'And though she be but little, she is fierce'. A nod to her small stature, but inner strength and courage, when taking a stand about something she believed in.

Some days, though, it wasn't so much about taking a stand, but more a sign of her own inner frustration with something or someone. Today she put it down to the small shreds of worry that Bruce's messages had left her with; still bothering her, like a stone in her shoe.

As she drove back towards Corfu Town, the sea on her left and the sun at its height, she decided to stop somewhere on the way back to St George South for lunch, to see another beach, another village, another taverna, and sit in soothing anonymity for an hour or two and watch the world go by.

Chapter 32

Dimitris stayed in town after his dinner with Alicia and her friends. The group had moved on to another venue and he'd found out more about each of them, particularly Alicia.

Her friends formed an enthusiastic entourage, rather than a casual friendship group, and took every opportunity to bring her into the conversation. Not that she needed any real help to be the centre of things; a girl currently unattached to anyone, but who could, he had no doubt, remedy that whenever she chose.

The company had been light and diverting, reminding him of the many nights and early mornings spent in London with Sally and their colleagues.

Colleagues, he reflected, a more accurate description of the people he had spent so much time with a decade earlier. His mind left the chatter and wandered off with annoying and unwelcome clarity into past revelries. As vivacious and charming as Alicia was, he recognized the character traits and expectations of a particular personality and lifestyle, and with his own unique combination of perception and self-deprecation, realized that on paper he fulfilled all the statutory requirements of 'holiday romance' material. He was Greek, tall, tanned, in good shape, and hadn't broken any mirrors recently. The fact that his quiet and natural charm made him more of a challenge placed him more in the realms of a *conquest* – not a scenario that Dimitris cultivated or looked for.

As he sat on the terrace bar of a hotel overlooking Garitsa Bay, he observed a large cruise ship, which had just left the new port, round the headland dominated by the Venetian fortress. The stone balustrade marked the boundary of the eyrie at the top of the hotel and featured two Victorian lamps, which framed the panoramic view before them like twin beacons. An inspiring and uplifting vista for even the most jaded and sophisticated traveller, he thought.

In his mind he was on the *Antiopi*, experiencing the lull of calm waters, lying back on the deck away from the light pollution staring up at the stars. He no longer did this as often as he used to – needed to – when he'd first come home. Then it had been like daily medicine, a dose of solitude, and he could admit now, a time to wallow in his grief.

On the moonlit terrace, the conversation had moved on to what everyone did at home. Alicia had placed herself on a chair arm next to him, balanced, cross-legged, nearly every sentence punctuated with a gentle touch on his arm or shoulder.

As a boy he'd been tactile and loving, never shying away from displays of affection, a live wire in company, never wanting to leave the party. It had been one of the things about him that people had noted when he'd come home: the absence of energy and natural warmth, replaced by a monochrome, two-dimensional version of himself. Present, but a spectator rather than a participant.

Now, he noticed when Alicia leant over and touched his shoulder lightly, but he didn't really feel it. As the volume of the chatter grew and the glasses of prosecco were refreshed,

Dimitris felt removed from the moment and the company he was in, drawn back to earlier that evening and his unexpected meeting with Penny, a woman in whom he sensed, without really knowing anything about her, someone he could talk to; a calming and warm presence.

Another cork popped and in spite of his polite protestations his glass was refilled.

As his eyes met Alicia's and cries of '*Yamas*' filled the air, Dimitris asked himself two questions: 'Why did I decide to come this evening?' and 'Why am I still here?'

He'd genuinely hoped that tonight would be a turning point, a chance to dip his toes in the water of the wider world, to say 'yes' instead of 'no'. It had soon become clear that this was not the right time, or the right crowd, from the moment he'd seen Penny sitting at the Rex. Or more precisely, the moment she had brushed past him as she'd left.

Without adding any layers of angst, self-denial, or practised indifference, he knew he wanted to follow her, to sit down, listen, be in her company. When they'd shared a drink at the Athena earlier, he had spoken to her on impulse; there was no plan, and the interruptions and busy atmosphere had made him lose whatever thread he'd had in his mind when he'd sat down. She too had seemed a little guarded, even distracted. But every time he saw her, he wanted to see her again, wanted to spend more time with her. As she'd brushed past him at the Rex the impulse to catch her, hold her, speak with her, keep her there for a minute longer had caught him by surprise.

He wasn't sure why or what that might mean, but it was the first real sensation he'd felt for a long time, when he'd been a different person, someone he had thought was never coming back.

Dimitri stood, stooped to kiss Alicia lightly on the cheek,

and said, 'Let me take care of the drinks. I have an early start, but thank you so much for inviting me. I hope you enjoy the rest of your stay on Corfu.'

And before anyone had a chance to comment, he was halfway across the terrace, speaking to the waiter, ordering another bottle of prosecco for the table, and settling the drinks bill.

He didn't look back.

Chapter 33

Nic had a window seat on the plane back from Athens and took the opportunity to follow the coastline below, as mainland Greece unfolded like a child's drawing of an imaginary place beneath him. He mused for a moment that this was the view the gods had enjoyed, whether from Mount Olympus or the clouds.

The invention of flying must have created more than a ripple of confusion and anger among them. He imagined them reclining, feasting, making love, fighting or mischief-making, interrupted suddenly by flashing phones and cameras from the passengers of a 737 en route to Crete for their holiday. An undignified scuttling for cover and a whirl of silken robes, and they'd be gone. The scene made him smile and it felt like a release. It had been a very intense twenty-four hours.

Looking back now, sitting in idle contemplation on the short flight back to Corfu, Nic was glad he'd been able to deliver some practical help to Melina. She would stay at the university; the crisis had passed.

As he felt the plane start its descent and the jigsaw puzzle of sea and shapes below began to look more like the picture on the box, his mind went to thoughts of home – specifically, to thoughts of Tess and Theo.

He'd take Theo to the olive press tomorrow and the summer routine, with no doubt an interruption or two along the way, would continue.

Then, there was Tess. There was always Tess.

He was glad he'd been able to catch an earlier afternoon flight and was eager to get back to the Mouse House, but he also wanted a little time to think and shake the emotional dust of the last forty-eight hours from his mind.

Stopping off for a late lunch on the way home felt like a good plan.

Penny soon found herself on the other side of Corfu Town, heading through Perama and approaching Benitses. Whichever radio station she was listening to had a playlist that defied description, but in its own way was quite addictive. One minute Lady Gaga, the next a traditional Greek song, then a Europop holiday classic. Eclectic and thoroughly entertaining. Even if she didn't know a particular song, Penny hummed or sang along.

As she approached Benitses, she looked at her watch. It was just after two and she was ready for a break and something to eat. Her taste buds remembered the amazing baklava.

The double row of tavernas and cafés was bustling and lively. Penny found a seat and placed her order, then took off her sunglasses and reached into her rucksack for her phone.

She hadn't rung Lizzie to discuss Bruce. Every time she'd thought of doing it, she'd worried about interrupting her friend's busy routine. Texting would be better; Lizzie could answer in her own time then. But what to say? Penny wanted to tell the story of the messages and how they'd made her feel, but as she tried to compose a text, the problem unravelled, diminishing and losing its power as she tapped away at her phone.

Looking up she saw Nic standing beside her. 'Hello, Penny.'

The waiter placed Penny's food on the table.

'I see you had the same idea.' Nic gestured to her lunch.

'Please, join me.'

'Are you sure? I'd like that.'

Nic sat opposite her and placed his order.

'The waiter's aunt makes the amazing baklava. The Athena is a customer,' Penny informed him

'How have you managed in such a short time to know so many people?' Nic said. 'In my time, I've eaten more of this baklava than I care to admit.' He patted his stomach self-consciously.

'Guy brought us here.' Penny took a sip of her water.

'Ah, but it's not just here. You seem to have become part of the Athena team, whether you wanted to or not. I half-expect to find you behind the bar when I arrive, and you've certainly become a firm favourite with Theo.'

Penny looked across at the man, who Lily was convinced was in love with Tess, and tried to read him. 'Theo's a lovely lad,' she said, watching Nic's body language as he listened to her warm praise of his godson. Quiet pride shone from his eyes.

'Yes, he's a good boy, clever too. He's interested in everything, although I'm not sure if that's just typical for someone of his age.'

'I really enjoyed our time together,' Penny confessed. 'He has such an imagination inventing animals. Has he done that with you?'

'Oh yes. My particular favourite was the Elepig – large, pink, and likes to eat cheese.'

Nic smiled and poured some water into his glass.

'So, you're here for most of the summer and in Athens at the university the rest of the time?' Penny asked. 'Is that the best of both worlds or do you miss seeing the seasons on the island?'

'Well, I've seen the seasons here since childhood, with the exception of the past decade at the university.'

'Do you miss the island through the autumn and winter?' Penny asked, digging as discreetly as she knew how and hoping Nic wouldn't discover her ulterior motive; waiting, hoping somehow that he would mention Tess.

'I miss the Mouse House, my very small villa here in St George South, and my mother still lives in Corfu Town. But you know that because you've met her parrot.' He grinned.

Penny couldn't help herself. 'I imagine you miss her, and Tess and Theo of course.' She took a sip of her water to make the question look casual and throwaway.

Nic stopped eating for a moment and turned his head to face the sun. He turned back, his eyes still squinting from the light. 'I hope Theo will be able to come and stay with me in Athens for a break during the school holidays, when he's older. There are many museums and other places of interest I think he would love.'

Penny nodded. 'It would be a nice change, a treat for Tess too perhaps. I mean, I've only been here for a couple of weeks, but I've seen how hard she works. She makes it look almost effortless, but I imagine a break in Athens would do her good, once the season has ended of course.'

She sat in silence for a moment, half-regretting her words, but at the same time reasoning that she had only spoken the truth.

'Yes, that's true. I just hadn't thought that Tess might like a trip to Athens. My apartment is in the middle of the city, close to a busy road and, although comfortable, it's not cosy.'

Nic's answer was practical rather than passionate, but Penny detected a note of warmth as he'd agreed that Tess was all of the things she'd noted. She couldn't work out whether he was remarkably good at hiding his feelings, or if Lily had misinterpreted the friendship between him and Tess. That was more than likely, and yet . . .

Her mind ran through what she knew already about her new acquaintances, including the fact that Nic had moved to Athens after Georgios and Tess had married. A coincidence, or a decision from a man who couldn't stay and watch his best friend marry the woman he cared passionately for?

Penny's flights of fancy were interrupted by Nic commenting on how good the salad was and asking her whether she was going to try some more of the baklava.

'I have made a habit of sitting on my little balcony, enjoying a coffee and a biscuit or two, so perhaps today I could take baklava home and treat myself.'

It was so relaxing to sit under the shade of the large parasol, with the marina and sea just yards away, and Nic proved to be a pleasant lunch companion. She sensed he preferred to chat to people individually, to speak more deeply and in detail about things, not necessarily about personal things, just not about trivia. Nic appeared to be a quiet, kind, and thoughtful man, not remotely frenetic or flamboyant. Clearly interested in people and what made them tick, his gentle questioning of her time in Corfu felt like more evidence of her rejoining the real worl, a lived experience rather than a long break in the sun.

Over coffee they chatted about the weather, but not the forecast. Nic walked her through the seasons and the changes, every nuance of the flora and fauna described in fascinating detail. He knew his island like a best friend he had studied with love and respect.

Penny sat spellbound, pulled into the layers of loveliness and a passion for the land that felt like the best story she'd ever heard, albeit true. A true tale of – as Gerry Durrell had called it – the 'Garden of the Gods'.

The last of the coffee was drained from their cups and the afternoon slipped by, marked by the movement of the sun across the parasol above them. Penny stretched, feeling the call of the cool apartment back in St George.

'Who'd have thought that an afternoon nap would become part of every day,' she admitted, as she yawned.

'Yes,' said Nic. 'I suppose I ought to be getting back.'

Penny looked in her rucksack for her purse. Nic saw her and put out his hand as a signal for her to stop. 'Please, let me. I invited myself to this lunch and you have very patiently put up with my endless chatter about the island.'

'I should be treating you. I would have paid to hear that lecture on Corfu. It's been a joy. Thank you.'

'My pleasure, but I insist on paying.' Nic wandered off, paid, and returned with two parcels of baklava.

They walked across the road together, Nic guiding her instinctively between the passing cars and coaches with a gentle hand on her elbow.

As she thanked Nic for lunch she instinctively leant over and kissed him on both cheeks.

He tipped his Panama hat. 'My pleasure. Safe journey home.'

His last words echoed in her head: 'Safe journey home.'

She switched on the engine, wound down the windows, and put her hands on the wheel. Looking in the rear-view mirror before she reversed, she caught sight of a tanned, open-faced woman. For the first time in her life her face reflected her inner strength and story. All the pieces that she usually looked at separately and critically, were bright and fused together – a complete picture of a whole person.

The bright sunlight highlighted the green flecks in her hazel eyes, adding a sheen to the wisps of hair that she pushed back from her face. It was as though she'd absorbed the life force of the island through every pore.

As every day passed, she moved in sync with the rhythm of the place: expecting, but not taking the sun for granted, letting the rhythm of her mind and body take charge. Even when her thoughts carried her to her little work studio, current projects, or new ones like the book idea Theo had inspired, a calm and warm sense of anticipation accompanied them.

Corfu bewitched and enchanted and she understood with sudden clarity why the Durrells had returned again and again. She'd discovered more than a location; she'd found the powerful source of their immortal words and zest for life.

Why then, she asked herself, as she gripped the steering wheel tightly as if it would comfort her, was she crying?

In that moment she realized that although this trip had been a shared dream, her reality here had no connection with her dad whatsoever. This was new, life beyond, unreal, unfamiliar, but also the answer on the road she hadn't wanted to step onto in case she left him behind.

Chapter 34

That evening when Nic walked into the Athena he was greeted like a returning hero. Spiro shook his hand and clasped a welcoming arm around his back, Theo ran to him from the kitchen and started asking about the trip to the olive mill the next day. Tess emerged from the kitchen, still wiping her hands and greeted Nic with a kiss on both cheeks. 'So, the wanderer returns. Good flight?' she asked, noting with surprise how relieved she had felt when she'd seen him walk in.

'The flight was fine. I had the chance to sit and think, and admire our country from the air. Always a special moment, however often I fly.' Nic sat down in one of the chairs at the entrance to the Athena and was immediately handed a drawing by Theo.

'The *Antiopi*?' he asked admiringly.

Theo nodded.

'I'd know it anywhere. That's a great drawing. You must show Dimitris and Aris the next time they're here.'

Theo high-fived Nic and wandered off, looking back to remind his mama that he was going to the olive mill the following day with Nic.

'He's not going to let you forget that,' Tess said. 'I don't know what he's expecting, but the donkey is getting top billing whenever he mentions it.'

'You'll be relieved to hear there *is* a donkey.'

'What time did you land?' Tess took an order for drinks from Lily as she flew past.

'Earlier than I thought, so I had a late lunch in Benitses.' Just as he was about to mention he had met Penny, she appeared.

'*Yasas*, Penny.' Tess greeted her from behind the bar where she was pouring drinks, adding, 'Rosé while I'm here?'

Penny nodded. 'Thank you, that would be great. Is my little table free?'

Lily, who was passing, answered: 'Yup, and it's got your name on it now.'

'Thanks, Lily. Perhaps I should carve my name on the chair.'

'Did you enjoy your baklava?' It was Nic.

'Yes. When I woke up from my nap, I sat with a cup of coffee, and it was as glorious as it was the first time.'

'Baklava that good can only be Benitses' baklava,' Tess remarked.

'Once is not enough,' Penny replied, as Tess handed her a glass of rosé.

'Penny was kind enough to allow me to join her for lunch today,' Nic said. 'I'm afraid I may have spoken at length about Corfu's hidden treasures and areas of scientific interest.'

'Oh, welcome to the family.' Tess winked at Penny, then felt an unexpected spark of jealousy that she shook off immediately, surprised to acknowledge that it had been there.

'It was a privilege and a pleasure. Really, it was,' Penny responded.

'So, you have a willing and appreciative audience at last,'

Tess teased Nic. 'He may never let you leave,' she told Penny. Tess patted Nic's arm as she passed him.

As she walked to her table, Penny thought that if one day someone smiled at her in the same way Nic did with Tess, she would be blessed.

Lily, she decided, was not wide of the mark when it came to the truth of his feelings for Tess. They clearly shared a deep bond of friendship and mutual experience between them, but Penny couldn't read Tess, to tell if there was something beyond – a chance of love growing beyond the platonic, the familiar. She made a mental note to steer her next conversation with Tess onto the subject of Nic.

After choosing dinner she sat back and watched the ebb and flow of the sea and the people at the Athena. Lily arrived with her vegetarian moussaka, with Theo trailing behind her.

'Penny, can I ask you something? Nic says I have to ask you, but I want you to come, so please, say yes. Will you come to the olive mill tomorrow? There's a donkey, and big stones, and machinery, and Nic knows the man who is in charge, so we'll see lots of things.' Theo barely paused for breath.

Penny looked at Lily for guidance, but Lily shrugged.

'Theo, did Nic send you over to ask or did you decide to do this yourself?' Penny asked. But before he could answer, Nic walked over.

'Sorry about interrupting your meal, but someone couldn't wait. Would you be able to join us tomorrow? Please, don't worry if you already have plans, but if you're free, I think you'd enjoy it.'

Nic stood with his hand on Theo's shoulder. If he'd removed it Penny feared that the small, excited boy would have defied gravity, floated away and had to be pulled down from the ceiling.

'Yes, of course, if you'll have me. I'd love to come.'

Theo threw himself at Penny and hugged her. Nic smiled. 'We're leaving around ten in the morning, from here. There's a lot of history to it. The family have been pressing olives on Corfu pretty much since people started making olive oil.'

'There are donkeys!' Theo had found his voice again.

Tess joined the group at Penny's table and catching hold of Theo's hand gently pulled him away. 'Are you sure you want to go on a trip with these two? It never turns out to be quite what you expect; it's always an adventure.' Tess kissed the top of Theo's head and walked him over to Spiro. Nic followed with a small smile. 'See you here in the morning. *Kalinichta.*'

After she'd finished her moussaka, Penny checked her mobile. There were no more calls or messages. Her text to Lizzie was still half-written. Sitting now wrapped in the warmth and chatter of the Athena, she almost couldn't remember why she needed to bother Lizzie with the news that Bruce had been in touch.

She was a world away, geographically and emotionally, from the places and people Bruce now lived and worked with. Whatever the reason, why he had sent the message, it was not her problem. And yet, even when people were no longer part of her everyday life, Penny almost felt responsible for their wellbeing.

The only residue of worry she had about the unexpected contact with Bruce was the remote but naggingly present one, that he was in some kind of trouble and only she could help or understand.

The sea sent a warm and wistful breeze which ruffled her hair and drew her gaze out into the darkness. The world had felt new and strange in a hard-to-accept and weary way before she'd arrived in Corfu. Now novelty held more promise and didn't feel like something lost so much as something found.

Chapter 35

The following morning as the cleaner washed and swept the stone paved courtyard of the apartments, Penny prepared for her trip to the olive mill.

Between Paxos and St George the sparkling sea was decorated with icing-sugar-topped waves that gently pushed and pulled the *Dora* as Dimitris and Aris paused and stopped the engines. On their return from dawn fishing, the stop had become an unspoken but special moment of calm before they re-entered the harbour. Sometimes their conversation involved the catch, or their plans for the rest of the day. Often it comprised soothing silence.

At the airport Guy directed new arrivals to their coaches as Rich, in the departures entrance, guided hot, tired, and mostly reluctant-to-leave holidaymakers through check-in.

It was another five days before they had an official full day and night off, and the weather, although miraculously predictable and glorious, was getting hotter and hotter, the crucible of mid-July and then August only a couple of weeks away.

At the Mouse House, Nic fed Ulysses and finished his first coffee of the morning. The car was ready: petrol, cool bag with bottles of water, and binoculars – essential items for a day out, whether exploring new territory or familiar byways.

For Penny, now past the midpoint of her holiday, the smallest, but truly important things were changing her world. When she woke up, the deep well of sadness in the pit of her stomach became shallower each day.

Chapter 36

Not sure what the tour would consist of, Penny had tried to cover all eventualities with flat pumps, knee-length shorts, a light cotton shirt tied at the waist, and a straw hat.

'Ready?' Nic asked, putting his sunglasses on.

'Absolutely.' Penny turned around to smile at Theo. As she did, Dimitris walked into the Athena with his father, carrying a box full of fish from the morning's catch.

As she settled back in her seat Nic started the car and the small white lanes of St George South led them out to the roads taking them north and then inland.

$\sim$

After driving for half an hour Nic pulled the car off the main road and into a small car park. There were just a few more cars and, a short stroll away, an old crumbling building that contrasted sharply with a smart white wall and glass visitor centre.

The smell as Penny stepped out of the car was an intoxicating mix of olives and heat. But before she'd had a moment to adjust to the landscape and the light, a man strode towards them.

'I should explain that Kostas and I were at school together and this is his family's business,' Nic said after exchanging greetings with his friend. 'For generations they've been pressing olives and making the best olive oil you've ever tasted.'

'Well, if it's the oil Tess uses in the Athena, I would have to agree with you.'

'Indeed, it is. I'm thrilled you think that.' Kostas beamed and looked at her more intently than he had when Nic had introduced them.

She noticed how very blue his eyes were, a stunning feature of a tanned, toned, lean face, topped by blonde hair, shot through with grey. He was without doubt a handsome forty-something man, and she supposed that when at school together Kostas had been the girl magnet and Nic had been the quiet one, always in the background.

For that reason alone, she felt more comfortable with Nic. There was no smoothness or flirting, no innuendo or pregnant pauses. He was simply Nic, which was perhaps why, she mused, if he did have feelings for Tess, he hadn't even hinted at them, let alone said anything.

Throughout the tour, which Penny conceded was excellent, Kostas's knowledge was impressive. One story particularly enchanted Penny. During the Venetian occupation centuries before, the Corfiots had been encouraged to plant and harvest olives, with the oil used to light the lamps of Venice. It conjured up romantic images of St Mark's Square and the Doge's Palace, their stone-carved terraces lit by hanging lamps, reflected in the canals. In her head Penny was already painting this scene.

Theo had to be patient until the end of the tour when the old millstone for pressing the fruits, which had originally been pulled by a donkey, appeared. In a paddock next to the ancient press a pair of donkeys stood patiently in the shade of the olive trees.

Before anyone had a chance to stop him, he was over the small fence and heading towards the animals. As Penny looked up into the hills and the groves beyond, the scream of the cicadas was constant. The shade that the donkeys wisely sought looked inviting.

'Thank you so much, Kostas,' Penny said, keeping her eye on Theo. 'This has been a real treat.'

'Well, as Nic knows, it's not over yet. Please follow me.' Kostas walked into the groves. Theo hugged the necks of the donkeys before he climbed back over the fence to join them.

As they strolled in the groves, the sun became dappled and kinder, the strong midday heat softened by the canopy of trees. Ahead was a large wooden table, topped with bottles of oil, goat's cheese, olives, golden-crusted loaves of bread, and a carafe of wine, all arranged on a white tablecloth, covered by a clear weighted gauze which, as Kostas pulled it back, revealed the sparkle of the wine glasses and beautifully polished knives.

A sylvan scene straight from a fairy tale. A banquet for elves, or fairies in a forest.

Kostas looked up and said, 'We usually have tastings in the mill, but I thought today you'd prefer this. Please, help yourself.

'The two unopened bottles of oil are for you, Penny,' he continued, 'to take and enjoy when you return home.' As he finished speaking his mobile rang and he walked away to take his call.

'Well, I didn't expect any of this,' Penny said to Nic, as she poured water for Theo and made sure he had what he wanted to eat.

'Neither did I. I've been a few times before for the tour,

but never had this special treatment,' Nic whispered back.

Kostas finished his call and made his apologies – he had to meet a business associate at the main building, but he hoped to catch them before they left.

To Penny he gave one last dazzling smile and with a nod to Nic, he was gone.

The three left in the enchanted landscape ate in comfortable and contented silence. The bread tasted like the best bread ever baked and the oil had a delicate nutty flavour that made Penny want more, to never be full, so that she could carry on dipping and enjoying the food of the gods. Penny felt she had to try the lightly fragranced red wine in the carafe, while Theo sat in the lower branches of a weathered old tree, his plate balanced on a knee and his eyes firmly fixed on a colourful, strange bird in the upper branches.

'Shall we?' Nic pointed towards a small incline of well-shaded grass.

They sat, side by side, watching Theo and sipping their drinks.

Penny looked down at her legs, now shiny and brown, like a pale hazelnut, and wondered idly what colours she would mix on her palette to recreate that hue.

Thinking out loud, she heard herself suddenly say: 'I never thought Corfu would be like this. How could I have imagined somewhere so perfect?'

It was a moment or two before Nic responded. It was not what Penny expected to hear. 'No place is perfect, because none of us are. We carry our hopes, dreams, hurt, and failings with us wherever we go. But when life brings you heartache, as well as good things, as is the usual way, Corfu does its best to either soothe you or celebrate with you.'

Without hesitating Penny asked, 'Is that how it works for you? Does it soothe you?'

He put down his glass and peered up through the sky at the interwoven tree branches, before answering. 'Yes, and sometimes no. There are days, moments, when it's easier to be away from here, with all its familiarity and memories.'

'I can see that,' Penny said. 'Is there something that feels more painful here than when you're in Athens?'

There, she thought, *I've said it. I've asked*; then immediately regretted prying.

'I'm sorry. I shouldn't have asked that. It's none of my business. I apologize. It's just that I know a little about wanting to be somewhere else, looking for answers that don't come when you're at home, thinking that somewhere else might have them.'

Penny stopped speaking as Nic gently put his hand on hers, patted it and said, 'Don't worry. You're only asking the questions I've been too afraid to ask or answer honestly for myself.'

She wanted to say, 'Is it Tess? Are you in love with Tess?' but instead, she tried frantically to think of something to say that wouldn't press Nic to reveal anything, but would offer the option for him to share.

'If there is something . . .' She paused. 'Whatever it is, if you want someone to just listen, I know we barely know each other and I'm only here for a little while longer, but – and I may be talking absolute rubbish, so feel free to forget everything I just said . . .'

The last few words came out in a rush and she sat hoping she hadn't gone too far and invaded the privacy of a clearly very private man.

She hadn't even considered that Tess might not feel the same way about Nic. Why should she? It was Georgios she had chosen originally, so why would she choose Nic now?

In the seconds that it took Penny to travel through all the

contradictions and possibilities in her head, Nic remained silent.

Then suddenly their attention was drawn alarmingly to Theo, who fell – not very far, but with spectacular comic timing – out of the tree.

They both rushed over to the small boy, who seemed unperturbed by his fall and, as though he was part of a circus act, still held tightly to his plate.

'Ouch!' he said, almost as an afterthought.

Theo asked if they could see the donkeys again before they left.

'I don't see why not. Are you ready to go now?' Nic asked.

'No, not just yet. I've got my insect box, but I haven't found an insect yet.' Theo ran to fetch his backpack.

'That's okay, we don't have to hurry. Take your time. That is, if you're fine with that, Penny? Can we stay a little longer?' Nic turned to ask.

'It's okay with me. I've no plans at all today except for this,' said Penny relieved at Nic's apparent lack of annoyance or embarrassment at her meddling. 'I can't wait to see what he brings back.' Penny raised her eyebrows.

Nic laughed and nodded. 'Yes, we've had some moments. The scorpion was one new friend he found when not much more than a baby. I think Georgios kept that one quiet. I'm not sure Tess knows about it even now.'

'Very wise.'

They sat back down on the grass bank.

'Penny, what you were saying before Theo decided to become an acrobat was very kind. You've only been here for a short time, but I think, hope, you know that you have settled into our small community very quickly. You will be missed when you go home. Tess, in particular, enjoys your company and for that, I am personally very grateful. So, while thanking you for your kindness to me just now, I want to offer you the same listening ear. I too, so I'm told, am a good listener.'

Theo came running back to them, transparent bug carrier in hand, which revealed a very shiny black beetle; then ran off again to find more.

'There was something I wanted to ask you.' Penny looked away into the sun as she spoke, afraid to look him in the eye as spoke in case he read something there she didn't want him – didn't want anybody – to see. 'Do you know Dimitris well?'

'Dimitris? I'm guessing you mean our fisherman-lawyer?'

Penny nodded.

'I've known him since he was a boy. Our paths didn't cross for a few years when he lived in England, but I've seen more of him since he returned, although of course, I'm away for a fair part of the year.'

'What's he like?' Penny asked.

'Well, he's quieter than when he was a boy. He was always lively, asking questions all the time . . . not unlike young Theo. He's certainly been quieter since he returned, but that may be maturity. Although . . .' He paused, as though wondering whether to continue. 'Well, no doubt you may have heard if you asked the same question of Tess – his mother died when he wasn't here and I believe there was a break-up with a partner over in England.'

Penny nodded.

'But if what you're really asking me is, is he a good man, then I'd say yes, but of course with all the reservations about faults and foibles that all of us have.'

Penny wondered if Nic was being discreet about Dimitris's conquests, which she imagined often, but of which she knew nothing for certain.

Theo ran back up to Nic.

'Now, what about those donkeys?' Nic asked his godson.

As they gathered up their things, Penny saw Kostas on the horizon. Before he got any closer, she said, 'Thank you, Nic, for what you said just now and about the listening. I appreciate it.'

There were thanks again to Kostas and more time with the donkeys, before they finally persuaded Theo it was time to leave.

Chapter 37

As Nic drove back on the road south, the sun was still high. Light filled the world as they passed by, making it difficult to imagine that in such bright and brilliantly beautiful surroundings anyone could be troubled or sad. A life force ran through the island that, if it couldn't make the hurt or worry go away, still seemed to lift the spirits.

From the moment Penny had stepped off the plane, the sheer exuberant, unashamed beauty of the place had embraced her, as though saying, 'You're not alone. Everyone here is dealing with something they never expected, or wanted, or dreamed. We may not have any answers, but while you're here, let's keep each other warm for a while.'

'Thank you for today.' She turned to Nic. 'It's been a real treat; an unexpected, lovely day.'

'So, was the invitation unexpected, or the fact that it was lovely?' he teased, as she added Nic Constantine to the list of extended family that had begun with Guy, Rich, and Lily. He felt more like an older brother in that moment than a holiday acquaintance she'd known for only for a couple of weeks. It was comfortable and comforting to be around Nic.

As she gazed idly out of the car window, she felt a pang as

she wondered if that was how Tess felt about Nic: comfortable, caring, platonic, but no more than that.

She hoped that wasn't the case.

Sometimes even the people who ultimately made you happy weren't the ones you immediately fell in love with. Where was Tess on this journey? Surely if Nic was in love with her, she had some idea of his feelings. Even his non-committal answers to Penny were, she thought, in some senses so telling. The two of them were obviously close.

She took the opportunity to look at Nic as he drove. His face was quite angular, his nose strong and well-shaped. His beard and moustache softened the face of the purposeful professor into a more approachable character. His olive complexion was topped with dark, now slightly greying hair, the sort of hair that had clearly never been tamed, and even when wearing his Panama hat, looked as though it was trying to escape from his head. He was an attractive man, who at over six foot was an impressive, albeit quiet figure when he entered a room.

He was, in every sense, a rock. Someone of stature and kindness, reliable, who wouldn't let you down. Nic Constantine was, in old-fashioned parlance, clearly a good man and an eligible bachelor – a catch.

The fact he had not been caught yet was a mystery to which perhaps only Tess had the answer.

⌒

Lily had been trying all the usual tricks to distract herself from some of her darker thoughts all day. Ever since she'd shared with Penny the story of Sophie's suicide, she'd felt as though pressure had been released from her head, but the memory hadn't lost its power to grab hold of her heart and mind, stop her in her tracks.

She knew too that the gentle questions from Rich and Guy – mostly from Rich – came from a good place rather than prurient curiosity. Rich, she'd noticed, had watched her as though she were made of glass and might trip and break at any moment. Guy had, in his usual bantering, self-mocking way, offered, if she ever needed it, an evening of poetry and wallowing. She'd smiled at that, knowing Guy well enough now to understand his unique ways of being a friend. Tess, as expected, had been kind and solicitous when she'd told her about Sophie, and every time Lily spoke about Sophie now it became a little easier.

A familiar voice brought her back into the moment. 'Lily, look. This is my new beetle. He's called Jet,' Theo informed her.

Lily stared at the large insect that seemed to be sleeping on a bed of grass and leaves. 'Why Jet? It's a good name though,' she added.

'Penny told me about a stone called jet that is very black and shiny, just like my beetle.'

Penny was one of those people who made you feel better just by being there. She and Tess were so similar in that respect; very alike, Lily thought.

She reflected on how lucky she'd been to end up in St George South, but more importantly, at the Athena. It was the best place she could be, with – and this was the miraculous thing – just the people she needed right now.

⟡

Guy and Rich drove back from the airport, having guided six planeloads of new holidaymakers either onto coaches, to their destinations, or through the departure lounge towards home.

They weren't on coach and destination drop-off duty, but had to deliver a welcome meeting in Kavos and then St George. After this they could blend almost seamlessly into the evening revelries, pausing only to take calls on their mobiles from holidaymakers who couldn't find a plug for the bathroom, or needed to know the name of a local dentist.

The attraction of Greek Night also dragged them towards St George. Although exhausting on some levels, after a long day with an early start of 5 a.m., it cast an almost hypnotic spell. The energetic and liberating Greek Night reaffirmed what life was about – or should be about.

As he drove, Guy tapped the steering wheel, uncharacteristically distracted and thoughtful. He had told Faith and Dee about the Athena and they had seemed excited about the idea of Greek Night. Having spent an evening with them, Guy imagined the warmth and welcome, the people and atmosphere at the Athena would appeal to them. Dee clearly loved shopping, but wasn't an all-night, hard-partying girl, and Faith seemed more at home in a quiet bar, chatting and absorbing the atmosphere of the never-ending pageant around her.

He then realized, as he directed the seemingly endless groups of people to their coaches at the airport, that for once he wasn't looking for new faces and new possibilities. He was thinking about Faith and hoping she'd turn up that night in St George.

Chapter 38

The red wine at the olive grove had been light and delicate, but by the time Penny got back to her apartment it had the impact of an opiate sleeping draught. Sleep descended, bringing with it strange, but not unpleasant dreams, which for once didn't feature her dad in distress.

Her new experiences on the island filled her head. Grief and loss lingered in the background, but seemed to be making room for life again, as they stood back and left space in the corners of her mind for fresh air and hope.

It was gone six o'clock when she woke up. The book she'd been rereading lay at her feet, about to fall off the bed. *Prospero's Cell* was a love letter to Corfu, but especially Kalami. The White House, the old fisherman's house in all its rustic and romantic glory, was still waiting to be discovered. For the hundredth time she promised herself she'd speak to Dimitris when she saw him next and book her place on the *Antiopi*. Time on her holiday was now telescoping, as it always did, running downhill to the finishing line. There remained less time on Corfu than she'd already enjoyed, and the rush and panic of a mid-holiday crisis assaulted her briefly, before she remembered she had come for a month and many adventures and days in the sun still lay ahead.

Penny swung her legs off the bed. Yawning, she unlocked the shutters onto the balcony and allowed the warm air to roll into the room. Tonight was the loud and lovable Greek Night, like a favourite maverick uncle, full of undeniable charm. An event which included and embraced everyone with its warmth and light.

She plucked a pale blue cotton shirt dress from its hanger. Its simplicity complimented her height and tanned skin. But Penny had no such thoughts as she chose it. For her, it was a lucky dress, the first thing she'd bought for herself after her split with Bruce. She'd never worn it, but this evening felt like the perfect time.

Her mind turned to Tess. It would be a busy night at the Athena. Everyone would be working, with little chance of chatting, except maybe at the very end of the evening. She suddenly recalled her grandmother saying to her, when she'd been trying on dresses as a teenager and felt swamped by their length, 'Good things come in small packages'.

'I hope so,' she muttered under her breath as she pulled her dress on over her head.

Bruce, she couldn't deny, was a striking-looking man, and she admitted that she'd been flattered by his attention. That said, it was strange that Bruce's good looks had affected her right from the moment she'd first seen him, as all her life her dad had focused on character being the thing that truly mattered, including having a good heart. She took one last look in the mirror that was still slightly misted over after her shower. This evening it felt as though her appearance mattered more than other days. She gave a tentative smile and moved her head from side to side, immediately pulling a face and laughing at herself.

'Who are you and what have you done with Penny?' she asked her reflection.

By 8 p.m. there was a lively mix of old and new patrons at the Athena. Two families who came to St George South every year had arrived that morning and were delighted to find that the Greek Night was happening on their first day. The air that night was full of the promise of what could be, with no shadows of regret or disappointment under the amber light that drew people into the restaurant. The sea below them, as always, took no notice of the proceedings. It had seen it all before, a million times.

Penny was touched when she arrived to find that they'd put a reserved sign on her little table. The colourful, lively tableau of guests, new friends, and live music comforted rather than daunted her. This place had become part of her luck and her life.

As soon as she sat down Lily was there with a glass of rosé, followed almost immediately by Rich, who asked if he could join her for a moment.

'I wanted to ask you something, if that's okay?' he said.

She had never seen him look so earnest or serious. 'I like Lily . . . very much,' he began, with a face that looked like that of a fallen angel about to enter Purgatory. 'I'm not very good at saying things – words in the right order at the right time don't always happen. I thought if I watched Guy, some of his charm and confidence might rub off on me, so I could speak to Lily in a way that lets her know I care about her, but doesn't frighten her off.' He sighed. 'She's just told me that she has a short break later and wants to have a chat, which is great, but also makes me feel pressured to say the right things and not look like a prat.'

As she looked at him Penny saw her own vulnerability at

the same age reflected back at her. 'Are you worried about what to say?' she asked.

'Yes. I don't know the details about why she's not going back to uni. So, how do I know what she needs to hear?'

'The most important thing you can do for Lily is listen,' Penny suggested. 'Forget about what you might, or might not, say; what's right, or what's wrong. The words will come if you listen.'

Rich looked at her as if trying to absorb what she'd said, focusing on every syllable so he'd remember her words like a mantra. He was about to thank her when Guy appeared.

'Hi, Penny, good to see you. How was the trip to the olive mill?'

She smiled, about to reply, when Guy saw someone at the entrance and shot off with a 'Back in a minute'.

'Looks like Faith and Dee have turned up. He'll be pleased about that,' Rich said, looking at Guy greeting two girls.

He stood up. 'Thanks for listening. Catch you later.'

'Good luck,' she couldn't help saying as he made his way through the tables to his friends. *Talk about physician heal thyself. I could do with a bit of relationship advice myself*, she thought.

⌒

After she'd eaten the usual Greek Night fare of mezze, Penny sat back and looked for Tess, who had whispered as she'd passed, 'Are you up for a drink later at the bar when it quietens down?' before being swept up in a line of dancers on a mission to pull more diners on to the dance floor. Nic had quietly fetched and carried, supporting Anna in the kitchen tonight rather than being out in the restaurant.

Signalling to Lily that she was going for a walk on the beach, Penny wandered out of the heaving but happy scene.

The moon was up. It always appeared larger and brighter on a hot summer's night, particularly in Greece, and it shone now, illuminating the wavelets at the edge of the sea.

Walking beyond the harbour so that she could stroll on the sandy beach at the other side, Penny passed wine bars, tavernas, and rustic cafés, all of them intermingled with larger establishments and supermarkets. Turning away from the busy, brightly lit road, she heard the sea before she saw it.

She untied her sandals so that she could walk on the wet sand and let the water fall over her feet, then looked back at the harbour.

Aris's little fishing boat was there, but she hadn't seen Dimitris since the morning, when she'd glimpsed him as he went into the Athena. As soon as she saw him, the Kalami trip was going to be the first thing she'd book. Even if she turned out to be the only passenger, she'd pay for the *Antiopi* for the day, throw caution to the winds, ready to spend more money than she normally would, and push away any reservations she might have about the journey, with potentially just her and Dimitris on board.

Let me think about this and take a step back, she thought. Dimitris was mysterious, even a little remote, but every time she saw him, she felt a warmth that she couldn't explain. She needed comfort, a physical presence, but wondered if endowing a man she barely knew with the attributes she want to see, to find, in a man was really a sensible idea. She knew next to nothing much about him. Their conversations had been short, perfunctory, casual. She needed him to be what she needed right now, but even as an object of desire, she couldn't even commit herself to a little light flirting.

'Penny?'

She knew his voice before she turned around, wondering if her face was showing any trace of the fact that she'd just been thinking about him.

'Beautiful, isn't it?' He looked at the sea and then up at the moon. 'When I'm out on the boat the stars are so bright, I can read the sky'

'That must be wonderful, to steer by the stars,' she said. 'I'm glad I've seen you,' she continued. 'I want to make a firm booking for your yacht, for the trip to Kalami, if that's still okay.' She stepped out of the water to face him, felt the sand move between her toes, and took a snapshot in her head for her memory bank.

'When would you like to go?' He stood alongside her now as they both began to walk.

'Well, I'm here for a while longer, but anytime that fits in with your fishing and your other passengers. There's nothing I have to do on any particular day. Although sometimes I wonder if, even on holiday, that's a blessing or a curse.'

'You like a routine then?' he asked.

'Mostly, although as any of my friends will tell you, I can be forgetful, erratic, and a little flaky at times. Although I never miss a deadline – if a book needs to have the illustrations finished by a certain day or time, I'll make sure it's delivered.'

As she finished, she realized she sounded like an advertisement, or worse, how she imagined a character synopsis for a dating website might read.

'I see,' he said, the tone of his voice giving nothing away. 'I could take you the day after tomorrow, or is that too early?' He stopped walking and looked at her. The truth was he wanted her to see the boat as soon as possible.

'That would be great. I wanted the day at Kalami to be near the end of my stay here, but now I realize that doesn't matter at all. Do you have some people already booked for that day?'

'Just a couple. There may be more, but the *Antiopi* never feels crowded, so please don't worry that it will spoil your trip if we're at full capacity.'

'I'm not worried at all. I can't wait. Will we be able to stop at Kalami for long? Should I book a place for lunch now? I don't want to be disappointed if it's full when we get there.' She bent to pick up a shell and cleared some of the sand from its corrugated surface, unaware that she was frowning a little, contemplating the thought of arriving at the White House to find the tables all occupied.

'I can make the booking for you. Part of the service.' Was he laughing at her? Amused by her practical, 'beans in a row' mentality?

'That would be wonderful, thank you.' she said.

He was standing between her and the sea. Behind him the waves rose and fell in gentle motion. His outline dominated her view.

Penny realized that her thoughts were taking over. This didn't feel like when she met Bruce. This felt unreal, as though she wasn't quite awake . . . and yet she'd never felt more in the moment in her life. All the common sense, all the reason and grown-up advice in the world couldn't stop her feeling like she wanted to reach out and touch this man. Be held and feel his warmth, smell his skin.

On impulse, so aware of his physical presence and intense gaze, she blurted out, 'This trip really matters to me. I've imagined it ever since I was a teenager, when my dad gave me *My Family and Other Animals*. He died last year and it felt like the right time to visit.' She paused, almost telling him about Bruce, but then thought better of it. Her words were just a diversionary tactic, a lifeline she was throwing herself to stop the ache that was becoming more intense by the second.

'I was pulled here by the world of the Durrells, their lives and writing, the strength of their characters, their way of living, and their attitude to life, especially on Corfu. I wanted to be where they'd been and I think I hoped some of the feelings, the joy they found here, would help me, give me some answers – or a map; a guide to living well.'

As she shared this, the sea flowed around their feet as though they were newly discovered islands. Dimitris turned away and then back, looking thoughtful and then grave, as though fighting a shadow that had fallen over him.

'Did you know that you were going to lose your father? Did you have the chance to spend time with him before he died?' he asked.

'Yes, I did, but the finality of loss was still a shock.'

He hesitated and then said: 'It's good that you could do that . . . be there, say the things you wanted to say.'

'Yes, but however long we have with our parents, with those we love, it's never enough. It's never exactly how we imagine either. How can it be? The only time we really have is now, this moment, the one that's just passed and a promise not to waste any of it, or wait for life to happen.' Penny paused, looked across at the edge of the harbour they'd just reached, before she continued.

'My dad used to say, "Life is what happens to you when you're busy making other plans."'

Dimitris seemed to be thinking out loud, talking to himself rather than Penny. 'Death too; that happens when you're so busy you don't notice, when you're so focused on your own life you don't have room for the lives of others, even those who are precious to you.'

Penny sensed pain in his words and thought carefully before answering. 'Even when you know what's coming, there's still the fear of saying the wrong thing, or saying nothing at all and then regretting it. We make judgements every day and every choice is about making things as easy as we can for the person who's leaving,' she said quietly.

They began to walk away from the sea, back towards

the road and the Athena. Then as they drew close to the restaurant she said: 'So, the day after tomorrow it is. Thanks, Dimitris. Tess asked me earlier if I was free for a drink, so I'd better get back. Though she might have changed her mind now.'

He smiled and looked at his feet before confessing.

'I was on my way there too, but then I saw you on the beach.' He stopped, thinking on his feet, with no plan . . . no clever, pre-planned smooth talk. He'd reached a point where he wanted to be in her company and that was all that mattered. 'Can I buy you a drink? It's still early and I don't think Tess will be finished for a while yet. It would be good to have more time to talk. I wanted to speak to you last night, when I saw you at the Rex. I just didn't want to be rude to the people I'd arranged to meet.'

She sat on the edge of the harbour wall and brushed the sand off her feet, then started to put her sandals back on, carefully wrapping the leather criss-crossed cords around her ankle and tying them in a bow.

'That would be lovely,' she said casually, but with a studied, controlled calmness.

Emotions coursed through her, of a very different kind to the ones that had drained and dogged her, for what seemed like a very long time. Her heart pounded. Her face flushed. The hairs on her arms tingled and stood on end. She hoped none of these things were visible in the darkness.

'Good. I'd like to hear more about you and what you do when you're not on Corfu,' he said.

'Fine by me, but only if you promise to tell me more about Corfu, which, trust me, will be far more interesting.'

As she stood up, she noticed Lily and Rich on the other side of the harbour. Lily seemed to be doing all the talking.

The Athena was still busy. There seemed to be more children in the restaurant that evening and they were, in turn, dancing around the restaurant or falling asleep on their parents' laps.

Sitting at her little table Penny and Dimitris found themselves in the middle yet apart from the merriment around them. Tess had fetched their drinks and told Penny that she thought it might be far too late for a nightcap by the time she was free, so perhaps they could do it tomorrow. Penny suspected that this was more to do with leaving her free to spend time with Dimitris.

'So, tell me Penny, what do you do when you're not here?' He opened the conversation, taking some of his wine. His hand rested on the table, cradling the glass.

Before she answered she made him promise to stop her talking if she went on for more than a minute or two: 'Because when I talk about painting, I don't know when to stop', she admitted.

He had laughed at that and warned her not to ask him to talk about the *Antiopi* because, he confessed, she was the love of his life. 'She costs me more money to keep at sea than I have ever spent on anything – or anyone – else. She has my heart.'

They discovered that they both loved cinema and had found the end of *Cinema Paradiso* intensely moving and yes, the music did make the film. One of Dimitris's favourite parts of Corfu was a small beach which you reached through an olive grove near Kassiopi.

'I'd like to show you it before you go home, if you're free,' he'd said and she had smiled, excited at the thought, but also noted the 'before you go home' and reminded herself that this was all happening on holiday and that their time together was brief.

As the Athena slowly began to empty and the carafe of wine on the table emptied, they both stood up, as Dimitris offered to walk with Penny down the lane. He would be up at 4 a.m. as tomorrow was a fishing day.

They waved their goodnights to Tess and Nic and walked across the street. From the karaoke bar down the road the not-so-dulcet tones of someone singing 'I will Always Love You' pierced the air. They both laughed.

'What would you sing? Do you sing?' He teased her.

'I don't, but you first. What would *you* sing?' she countered, with raised eyebrows.

'I don't sing either, so it wouldn't really matter, as the results would be so bad people would leave.'

'So, let's make a pact never to do it.' She held out her hand for him to shake it, which he did, but he didn't let go.

'That sounds fair,' he answered. The look in his eyes was new. Questioning, but glowing with a warmth she hadn't seen before.

The effect it had on Penny was immediate and strong. They carried on walking, their hands still interlocked. As they reached the lemon trees halfway down the path she stopped and he turned to her.

'I'm fine from here.' The need to take back some control overwhelmed her. 'I've had a lovely evening. Thank you. I can't wait to—'

But before she had the chance to finish the sentence, he had taken her head in his hands and was kissing her gently. It felt so natural to lift her head to meet his mouth.

'I've had a lovely evening too,' he said, releasing her and tracing his finger over her mouth with the gentlest movement. 'So, 9 a.m. at the Old Port, the day after tomorrow. Will you be there?'

'Yes, I'll be there. I can't wait.' she replied and kissed him lightly on the mouth, then with a squeeze of his hand, she let him go and walked the few yards home, feeling more whole than she had for a long, long time.

Minutes later, sitting on the single bed in her room, Penny glanced across at empty side of the bed that seemed to stare back at her accusingly. How easy it would have been to have invited him up . . . to spend the night together. *Really?* she thought, as she threw herself back on the bed. *Easy?*

Nothing felt easy any more and she wondered when she had become so terrified of living.

Chapter 39

In the day that followed, Penny found herself thinking less about the days that were left and more about her impending trip to Kalami.

The idea of the cruise up the coast would have been thrilling in itself, a highlight of her holiday, but had now taken on more significance than a much-anticipated day on the water. She had to admit to herself the reason was Dimitris – or more honestly, the idea of Dimitris being more than a holiday acquaintance.

Her mind seized cruelly on the narrative of a holiday romance, a story that ended at the airport with an embarrassed farewell, mired in a mixture of sadness and relief. And she considered, albeit briefly, backing out of the Kalami trip.

The one thing she couldn't talk herself out of was how he had made her feel last night. Just one kiss, a little hand-holding, and shared laughter and she had felt totally true to herself when he'd kissed her, sure of who she was, who she wanted to be. She had come to the conclusion that perhaps the reason this felt so daunting was the worry of something going wrong. She wanted to go carefully, to find out who he really was. Was this just a fierce and fleeting attraction, or something more?

It hadn't been the same when she'd met Bruce, when she'd equated love – or falling in love – with a loss of her sense of self, or the fear of being hurt.

If she loved, at some point she was bound to lose, she had decided. So, it mattered that the bits in between, the life she had together with someone else, was worth it; that the love was real, because grief and love, she now believed, were the same thing – each an expression of the other.

So, whether a holiday romance or something finer, stronger, and more layered, Dimitris was an unexpected element in a trip originally designed to heal and give her new hope. Was he part of the healing? Was he the hope?

Dimitris had been curious about her work, her family – only two aunts and their offspring were left – her friends and her home. She asked him about the yacht and the seasons on Corfu, what he did in the winter, about his father and wider family. His mother had died two years before, but more than that he was obviously reluctant to say.

She understood this and had chosen to keep the story of Bruce to herself, for the moment.

He hadn't asked her anything about a partner or boyfriend, but as she didn't mention one and was travelling on her own, he'd concluded she was single.

The scene in the bar – Nic, Tess, Guy, Rich and Lily – had seemed nostalgic even before it had passed. Penny's eyes had taken in each little vignette of life as she scanned the room, marvelling at how many people she knew or at least knew of, as she did so.

It was a painting, but not a *still* life. It was life. And at the moment, it was hers.

Chapter 40

The day on Corfu dawned like all the others, inviting relaxation but reminding the visitor that their time there was brief and fleeting. The heat continued to manage the day, with the afternoon only occupied with anything that needed minimum effort and every opportunity to cool off, doze, or read.

Penny spent a little time caught up in the world of home and work, answering a couple of emails about future commissions, which made her think about the book developing in her head, inspired by Theo. She was in the process of creating or photographing images that would be her main resource for a children's book about Corfu, the animals, the landscapes, the sea, and a boy who loved every part of his island.

The overall idea involved the fact that each animal the boy met would lead him into a new adventure. The details were still sketchy, as it was very much a work in progress, her personal project for now . . . something for herself.

She'd also decided to take a couple of watercolour paintings into Corfu Town to be framed as a farewell gift: a thank you to Tess and the Athena, to Saint George South, to Corfu – to Aris and Dimitris

There was so much familiarity and gentle routine to each day now. She was still Penny, the girl who'd stepped off the plane, wishing her dad was with her, but life had taken over in a dazzlingly short span of time and grown around her like a hothouse plant.

As she lay on the bed in the apartment the night before her trip to Kalami, she realized that in the 24 hours since she'd seen him, she had replayed the moment he'd kissed her a hundred times. Each time it left her with a longing for more.

He had left a message at the Athena for her before he went out fishing with all the details of when, where, and what to bring. She had the impression it was a busy day for him and reminded herself that she was on holiday and he was not.

As she fell asleep, images of Dimitris, his yacht, the coast, and the White House all blended together in a fast-moving film reel. As she tried to focus on one scene it melted into another.

After turning on her side and setting the alarm on her phone for the first time since arriving on Corfu, tiredness finally won and she fell asleep.

Chapter 41

Dimitris had been up since 6 a.m. He'd stayed in town the night before at his own place, wanting some space and to make sure he was ready for a full day's sailing.

Sailing was a pleasure, when he felt happiest, but he'd never quite got used to the hosting part of the days out. The boat was immaculate and the cabin stocked with chilled wine, water, and mezze, everything a generous and hospitable guide could provide.

He greeted every passenger at the old harbourside and guided everyone aboard, offering a steady hand to those who needed it as they stepped across the side of the yacht and a smile and nod of the head to those who didn't. The only other crew member of the *Antiopi* was Basil, who acted as lookout, plus drink and food distributor on deck.

Today, Dimitris felt different, because Penny would be onboard.

He wasn't really sure why this was the case, although perhaps meeting someone who felt real and warm had, without even trying, spoken to him in a way that had both calmed and lifted him. He had been moved to kiss her to find out how that felt, and had been thinking for days how it would be.

Their brief conversation on the beach had made him think too, woken him up, introduced him to a different way of thinking about his own grief. Whether he was ready to take a step towards mending or letting go of something that had ultimately become so entrenched in his world and psyche was another matter.

Just before 9 a.m. the couple that had also booked for the Kalami cruise arrived, dressed in khaki-coloured cotton shorts and T-shirts, with a backpack each, as though they were about to go on safari or a route march.

Harry and Mary were in their late sixties and, as seasoned travellers who liked to hike, always carried supplies and items with them to deal with anything from a cut knee to a siege. At least three times a year in the early years of their so far euphoric retirement, they had randomly chosen an island or country, booked a flight, and spent an adventurous week or two abroad.

It was their first time on Corfu and they had spent as many hours of the day as they could walking. The cruise was a little treat to themselves, where they could sit back and let someone else take them to their destination.

Mary passed her backpack to Basil, who stowed it in the cabin and was chatting to Dimitris about the route and the conditions at sea that morning when Penny arrived. Dimitris saw her wander over from the bus stop, watched her as she spotted the yacht and adjusted her rucksack to walk towards them. She wore dark blue shorts, a white cotton shirt with the sleeves rolled up, and white pumps. Her hair was scraped back, with a scarf tied up like a headband. Her sunglasses looked a little too large on her small face. The overall impression was of a blithe spirit carried in a petite frame. Dimitris wondered if she'd been a water sprite in another life.

He waved from the helm and, excusing himself, moved

from Mary's side to help Penny aboard. 'Welcome to the *Antiopi,*' he said, as she reached out for his hand.

As he took it, the softness and smallness of it moved him in a way he hadn't noticed two nights ago. Once again, he found himself reluctant to let go. She smiled back at him, adding, '*Kalimera*', and in that moment he felt that he'd known her a long time. Was she part of a past life, a vision of what might have been once, or a harbinger of the future? He wasn't yet sure.

As she jumped down onto the deck and greeted Harry and Mary with a handshake and a hello, he knew he needed to find out. The kiss had not been an illusion; what he'd felt when he'd touched her face and felt her move towards him had not been a figment of his imagination.

The *Antiopi* glided out of Garitsa Bay to the accompaniment of church bells in the town. The old Venetian fortress rose above them and the coastline of mainland Greece shimmered in the morning heat haze. A ferry and a large cruise ship moved towards each other in the channel between.

Penny chatted with Harry who, although he'd never been to Corfu before, was a huge fan of anything Greek, particularly the myths and legends. Odysseus featured heavily and she found herself drawn to the lyricism of the story and loved hearing about his connection with Corfu. Once they'd cleared the bay and then the new port, they hugged the coastline more closely as they sailed north towards Gouvia.

The beaches and coves, churches, marinas, and clusters of houses along the shore reminded Penny of a continuous show reel of cinematically beautiful things. The white bell towers of churches with their robin-redbreast roofs, the inviting and cosmopolitan marinas, all bathed in the radiance of a sun that was enticing people to their shuttered windows and balconies. Blue, yellow, green, and crimson fused on the shoreline as they passed.

At the helm Dimitris looked relaxed and calm. Mary regaled him with tales of her previous holidays, the key theme of which seemed to be narrowly avoided disasters. Most of the stories seemed to end along the lines of, 'Luckily, we managed to get out before that happened.'

Basil appeared with coffee and doughnuts, handing out espresso or cappuccino as requested. In a short time they passed Gouvia Bay, where the old Imperial Airways flying boats had landed in the 1930s. Behind the marina lay the ancient Venetian shipyards.

Margo Durrell had left Corfu from here at the close of 1939, returning home to England, where her mother, Leslie, and Gerry waited. The Second World War had already begun and the days that lay ahead would be filled with peril and partings. What had run through Margo's mind as she'd looked out of the window of the seaplane and watched the island below grow smaller, until it was no more than a memory lying below the clouds?

She couldn't have known then that she would return one day in happier and more convivial times. In that instant, the last whispers of adolescence and teenage years must have felt as though they'd slipped through her fingers.

Penny didn't think that anyone could let go lightly of any time spent on Corfu. She leant over the side of the yacht, her head resting on one of the rails so that the sea spray caught her face and hair. It was hot already. She checked her arms and could still feel the sunscreen she'd put on before she left the apartment.

She pulled her shirt collar a little higher up the back of

her neck, thinking of childhood days when her neck had been red and sore from playing too long on the beach.

It was magical to sit near the front of the boat, with a cup of coffee and a doughnut that was still warm. Her hands were sticky with sugar and she laughed when Basil handed her a wet wipe.

The sensation of the boat and the moving seascape were intoxicating. She looked back over her shoulder to see Harry and Mary studying a map together. Basil stood next to Dimitris, who was saying something to him.

Basil returned to Penny's side and said, 'Dimitris wants you to know that we'll be coming up to Kontokali in a minute. You can see the Durrells' house, the one used in the TV series. He thought you'd like to see it from the water.'

Penny turned and smiled and gave the thumbs-up, mouthing, 'Thank you' above the sound of the waves and the *Antiopi*'s effortless movement through the water.

Seconds later the house was there, clear and close, as Dimitris steered the boat past the villa. Although not part of the real Durrell landscape, it captured the spirit of the family whose echoes Penny had come to listen to. The Venetian villa embodied a rustic doll's house of grandeur and familiarity, seen by millions and forever associated with a dramatized Durrell family. She held the image in her mind to play back to herself on other less sunny days, or when she needed uplifting. She could see the characters carrying a wooden table to place in the shallows, in order to dine and stay cool, with their feet dangling in the sea.

The Greek mainland turned into Albania and the hour to reach Kalami passed far too quickly for Penny. Since they'd left Corfu Town she'd not really had the chance to speak to Dimitris. She didn't want to distract him from piloting the boat and assumed that Basil was there for the passengers, to chat and look after their needs.

In this new environment for her, but in Dimitris's comfort zone, on his boat away from the Athena, she felt a little shy and realized once again how little she knew about him.

She decided to put more sunscreen on and wash her hands. As she passed Dimitris she stopped. 'This is wonderful. How long before we reach Kalami?'

'We're about fifteen minutes away. We'll anchor in the bay and I'll be able to take you ashore in the dinghy. The White House has a jetty, so you can step straight onto it and you're there. I booked a table for Mary and Harry too, but I booked you a separate one. I hope that's okay? I thought you might want to be on your own, have your own space.' He kept his voice low so that the couple, who were now at the front of the boat and taking photographs, wouldn't overhear. 'I know this is a special trip for you, so I wanted to give you your own space to enjoy it. I'll be around . . .' He paused. 'It's good to see you.' He smiled at her again, his eyes telling her that he hadn't forgotten the kiss.

'That's great. Thank you. And it's good to see you too. Yes, I'm looking forward to soaking up the atmosphere. Perhaps even making a few sketches. How long have we got there before we travel back?'

She looked up at him, waiting for his answer, but drawn to his face once again. 'We can negotiate that.' He smiled. 'I have no idea if I'm going to have to go looking for Harry and Mary up in the hills. They seem to have lots of maps and enough kit to climb Mount Pantokrator. If they wander off, who knows when we might be able to leave.'

She laughed, resting her hand on the cabin roof as the boat changed course and she had to step down the cabin stairs to steady herself. His hand automatically held her arm to stop her falling. She steadied herself and held the rails a little tighter.

'Okay?' he asked, his face concerned. She nodded, aware again of the effect his touch had on her – the electricity. 'I usually leave around 2 p.m., so we're back in port for just after 3 p.m. That gives you nearly four hours in Kalami. As well as the White House, there are a few shops, bars and, of course, the beach – much more than there would have been in Larry Durrell's day.'

'Yes, the remoteness that seems to have appealed to him probably isn't so remote any more, I guess,' Penny said.

'Not remote, no, but still very beautiful. I think you'll still find him there if you want to.'

She looked at Dimitris, surprised but more intrigued by his answer. He seemed to really understand why she was here, what she was looking for, what she wanted to feel.

'Will you come back to the boat when you've taken us ashore?'

'I will when I've been to see a friend I promised to drop in on. I have something I need to pick up from her.'

He took a swig of water from a bottle next to the wheel and looked ahead intently.

'Thanks, Dimitris, that's perfect,' she said, beginning to climb down into the cabin.

'No problem. The table is booked in your name for midday. They have a great team there. You'll be well looked after and the food is terrific. I'll also give you my mobile number – Harry and Mary already have it – so if you have any problems at all, you can call me.'

'Thank you,' she replied, but all she could think about was who the female friend was. The fact that she gave it a thought was more telling than she wanted to admit.

Chapter 42

In 1936, as spring established itself and the gentle weather carried the promise of halcyon days of heat and light yet to come, Larry Durrell and his wife Nancy moved into the two rooms that were part of what is now known as the 'White House'. They were searching for wild, remote Corfu, a sanctuary and solitude, where Larry could write and Nancy could paint.

They did both in abundance, but more importantly, it was the time and place where the rebirth began that Larry spoke of in later years; the place he discovered himself, a way of life and being that he would recall and return to in his heart and mind for the rest of his life.

The originally humble and sparse building, once a fisherman's home, still looked as though it had been gifted by the sea that might at any moment claim it back, and possessed an organic, elemental aura. It had grown, even in the Durrells' time, and now boasted another storey and a window out to the sea.

Today visitors could stay and dine there. Few places in the world existed in a more inspiring location, whether choosing the shade of the terrace, or a table on the sun-bleached, white flat stones as moonlight filled the bay with unforgettable iridescence.

This was the visit that Penny had anticipated the most, a few precious hours to immerse herself in the place that had played a vital role in the growth and psyche of a writer with unique and special gifts.

With the *Antiopi* anchored and Basil left on board, Dimitris guided the small motorized dinghy to the wooden jetty. Harry and Mary set off along the beach road with the intention of walking to Kouloura, the next bay along. They had kindly asked Penny if she wanted to join them, but she'd declined politely, explaining that she was going to sketch and read.

Dimitris told her where she could hire a parasol and sun lounger, but seemed to be reluctant to leave her as she stood on the white dusty road by the beach.

'Have a good day. I'll see you later,' she said eventually.

'Please, call me if you need anything. Whether I'm here or on the boat, it doesn't matter. I can be there. Okay?' he said.

'Dimitris, I'll be fine. How could I not be? It's incredible here.'

He nodded and said, 'Great. See you later.' Then, with a wave, he was gone.

She watched him go. He walked away without looking back, the backdrop of the rising hills behind him, the olives, cypress trees, and pale houses like a painting.

It was Nancy's painting spirit that she tried to find, carried on the sea breeze, as she paid for her sunbed and established herself on the beach. It was so hot, the parasol's shade felt like a friend.

Dimitris had passed her a folded A4 copy of the White House menu, in case she wanted a preview and extra time to study it. It fell out of the pocket of her shorts as she sat down. She would look at it later.

Glancing at her watch she saw she had just under two hours before her lunch reservation, so she decided to paint a few loose pictures of what she could see from this spot and then wander for half an hour or so, along the beach, before noon. She could then spend the rest of her time in and around Larry and Nancy's home, either at her table, in the lounge, or out on the rocks.

Squinting from underneath her sun hat and with her hand shielding her eyes, she stepped out from the shade to get a clearer view of the *Antiopi* across the bay. The becalmed yacht looked like a sleeping sea creature, rocked gently by the calm water around it. How had Dimitris bought his beautiful boat? Did he get a mortgage? Perhaps not, as he said he had a place in Corfu Town; but was that rented, she wondered idly?

Laying out her paints and pencils, from her rucksack she pulled two small wooden boards she'd prepared the night before, with stretched watercolour paper.

The White House was to her right, framed by smaller boats along the jetty, the hills, and edges of a green and lush bay. She told herself it didn't really matter how she captured what was in front of her. Whenever she looked back at the little paintings, they would instantly carry her back to this day, this experience. More potent than a photograph, her paint carried all the emotions she was feeling, right down to her fingertips.

Idly she thought about painting Dimitris. Which features would she find difficult to translate onto paper? Would he be a good sitter?

She laughed at herself then, imagining the double pressure of remaining detached and professional, studying every inch of that remarkable face. 'So, you're conceding that today, are you?' she spoke to herself, adding. 'A remarkable face, eh? That's a neutral endorsement. What you really mean is beautiful, handsome, and magnetic; a face you want to reach out to and touch. More than a muse, or a model; a face you could fall in love with.'

Out loud she answered herself with, 'Yes, you could . . . *I* could. Perhaps I am.'

Chapter 43

Just before noon Penny sat on the wall outside the White House, checking her phone and glancing back through the photos she'd taken that morning. She'd had no response from Bruce to the message she'd sent, and hoped that would be the last of it; but she had a niggling feeling that, once she returned home to England, she might hear from him again. When Bruce wanted something, he was usually persistent and single-minded. If he wanted to talk to her, he would find a way. But that was something for another day, another place.

Before lunch, in a setting anticipated with such joy, she cleared her mind, creating a blank canvas ready for all the sensations and images to fill it up.

'Hello, Penny,' Harry said, with Mary two steps behind, still studying a map.

'Hi, have you had a good morning?' Penny stood up, ready to walk into the restaurant.

'Really great,' enthused Mary, taking off her backpack to put her map away. 'Nothing like a good walk to get you ready for a big lunch.'

They didn't ask her if she'd like to join their table, for

which Penny was grateful. They must have picked up that she wanted to be on her own.

Guided to a table on the small stone terrace that ran along the front of the restaurant's sea-facing walls, Penny ordered a small carafe of rosé. She'd travelled into town that morning on the early bus so that she could have a couple of glasses of wine, and was thinking of treating herself to a taxi home. Harry and Mary sat a few tables away. She'd seen nothing of Dimitris since he'd wandered off to see his friend.

Lunch ordered, she rested her arm across the back of her chair, so that she could see the bay in front of her and the sea at her feet.

Dad, you would have loved this, she thought wistfully, putting down her glass for a moment and reaching into her pocket for a tissue.

Her face felt warm, but the tear that fell before she could check it was hot, carving a channel down her face, like lava. She dabbed discreetly at her face, making it look as though she was wiping rivulets of sweat away.

It was good to be here at last, in this magical place, but this place needed to be shared with someone. Harry and Mary were a fussy, slightly eccentric couple, but they were very much a couple. They operated as a unit, a duo, friends and companions, sharing experiences, good and bad, still delighting in each other's company.

The splendid isolation that she'd imagined the holiday would bring her, a time to heal, had turned out to be more about other people than any other break she'd been on. So many lives, loving, complex, and beautifully imperfect, had become part of hers in so many ways.

Other human beings were so important to her wellbeing, and the main ingredient of an enriched and loving life. But she also needed someone special to share it with.

Looking around, she saw that the tables were full of couples, families, and groups of friends.

Remembering why she'd wanted to be here, on Corfu of all places, she turned to the stone house and placed her palm flat on its cool exterior. On the other side of this thick and seemingly impregnable wall, two creatives had lived, loved, laughed, and discovered life and each other, in a moment in time, never to be repeated, punctuated by naked moonlit swims and the realities, as well as the wonders, of life far from the madding crowd.

The love hadn't lasted, the parting of ways had come, but it had been a life, an experience, something rich and unique that had shaped them. All the old wives' tales and sayings about love and life started to flow into Penny's head. As with all these things a thread of truth was woven through them.

When the salad arrived, it looked like a still life: green peppers and shiny purple-black Kalamata olives, crumbling, creamy feta, tomatoes that looked like they'd been grown in a giant's garden, and red onion glistening between the cucumber, all touched with a delicate herb-infused dressing. The rosé complemented it perfectly, making Penny feel as though she could eat this meal every day for the rest of her life. She closed her eyes to savour the moment again.

When she opened them, Dimitris was standing in front of her.

'Hi,' she said. 'Do we need to get back to the boat?'

'No, not yet. There's plenty of time. May I join you?' He gestured towards the chair.

'Yes, of course. Please do. Would you like a drink?'

One of the waiters had clearly seen Dimitris arrive and looked over to their table.

Dimitris turned and the waiter came over and a jug of iced water was ordered.

'I was half-hoping you'd help me finish this carafe of rosé, but you're our pilot, our captain, and need to keep a clear head.'

'I can't drink, but whether or not I have a clear head is another matter,' he said, leaning on the table, his chin resting on his hands.

Penny suddenly felt as though he was studying her more closely than he had before. Having finished her salad she leaned back, hoping an inch or two further back would lessen the intensity of the stare.

Before he could say anything, she chatted nervously, curious but vaguely anxious about what he was going to say, subconsciously wanting to delay it.

'In case I forget to tell you, I'd just like to say that the *Antiopi* is exquisite. She's a thing of beauty. How long have you had her?'

'I bought her about eighteen months after I came back from London. I wanted to sail when I wasn't fishing – any excuse to be out there, at sea.' He paused.

'Then throughout the first summer I was asked over and over again if I would take people up or down the coast, or around the island, and that's how it started. From April to October I am on the water most days, whether in the *Dora* or *Antiopi*.'

Penny wanted to ask how much the yacht had cost, but kept quiet.

'Do you love the sea, or *need* the sea?' she asked instead. 'Or both?'

He watched her closely, drinking his water and then looking over her shoulder to the bay. 'Both, I think. It has been my life for a long time now.'

'You make it sound like you're 100 years old, but you can't be 40 yet.'

'No, not quite. I was 35 when I came back from England.'

He looked vaguely amused now and Penny let the silence carry on, wondering what was coming next.

'Can I buy you a drink? They have some amazing cocktails here.' He smiled.

'No, thank you very much. I've had enough alcohol. The wine is wonderful but heady and I think there are probably maritime laws about tipsy passengers. Coffee would be great though.'

Penny took out her phone to show Dimitris some of the photos she'd taken.

'Would you like me to take a photo for you, to prove you were here?' he asked and when she started to shake her head, he insisted firmly, but with good humour.

'Don't move, Penny. That's perfect,' he said as he took the shot. 'You have to have at least one photo of yourself on holiday.'

'Thank you,' she said putting the phone back, changing her mind about showing him the photos. 'I'd like to take a few more on the *Antiopi*. As an illustrator, I have so many photos, like a library where I can find any object if I need to draw it. Even a yacht.'

Then before he could say anything else, she said: 'Did you have a nice catch-up with your friend?'

'With Maria? Yes. She's a very special woman. My time with her always feels like a gift. I'm lucky to have her in my life.'

The coffees arrived, the clock moving ever closer towards 2 p.m. It had been thoughtful of him to give her time on her own today, but she was glad now he was here. It felt good, it felt right.

'Have you known Maria long?' she asked.

'Yes, years.''

'I see.' Penny hoped he couldn't read her face. Maria had in nanoseconds become the worshipped, but coy, exquisitely beautiful, potential girlfriend he had pursued on and off since his youth.

She sipped her coffee, inhaling the fresh, aromatic smell as she did. Then seeing he was doing the same thing, she laughed and said, 'We look like one of those terrible adverts for coffee, where everyone takes their coffee far too seriously and the message is if they choose a particular brand, they will lead an enchanted life full of glamour, riches, and romance.'

Before Dimitris could reply, Harry suddenly appeared. 'Hello, both. I don't want to interrupt, but Mary and I are finished now and we're going to sit on the jetty. So, no hurry. I know it's not quite 2 p.m., but whenever you're ready to get back on the boat, we are too.'

'Five minutes,' Penny said, almost as though she were pleading for more time visiting a loved one in jail before execution.

She wanted to be with this man, suddenly feeling brave enough to go with the flow of whatever it was, or could be. Less about feeling confident and sure, and more about not closing the door on what life could bring.

She even felt courageous enough to fight the unseen Maria for him, who in her imagination was already indignant about her spending time with Dimitris.

Chapter 44

The journey home to Corfu Town had a quieter feel. Harry and Mary planted themselves near the front of the boat, sitting on the deck to enjoy the feel of the sea breeze as the *Antiopi* cut through the waves like a flying fish.

When Penny looked over at them, she couldn't tell behind their sunglasses if they were dozing, but Harry's hand had fallen to one side and the pages of Mary's book remained unturned.

Basil was cleaning the cabin below, after offering everyone refreshments once again, which were declined with thanks. The lunch at the White House had left them all comfortably sated and content.

Penny felt a little dozy herself and edged her way to the back of the boat behind Dimitris, where there was a small seating area. She'd taken a few photographs of the boat as they'd approached it from the water and then as they'd left Kalami behind.

She breathed in the sea air and let the rise and fall of the boat lull her into, if not sleep, then a state of calm and peace.

As she passed Dimitris, she smiled and pointed to where she was heading. He nodded and returned the smile. She understood why the sea pulled Dimitris out onto a boat every day.

The light now was golden, and gilded the polished metal and sleek sides of the yacht, making each cove along the ever-changing shoreline look like an undiscovered Shangri-la. Penny watched Dimitris from behind her sunglasses. He had his back to her as he steered, but she could see his profile, just as she'd seen him for the first time in the Athena.

It felt different now. *He* seemed different, less mysterious and more real.

These thoughts and many others danced around in her head as she closed her eyes and the *Antiopi* carried them home.

Basil's voice made her open her eyes as he came up from the cabin and Penny spotted the old fortress ahead.

She stood up to get the best view for the last few minutes on the boat, slipped, and banged her arm as she steadied herself.

Dimitris turned around to see what was happening.

'I'm fine, really. Just a daft thing to do. I forgot I was on a boat.'

'How are you on the back of a motorbike?'

'Motorbike?' she asked, thinking for some strange reason of stunt riders in action films. An image of her clinging on and Dimitris careering around corners flashed before her eyes.

'Yes. You said you took the bus into town this morning. I have a motorbike and when we get into port, I'm riding back to St George. So, I can take you, if you were planning on heading straight back.' He checked her reaction, wondering what she was going to say.

'Well, I was planning to get straight back, but I haven't been on a motorbike before, so if there's a knack to it and I don't have it, you might regret making the offer.'

'There's no knack. You just hold on to me.' He turned back to concentrate as they came into the port.

Harry and Mary stood, ready to disembark. Basil handed them their backpacks.

'Okay. Thank you. That would be great.' Penny tried to sound more confident and cooler than she felt inside.

'Great.' Seconds later the *Antiopi* was safely back at her berth.

⌒

After farewells to Harry and Mary and a handshake and tip for Basil, Penny found herself walking across the car park with Dimitris, who was carrying two helmets, one of which he handed to her as they reached his motorbike.

The next forty-five minutes were both thrilling and terrifying. She got used to the sway and manoeuvres of the bike, the press of air, and how close she felt to the road rushing by.

Even at just 30 miles an hour, the bike felt fast to Penny. They reached Benitses in what seemed like five minutes and Penny was able to glance quickly at home of the baklava, but was then distracted by an aircraft overhead.

The sensations she remembered most, though, were her arms around Dimitris's body and the sheer terror and speed of it all. She'd never been close enough to him before to feel his warmth, to hold onto him for this long. She felt like a twenty-first-century version of a Regency heroine riding behind her sweetheart on horseback.

Closing her eyes, she tried to memorize the sensation in

her mind in case it never happened again. She felt about 16, giddy, uninhibited, and part of the world she had, until a few minutes ago, felt as though she was just visiting – a tourist. Her face glowed, her arms still had a salty, suntan-lotion feel. She laughed out loud at the thought of what she was doing, where she was, who she was with. The joy of the moment bubbled up from inside like champagne.

As they turned onto the Main Road in St George South, Dimitris slowed down and they glided to a halt outside the Athena.

As he switched off the engine Penny unbuckled the chin strap of her helmet and took it off. She shook her head to revive her hair, before even thinking about trying to climb off –hopefully with as little fuss as possible.

Putting one leg to the floor, it was easy to dismount.

She stood on the steep pavement, but Dimitris didn't move.

'Thanks, that was an experience. I mean exhilarating,' she added in case he thought she was being sarcastic. She smiled broadly at him, and handed back her helmet.

He took it and looped it over his wrist. 'You're welcome.'

'And thank you again. I've had a wonderful day.'

'Good,' he said. 'I'm going to my father's now, as we're out in the *Dora* early tomorrow, so I'm staying here tonight. Are you eating here later?'

'I think so.'

'Do you know the little bar near the harbour? The Mediterranean?'

'Yes, I do. I had a drink there the other night.'

'Would you like to meet up for a drink, say around 7 p.m., before dinner?'

She felt a pull towards him in that moment, an urge to lean towards him and kiss him goodbye. So, she did. She could taste the salt on his mouth. 'See you at 7 p.m.'

He rode off and she stepped across the road and walked slowly down the lane to the apartments.

It was just after 4 p.m. She felt tired and yet more alive than she could ever remember. There was an inner lightness, a skipping sensation in her middle, and an impulsive need to giggle, like a teenager.

The sensible Penny who would have told herself to 'Get a grip' and 'Behave' had left the building.

In the apartment, she plugged her dying phone into the charger next to the bed and set the alarm on a little bedside alarm clock for 6 p.m.

Chapter 45

In July the sun rose in St George around 6 a.m. The hours in between before the sun set at around 9 p.m. were usually filled with intense light and rarer, but spectacular, thunderstorms.

After 7 p.m., the sun began to think about departing and the feel of the day changed, imperceptibly at first and then more confidently, bringing with it the 'Golden Hour'. Penny stepped out into this luminous world a few minutes before 7 p.m.

She measured her steps, trying to slow her usual fast pace, wanting to be on time, but not early. As she approached the Mediterranean Bar, she saw that he was already there, talking to the owner, who was probably describing the wine he was so proud of. The conversation was certainly animated.

As soon as he saw her Dimitris stood up and introduced her. Penny immediately complimented him on the wine she'd had on her first visit, which delighted him and he immediately went away to fetch a couple of glasses.

'*Yasas*.' Dimitri pulled a chair out for her.

'*Yasou*,' she replied and they both moved forward to exchange a kiss on each cheek.

'Is this one of your favourite bars?' Penny asked.

'Yes, I've been coming here since I was a boy. You can

always rely on the wine being good.'

'It also happens to be in one of the most beautiful locations in the world,' Penny noted, looking through the palms and the flowers to the sea and harbour. The *Dora* was moored in its usual place, and she remembered sitting here and seeing it the first time, just a couple of weeks ago.

'So, you've fallen in love with our village, our island?' Dimitri leaned back as he saw the waiter approaching with their wine.

'I think you know the answer to that. How could I not fall in love with such a place?'

'Did you have a good idea what it would be like, and has it lived up to your expectations so far? The food, the climate, the landscape?' He paused. 'The people?'

'When I came here it was a leap of faith really. I had wanted to come here since I was a teenager. It started, as you know, with books by Gerry Durrell and then Larry Durrell's work, and then became a fascination with the whole family. My dad and I never made it here together, but when he died last year, the idea of a pilgrimage if you like – something more than a holiday – took hold. And here I am.'

She paused. 'I was expecting a lot of Corfu. I was hoping it would help me to move on, to build something new and hopeful around my grief, which had become a way of life for me, but letting go of it felt like letting go of my dad. Since I came here, I've realized that letting go isn't about loving less, or forgetting. So yes, it has lived up to my expectations in more ways than I could have anticipated before I came. It's taught me many things.' She looked at him to study his reaction, before adding. 'Also, the baklava is terrific!' She laughed.

He didn't say anything for a moment or two, but then asked, 'Did you want to be here on your own?'

'Yes, I think so. I wanted the freedom to go where I wanted, read when I wanted, paint, sleep . . . be selfish, I suppose.'

'But you haven't been selfish, have you?' he said.

'Why do you say that?'

'Because you've helped people, made friends, and listened to their stories.'

'Has Tess been talking to you?' she asked, wondering if Tess had mentioned Bruce.

'A little, but she has shared nothing with me that you haven't told me. Tess is not a gossip.'

'I know. She's a lovely person.'

'I can see the effect you've had on Tess, Lily, even Nic. I've seen enough of who I think you are to know that "selfish" is the last word I would use to describe you.'

She looked down, not sure where the conversation was going, but feeling, understanding now, that he had spent more time than she had imagined, hoped, thinking about her.

'I have my moments.' He grinned back at her. The effect of this spontaneous and utterly natural smile was like the sun coming out on a rainy, February day.

'It's my turn,' she said, her head full of so many questions for him she hardly knew where to begin.

'Go ahead,' he answered.

'You've been back here for two years now. I heard you were a lawyer in London at one of the top firms, so why did you come back? Was that always the plan? And why didn't you carry on practising law when you came home?'

Even as he finished the sentence, she hoped she hadn't asked too much too soon.

'I was in London, working for my Uncle Theo's firm. I wasn't a partner, but I was lucky enough to get a place there after my studies. I stayed long enough to buy a house, find someone I wanted to spend the rest of my life with, and then lose them.' He took another sip of his wine before he continued.

'But that's all part of life's rich pattern when you're in your twenties, even thirties, isn't it? You love, you lose, your friendship groups grow and change, as do your colleagues, and all the while, your connection with home, with your roots, can become more and more tenuous.' He stopped for a moment, then continued.

'By the time I realized how completely detached I'd become from home, from my parents and my life here, it was too late.'

'Too late?' Penny asked, moving towards him as though she might need to catch him, as though while the words flowed, his heart was still catching up.

'My mother died suddenly, when I was in London. I hadn't seen her for months. I'd cancelled trips over here because I didn't want to interrupt my life, my lifestyle. Even the Skype calls had become a chore, a box to tick. I couldn't be bothered, I was so full of myself in my new world that I forgot what was important – *who* was important.'

'Is that when you came home?' Penny tried to keep her voice neutral and calm. She wanted him to share without feeling judged or hurried.

'Yes, I came home the next day. My father met me at the airport. He has never rebuked me or brought up any of what I've just told you. I was home; he was glad. So was I. I have spent as much time with him as I can, helping with the fishing, staying over a few nights each week. Even so, it will never be enough, as I said last week.'

He looked at her again. 'You are only the second person I have spoken to about this. I went to see Maria today because she has known me since I was a child. I wanted to talk to her about this – about you too – as she was my mother's oldest friend.

The speed with which Maria became a heroine rather than a threat astonished Penny. She felt her stomach lurch a little, but her face gave nothing away, the revelation more of a relief than she could have imagined.

Penny looked down at her hands. The silence was contemplative rather than uncomfortable. Then she said what was in her mind and heart. 'I didn't know you existed two weeks ago, Dimitris, but I can only think that your father loves you very much and your mother did too. Any parent, whether they're still here or not, wants their child to be happy, to live every year that's left to them well, and to follow their dreams. Whether you're 14 or 40, the same applies.'

She realized she was talking to herself, as well as Dimitris. He looked away for a moment. 'That's exactly what Maria told me this afternoon,' he said finally.

Chapter 46

An hour later Penny and Dimitris walked into the Athena together, to be greeted by Tess.

'Good day?' she said, as though seeing them together was an everyday occurrence. 'Table?'

'That would be great. It looks extra busy tonight,' Penny said, wondering how Tess would fit them in. She wasn't sure if it was full-moon madness or just the numbers increasing each week as the summer season reached its peak. The noise level was quite high, the chattering louder than usual, and the music, although always subtle, was tonight fighting for airtime. It was joy escaping from people who had found their very own marvellous and life-affirming Nirvana for a week or two.

Lily bounced by, tray in one hand and a new drinks order in the other. Rich followed, carrying dirty glasses and a knife someone had dropped on the floor. She gave Penny and Dimitris a quick wave, as did Rich. They went into the kitchen together.

Guy was sitting at a table with Faith, Dee and a new lad, who seemed to be with Dee.

As Penny and Dimitris passed by en route to their table,

Guy stood up and to her delight kissed her on both cheeks and shook Dimitris by the hand, as though he was saying thank you for something, but she wasn't sure what.

Sitting at her usual table, now with an extra place for Dimitris, Penny looked out at the moon, unable to remember whether it was a new or full moon she should make a wish on. Either way she had nothing just then that she needed, but looking across at the man opposite her she wished him the peace of mind he had been unable and unwilling to find for the last couple of years.

She couldn't see Nic, but assumed he was in the kitchen helping Anna, perhaps even washing up, which made her smile.

'What are you smiling at?' Dimitris asked.

'I was just thinking about how everyone here has a way of working together in a kind of organized chaos. There's sort of a plan, but there's also a sense of family, of everyone mucking in and being happy to do it.'

'That's Corfu,' he said, just as Nic arrived with a glass of rosé and a glass of red.

'*Yasas* and compliments of the management,' he said, placing them on the table.

'*Efcharistó.*' Dimitris picked up his glass and toasted Penny and Nic.

'Lily will be over in a moment. There's mezze, of course, but if you want anything else, just ask.' Nic left with a smile.

Penny watched him go, thinking that she still hadn't really got to the heart of his feelings for Tess, or Tess's for Nic.

Turning back to Dimitris she said: 'Do you dance?'

'That's a very broad question. It could mean anything from a tango to the twist. Or did you mean traditional Greek dancing?'

'I'm not sure. I suppose I was wondering.'

'Sometimes.' he said. 'How about you?'

'I don't dance so much as try to avoid injury. I can trip over air, or my own feet.'

'I shall have to hold onto you then.' He spoke matter of factly, as though their dancing together was a natural thing.

There was a lull in the chatter and music, and in the quieter air Penny suddenly heard a familiar voice.

'Hello, Penny. You're an elusive woman to find.'

Bruce.

When she looked back later at that moment in the Athena, she was struck by the support her newest friends showed her.

Looking around and seeing Bruce towering over her had been a shock. More than a shock. It had felt like an intrusion, an unwelcome and uncomfortable meeting that made her feel vulnerable and exposed.

Civility and calm had been maintained.

She'd greeted him with a cautious 'Hello, Bruce', and caught a glimpse of Tess, who looked concerned but also calm. She had clearly guessed who he was.

Then she'd introduced Bruce to Dimitris as 'a friend', but he'd corrected her with, 'Penny and I were engaged for a while.'

It was easier, she thought, to excuse herself and find out what Bruce wanted without an audience, particularly Dimitris. She knew Bruce well enough to know that he wouldn't have tracked her down to Corfu without a good reason – or at least a reason that made sense to Bruce and was principally about Bruce.

Dimitris had given nothing away, standing to shake hands with Bruce; and when Penny excused herself and Bruce, with profound apologies, he had waved away her concern.

'I'm staying here, Penny. I'll be at the bar with Nic. You have my mobile, don't you?'

She knew he was saying, *Call me if you need me*, and she was grateful for that.

Penny looked at Dimitris, but could think of nothing more to say. *What is he thinking? What must he think of me?* she wondered.

Tess nodded at her as she walked out with Bruce. Nic said '*Kalinichta*,' adding that he would be staying until late to help Tess clear up, if she wanted to come back for a nightcap.

She knew they were all touching base with her, aware that something was up, not wanting to intrude but needing to make sure she was safe.

She asked Bruce to wait on the pavement for a moment and slipped back into the Athena. Tess came to her.

'Tess, you've probably guessed that's Bruce, my ex-fiancé. I have no idea why he's here. I'm taking him to the little bar down the road, the Aphrodite, I think it's called, so I can find out. Please don't worry. Can you let Dimitris know I'll be back later if I can? But please tell him not to wait if it's too late. I will explain, but this is a huge surprise to me. I had no idea Bruce would be here.'

Tess nodded and kissed Penny on the cheek.

Outside Bruce waited, clearly impatient to leave, and ready for a drink.

As she led him down the road to the little seafront bar, there were a hundred different scenarios running through Penny's head. Ten minutes later they sat on bar stools, a pint of Mythos in front of Bruce, and Penny nursing a coffee.

'It's a little bit too quiet and rustic for me here, but not bad. The beach looks clean.' Bruce opened the conversation.

'Why are you here?' Penny put her head on one side as she said this.

'I wanted, *needed*, to see you. You obviously didn't want to talk on the phone. I rang you twice earlier, but there was no response.'

Penny realized she'd left her phone on charge in the apartment.

'But how did you know I was here?'

'I rang Lizzie first, who was vague and protective. Then the writer you work with was very chatty about Corfu and the little village you'd found, so it didn't take long to work it out. I flew in this afternoon. I'm staying in Corfu Town.'

She noticed she was biting her lip, an old habit from childhood, something her grandmother used to tease her about.

'You look fantastic, Penny. The warm climate must suit you.'

'It does. I love it here. But why are *you* here?'

'First of all, there's nothing to worry about. No one's died or become ill. It's all good – or could be. Now before I start, hear me out on this one, Penny.'

She put down her coffee and, uncrossing her legs, sat on her hands, straightened her back and her resolve.

Bruce bumbled on. 'I don't think we should have parted. Being in Italy these past few months has given me time to think. You're still on your own – I did manage to get that out of Lizzie – and so am I. I missed you.'

He stopped for a moment and Penny was glad her hands were out of the way, as she sensed he would have grabbed one at this point in his monologue.

'We had some great times, Penny. You were always there for me and I know now that whatever comes to me in Italy, whatever turn my career takes, I want you to share it. I know we've been here before, Penny, and maybe I wasn't always the most supportive partner, but I really didn't appreciate how special you are.'

He stopped speaking and looked down. When he lifted his head up his eyes were full of tears. She didn't know what to say or where to look. This was a first for Bruce. She had never seen him so emotional, so distraught.

'I panicked, Penny, when your father was dying. I'm ashamed to say I couldn't cope. All I could think of was taking myself away from the pain. It was so hard to watch you, to see the realization that you were going to lose your dad hitting you so hard. I wanted to make it all better for you, but when I couldn't and the opportunity in Italy came along, it seemed like a solution. To take myself out of the equation because I knew I was making it worse for you, and I couldn't bear that.'

He paused, watching Penny closely, then wiped his face with a tanned hand, brushing away a tear.

'As you can see it's not easy to say all these things. When I realized you'd gone, that I was in Italy without you, I knew that what was ahead wasn't going to mean anything without you.'

Penny looked away out at the sea. Out of the corner of her eye she could see the lights from the Athena and figures moving along the terrace there. She wondered what Dimitris was doing. She imagined him sitting with Tess and Nic at the bar. What was he – what were *they* – thinking?

'Penny, will you give me a day, please? That's all I'm asking: a day to give me the chance to show you, to begin to show you, how much I love you. A chance to hope that you'll let me make it up to you.'

Penny realized she was still in mild shock, still absorbing all that Bruce was saying. It was overwhelming, like a tsunami of emotion and words.

She looked at him, his face still beautiful, his eyes fringed with the soft dark lashes that had always given him a look of vulnerability in repose. In the warm night air, she could smell his familiar aftershave and it opened the box of all the things about him that she'd loved and had sealed away because it was easier – the reasons why she'd been with him for three years.

'I'm not expecting an answer now, Pen. I wouldn't do that to you. I hired a car at the airport, and I've got forty-eight hours before I need to be back at the university. Can I see you tomorrow? Pick you up in the morning? We could drive somewhere up the coast, talk, eat. Even if you need more time, Penny, or you never want to see me again, please, just give me this.'

'I have to go now, Bruce. I don't know what to say to you. I'm tired. I've been out on a boat all day and I need to sleep. But I'll give you tomorrow. You can pick me up and as you said, we can drive somewhere and talk.'

She stood up and started to walk away, feeling uncomfortably as though she had not been kind, but simultaneously, that she had been cornered. Conflicted and discomfited, her apartment and her cool bed beckoned. *Why are you really here, Bruce? Are you telling the truth? Why do you feel more real than Dimitris? Is it because we have three years of mutual history and not two weeks?*

'I'll text you when I set off and meet you outside the place where I found you this evening.'

She didn't look back to acknowledge him again. One more look at him standing there alone would not have helped her confusion and disquiet.

Chapter 47

Dimitris, Tess, and Nic were at the bar when Penny walked back into the Athena.

They all looked at her. Tess put down a bottle she was pouring from and moved towards Penny. 'Can I get you a brandy?' She patted her arm and guided her to a barstool.

Dimitris said nothing, but waited for her to speak. 'Thank you. That would be great. Just what I need,' she replied.

She smiled at him, almost to reassure herself that he was real, was there, wasn't a figment of her imagination.

Laughing as a release she said, 'Well, I wasn't expecting *that*.'

Tess put the brandy in front of her. 'Where is he now?'

'He's staying in Corfu Town. He's driving back there now.'

Dimitris stood with Nic. She wondered what on earth he was thinking about what had happened; what he was thinking of her.

There was anger too. How dare Bruce step into her new world, even for a moment? He hadn't considered how his unburdening himself might affect her, how she might feel about that.

Penny climbed off the bar stool and Tess went to fetch the mezze she'd promised Penny.

"Goodnight,' she said to Dimitris and Nic.

'Take care,' said Dimitris, his face giving nothing away.

'I will. And thank you for today. It was lovely.' She held his gaze. 'I'm sorry about my unexpected visitor. I had no idea he was coming. Can we talk, perhaps tomorrow?'

'I'll be in Corfu Town for most of the day, but I might be free later.'

Penny tried to read his face, but it was closed and she recognized the man she had met on the first day of her holiday. He had returned, with the cold stiffness that had made her think of him as a sculpture.

An hour earlier it would have felt like the most natural thing in the world to kiss him goodnight, but now it felt as though a spell had been broken.

Once across the road and walking down the quiet lane, Penny began to cry. It was a release, a mark of her confusion, and the return of a deep sadness.

Dimitris watched her quietly until she disappeared into the velvet darkness of the still warm night. The day had not ended how he had expected either.

Back in the apartment, sitting on the side of the bed, Penny noticed her phone was still charging. She picked it up and saw three missed calls, all from Bruce, and a text from Lizzie.

Hi Pen. I just wanted to let you know that Bruce has rung me. He seemed to know you were abroad, but wanted to know where. I didn't tell him. I hope that was the right thing. He seemed keen to chat to you and was full of how marvellous Italy is. I couldn't make it out. If I'm honest, our conversation was a bit odd. Hope you're ok and still soaking up that glorious sunshine and drinking

the wine. Text me back if you can to let me know how you are.
L x

There was also a voicemail, from Bruce, but she put down her phone without listening to it.

It wasn't midnight yet and she heard movement outside as people returned from dinner.

Soon, though, there was silence and it was in this quiet she fell asleep, still dressed, on the bed, falling into a series of fitful dreams and a strange, surreal replay of the day's events.

Chapter 48

The air was richly perfumed with the scent of geraniums and the sea. The lemon trees that lined the little road that led to the Athena looked like illustrations from a children's storybook, vivid yellow with bright green leaves, framed by a clear blue sky. The early-morning scene breathed serenity, as well as a freshly washed feel.

Tom, the ginger cat that Theo liked to play with at the Athena, lay in the shade, preparing, with lazy acceptance, for a day of being petted and stroked. Tess stood with her first coffee of the morning, her eyes on the horizon where a yacht moved slowly south.

Tess had been thinking of Penny and Dimitris that morning. Grateful for the love she'd had, she recognized two people falling in love. Now, after the appearance of Penny's visitor last night, it seemed all bets were off.

Sometimes people just keep each other warm for a while, Tess thought. It crossed her mind, not for the first time, that that phrase could have described her friendship with Nic.

She worried about him sometimes. He had never found anyone to share his life with, to share all the wonderful things she knew he embodied, and could offer.

What she didn't admit to herself was that when she followed through the idea of Nic finding someone and settling down, she was not sure that was what *she* wanted. Nic with a partner of his own, perhaps even a family, was a Nic that wouldn't be there so much for her and Theo. He would be missed, as he was missed during the winter, when he was in Athens.

She'd surprised herself with how unsettled his day away in Athens, unusual in their summer time together, had made her feel the week before.

She put down her coffee cup and straightened the table and chairs next to her. There was a lot to do before the first breakfasts were served.

⌒⌒

It was just after 11.30 when Penny strolled down to the end of the little lane and saw Bruce waiting there. The new day had washed away the shadows from St George. She'd worried that the incident with Bruce might have tainted the place, covered it with a pall of misery, and squeezed out the joy.

Wherever you went, you always carried your baggage with you, Penny decided, remembering that Nic had said that Corfu either soothed you, or celebrated with you.

As she got into the car, a smiling Bruce reached across and kissed her on the cheek.

'Good morning. Thank you for agreeing to come. I've found just the place. I think you'll love it.'

He set off before she had a chance to fasten her seat belt properly, and they left St George at pace. She looked over at him and saw no trace of the distraught man she'd been with the night before. Here was a taste of the usual, self-confident Bruce of old and here was she, starting to feel all the old feelings – the confusing ones that made her feel unsure, made her feel that she was giving up something of herself.

There was still unfinished business between them, she thought. The door hasn't closed on this. He felt so real, sitting there next to her. Maybe she was wrong she still loved him. Was there anything he could say that would make her want to be with him again? What did she want?

She wondered how she might have felt, if he'd turned up in a few days' time when she'd had a chance to be with Dimitris that bit longer – long enough to know and feel where that was going. Instead, here was the old and familiar – if far from perfect – calling her away from the new. The new – Dimitris – was exciting, promising, but as yet unspoken and untried. Their connection might even, after last night, have no future at all. What must he be thinking?

Was what she thought she might have with Dimitris a mirage, based on a kiss – albeit a tender kiss – and a need to feel love and be loved? Or was it just a holiday romance?

Twenty minutes later, off the main road to Corfu Town, Bruce pulled up. It was the restaurant with the wooden pier that Lily had spotted on their trip to the Strawberry Villa.

Once seated, Penny waited for Bruce to speak. Surely, he had another speech prepared, she thought cynically. But he didn't say anything. He just looked at her as though she was the most precious and fascinating thing he'd ever seen, which made her feel pinned down like a butterfly, caught and displayed in a glass box.

'So, what have you been doing for the last two weeks? Sunbathing? You look fantastic. The sun suits you, Pen.' She didn't answer, so he smiled broadly and looked around him, taking in the rocky headland, softened by gently swaying pine and cypress trees and an old Venetian manor house hidden through the trees. A few seabirds were circling and a motorboat purred past, swirling across the bay. Under the pier, the sea sparkled.

'This bit is a little more sophisticated. More us, don't you think? I'm not sure I'm into getting away from it all so much. There's nothing to do. You really have to like scenery here, don't you? You said you'd been on a boat, yesterday? Where did you go?'

Penny put down her glass.

'Kalami. It's up on the north-east coast, where Lawrence Durrell lived and wrote. I came here to see where he and the rest of the family lived in the 1930s. You remember how much I love their books? I was reading one of them to Dad when he was dying. There's just one more villa to see – the Snow White. It's not far from here actually.'

'So, who was the guy – Dimitris, was it? – that you were having a drink with?'

'Dimitris? He took me, and another couple up to Kalami. He has a yacht and you can charter it for trips.'

'Ah, so a sort of tour guide. I bet he was charming. It's part of the job, isn't it? I bet he's popular with women of a certain age.'

Penny looked down at the table, trying to keep her trembling hands still, and then looking directly at Bruce, she said, 'Bruce, why are you here?'

He put down his drink so that he could lean back and use his hands and arms to emphasize his words.

'Okay, here goes. So, it turns out that I've caught the attention of the university board and in the autumn, I'm applying to be Master – head – of one of the colleges, which is where you come in.'

She raised her eyebrows quizzically.

'When I apply for the post in the autumn, which would be a really big deal for me, I've been told that applications are looked on more favourably if you're married, or planning to be. Quirky, I know, but there it is. Southern Italy, it turns out, isn't so different from Oxford in the 1950s.' He looked rueful, then amused.

'So, it all seemed to make sense, Pen. I've been missing you, and we're both still single. We were planning to get married . . . These last six months have been a test, but we've found each other again. So, what do you think?'

As he finished, Penny wasn't quite sure how to arrange her face. She'd never felt so detached from someone who was sitting so close to her.

All that they'd ever been to each other seemed like an echo from another time, another world. What she'd just heard was less of a declaration of love and more of a business arrangement. She felt a frisson of anger that he clearly had so little respect for her, that he thought she'd jump at the opportunity to marry him.

You don't know me at all, Bruce, you never have, she thought. *But I know you and that's all that matters now.* Still, she said nothing.

Bruce began to talk again.

'I appreciate you weren't expecting to see me yesterday, but I hope it's a good surprise. Italy is amazing, Penny. You'd love it. You should see where I live, the rooms. It's like living at the Villa d'Este. And as for the wine . . . I have my own cellar.'

Penny held her hand up to make him stop, before he moved on to a description of the furniture and his car.

'Bruce, please, don't say any more. There are two very important things you need to know. Firstly, breaking off our engagement was the right thing to do. That decision is still the right one. Secondly, the life you have found in Italy sounds perfect for you – as perfect for you as Corfu is for me.' She held up her hand again as he was about to interrupt her.

'I don't want to be unkind. You do at least understand that about me, that I don't like hurting anyone, but I won't marry you to make the world right for *you*, to make things happen that work for *you*. I have as much right as anyone to live my life and enjoy it. I owe you nothing, Bruce, just as you owe me nothing. I think that's all I need to say.'

She watched as the truth began to filter through to him, as the realization dawned that he wasn't going to get his way.

'You shouldn't have come, Bruce, and I shouldn't be here. I have somewhere else I need to be.'

'Penny, wait.' He reached into his shirt pocket and fetched out his wallet, pulling a photograph from it.

'Do you remember this? What a night that was, Penny. I never felt more sure about anything, or anyone in my life.'

He handed her the photo of their engagement party photo. She saw herself, all shiny hair and eyes, smiling broadly and presenting her hand with the flashy ring towards the camera. Bruce had his arm around her waist, but wasn't looking at the camera, or at her. For one terrifying moment, she couldn't recognize herself as the woman in the picture, who seemed lost in another time, someone from another planet. She wasn't sure yet whether the new Penny was real either, but she also knew she couldn't go back.

She got off her chair and stood next to a now silent Bruce.

'You've changed,' was all he could find to say.

'I don't think so. I think I've just had the space and the courage to be who I really am. This is who I've always been.'

He shrugged, as if to say, 'So what?'

She was strong enough to smile to herself. His blatant disregard for her feelings when they didn't fit in with his plans had always been there. Was there still. Always would be.

He might turn heads when he walked into a room or a restaurant – he was a handsome man – but the fact that he had thought that just strolling back into her life was enough to pull her back to him, that she could be gulled and flattered into hitching her wagon to his star, made her pity him.

The spell had been broken, truly broken now.

'Goodbye, Bruce. I'm going home.' She walked away.

He stood up and, throwing some money on the table, followed her. 'Penny, at least let me take you back. Don't walk away like this. Stop. We can be civilized.'

She carried on walking.

Chapter 49

As Penny stepped into the Athena, the smell of coffee and the chattering customers enjoying lunch lifted her. The local green bus had been an adventure – she hadn't been sure she was on the right one until about five minutes before she got off – but it had brought her back in one piece.

Lily popped up from behind the bar, where she'd been fetching bottles of orange juice out of the fridge.

'Hi. Usual table?' she said. 'Tess asked me to put a reserved sign on it.' She raised her eyebrows as though this was a special and unusual thing.

'Yes, please,' said Penny.

A few minutes later she was staring out at the sea and the rocks below, sipping coffee.

She felt about coffee the way some people felt about tea – there wasn't much a cup couldn't put right. Even the thought that Bruce was still somewhere on the island wasn't enough to dampen her mood. He had left her life, finally, irrevocably,

She put the fact that he had been in it at all down to life and experience. He was just part of the journey that had brought her here, that had shaped her. Even if that shaping had been more about knowing herself and what she *didn't* want, it was still in progress. She was growing.

Tess wandered over.

'I bet that felt good.' She brought another cup of coffee for Penny. 'Here you go. One is good; two even better'

'Thanks, Tess. just what I needed. Thanks too for the brandy last night. It was quite an evening.'

'How are you?' Tess took a chair and sat down.

'I'm relieved. In a way Bruce was unfinished business. He hadn't been in my life for months, but I still wondered when I felt low, or lonely, if I'd done the right thing. It was the best thing that could have happened in a way, as it gave me the chance to say some things I needed to say and to know that, whatever comes, I know myself well enough now not to let another Bruce into my life.'

Penny looked at her before Tess added, 'My dad said real love was about being with someone who is there with you through all the difficult times, sharing the load. He had that with my mum. They didn't have long together, but every minute was worth the pain that losing her brought him. I suppose that's what I'm looking for and I know it's worth waiting for. More importantly, I know what it isn't and I now have the courage to say "no" to that.'

Tess squeezed Penny's hand and stood up, as she heard Lily calling her from the bar.

'Your dad was right,' she said, then added, 'Dimitris was in this morning. He asked me to pass a message on. He's gone into town but will be back after lunch.'

'I'm going into Corfu Town after this coffee,' Penny said. 'If you see him, will you let him know I'll be back later, please?'

Tess nodded and after touching Penny on the shoulder, walked back into the kitchen taking off her apron as she went.

The Liston exuded its usual timeless, cosmopolitan air. Penny sat at one of the tables under the cool stone canopy, with two parcels at her feet.

She'd been to the art shop to collect the two paintings she was leaving as farewell gifts. The mounting and framing had been done beautifully, with real craftsmanship and quality in the work. One was of Theo – that was for Tess. The other, for Dimitris and Aris, was the painting of the *Dora* that Tess had admired. She hadn't decided yet when to hand them over.

There remained six full days left on the island and she already had a feeling they would be even more precious than the ones she'd had so far. Being on her own in town felt different today. When she'd first arrived, she'd imagined spending most of her time on Corfu on her own.

Yes, she'd had lots of time to do her own thing, relax, make her own plans, or choose to have no plans at all, but she'd never been lonely. Every person she'd met had become part of the jigsaw of her life. Whether a small or large piece, they mattered, had become part of her story.

She felt she understood now, more than ever, what the Durrells had experienced here, the impact the island had had on them all.

It wasn't just beautiful, idyllic – all the things that you'd expect from a Greek island with a climate the gods themselves must have designed. Beyond the holiday brochure descriptions were the things that a person could only experience there. Corfu was ready to change a person's life and help them discover who they really were.

Penny could resist, ignore what the island had taught her, or when she returned home, choose to forget. The wise let the new feelings and revelations in, absorbed them and were grateful to the island and its people for what they so generously revealed and shared.

Penny parked the car opposite the Athena and clicked open the boot, walking around to the back to take the paintings out. Wedging them under her arm she locked the car and started walking down the lane to the apartment. Halfway down she saw a man walking towards her.

She stopped for a moment to hitch up the paintings under her arm. She then carried on walking, as did he. When Dimitris reached her, he didn't say a word for a moment.

When people said that their hearts were in their mouths, she now knew what they meant. She braced herself for a goodbye, the end of something before it had really had a chance to get started.

'I've been looking for you. I looked in the Athena, but didn't see you,' he said.

'I mentioned to Tess that I was going into Corfu Town. Did you see her?'

'No, I just stepped inside. She must have been in the kitchen.'

As he studied her face, she felt the paintings she was holding become heavier.

In one swift movement he took the parcels from underneath her arm and then leant them against the stone wall beside them.

'Penny,' he began, 'we didn't finish our evening out. Are you free?' He smiled as he spoke, resting his hands on her upper arms.

It felt to her as though he was asking about more than

whether she could go out that night. *Yes, I am free*, she thought, *and tonight is a good place to start enjoying that.*

'No, we didn't. We were rudely interrupted,' she replied. 'But I know it won't happen again.'

'Shall we risk it and try again this evening?'

'I'd like that very much.'

'Great. Shall we say 7.30 at the Mediterranean?' He picked up her parcels. 'Can I help you with these?'

'I'm fine. They're not really heavy, just a little awkward. Honestly, I'll be fine.' She didn't want him to ask her about the parcels, in case it spoiled the surprise if she gave him even a hint about the paintings. 'See you at 7.30.'

As he placed the parcels under her arm, he looked at her intently for a moment and said, 'Yes, 7.30.' Then, because she was smiling and lifting her head, so invitingly, he bent down and kissed her. Half-laughing, a little clumsily, they rested their foreheads together for a moment and then parted.

She walked back to the apartment, aware as she did that something else had changed again between them. Another marker had been reached on the journey of whatever was happening, wherever they were heading. Whatever it was, could be, wasn't over.

Chapter 50

Nic sat in the Mouse House trying to focus on some notes he was writing up for a new university course planned for September. He'd been putting it off, but knew that there was never as much time towards the end of the holiday as he thought there would be. The work began to outrun the days and with that came the frustration of not being able to spend as much time with Tess, Theo, and Spiro.

He got up to pour himself a glass of water from the large bottle in the fridge, looking out at the rear garden as he did so. It needed a little taming, but there was a luxuriant beauty about it at this time of year that he loved.

It crossed his mind too that it was just the sort of half-wild territory where Theo could spend a happy afternoon watching and studying a variety of creatures, but sadly not Ulysses now. Nic had picked his mother up from the airport that morning and taken Ulysses with him. She couldn't bear to be in the house without her parrot and he was always there to greet her when she came back from Athens.

The Mouse House felt strangely quiet and emptier without the chatty bird. He thought for a moment about the times, not so long ago, when he had shared a few glasses of ouzo and much laughter with Georgios. For a time, Tess had joined them at their get-togethers and he had seen his oldest friend happy and secure in a loving marriage, occasionally slightly bumpy but a good one.

After Theo had been born the focus had been very much on the Athena, home, and family. Nic was still warmly welcomed into the circle, but they all knew it was a new chapter in their lives.

On the wall in the kitchen was a small framed photograph of Nic and Georgios aged about 20, arms around each other's shoulders, raising a glass, celebrating their first summer back from university and being together again for a few glorious weeks.

Another world. Another lifetime.

As he put down the glass he looked out at the terrace and saw Tess standing there.

'Hello,' she said. 'Are you receiving visitors? I've escaped for half an hour.'

Nic, surprised but delighted, offered Tess a drink.

This never happened. Tess never came to the Mouse House. She never had time.

'This is an unexpected pleasure. Is everything okay?' Taking a seat next to her, he looked across with a little concern at Tess.

'Everything's fine. Ina arrived at work when she wasn't on the rota, so with Spiro, Anna, and Lily holding the fort, I didn't think I'd be missed and so . . . well, here I am.'

Nic was glad all was well, but it still didn't really explain why Tess had come to see him. He would have gone to the Athena later anyway.

'Well, have five minutes on me. If you want to close your eyes and drift off, that's fine. I know how rare these moments are for you.' Nic sat back in his chair and gazed across the garden.

'I'm not tired, or no more than usual.' She paused, looked at her hands, then picked up her orange juice and sipped it. 'I was chatting with Penny earlier, when she came in for a late breakfast.'

'Is she all right after her surprise last night?' Nic asked.

'Yes, in need of coffee and toast, but good, I think. Last night's unexpected visitor won't be returning. And I'm guessing that there may well be something developing between her and our friend Dimitris.'

'I did wonder when they arrived together last night.' Nic smiled, thinking of the girl who'd been very much on her own when they had first met in the shade of the Liston.

'She said a few things this morning that made me think, and that really resonated with me.'

'That sounds intriguing.' Nic leant forward,

'She talked about her dad and something he used to say.'

Nic wondered where Tess was going with this and if it was a bad day, crowded with memories of losing Georgios.

'Penny said he told her that real love is being with someone who's there with you through the worst things life throws at you, to make sure you don't give up, and to share the load. Someone who never gives up on you.'

She looked at Nic and watched his face closely as she spoke.

'Nic, I don't know what this means, what difference it might make to our friendship, but I realized this morning that for me *you* are that person: the person who never lets me give up, who has been there, uncomplaining and constant – even when you're not physically here – for me and Theo.

'I'm not sure what I'm saying or whether it's a good idea to say it, but I can't imagine a time or a world in which you won't always be that person. More importantly, I don't *want* to think about a life where you won't be with me, with us.'

Tess stopped and tried to read Nic's face, wondering what he would say, if anything. What could he say? Had she just upset the balance of their friendship irrevocably?

'You don't have to say anything,' she added, wanting to give him time to absorb what she'd said. She wasn't too sure herself where some of it had come from, so how could she expect Nic to understand what she was saying?

The air was sleepy and heavy with the noonday heat as Tess's words glided over to Nic and he began to unravel them in his head.

'I want to say something, Tess, but like you, I don't want to say too much, or anything that changes a friendship I care about more than any other in the world. I hope you know how much you and Theo mean to me.'

Nic's normally steady-as-a-rock demeanour was clearly struggling to stay in control. What was Tess really saying and why was she saying it now?

'There is nothing that you could say that would change how I feel about you, Nic, or change what you mean to me. I don't think I'm saying I'm *in* love with you, but I do love you, and if that's enough for you, then it's more than enough for me. If you feel some of what I feel, then perhaps we have a chance to make something deeper and different out of what we already have.' She paused before adding, 'If that's close to anything that you might want . . .'

She felt the relief of someone who didn't realize that they'd needed to share something, but in the sharing had finally realized its truth and importance.

Nic seemed to be in suspended animation, barely moving, as though if he said anything, he might break a spell. Without thinking she reached out to touch his face, moving out of her chair as she did so. He put his hand over hers, moved it to his mouth, and kissed it gently. Tess sat at his feet and put her head in his lap.

As he stroked her hair Nic looked down at the woman he loved, he said simply and tenderly, 'That works for me.'

Chapter 51

Penny was still undecided about when to hand over the paintings to Tess and to Aris, thinking that the best thing would probably be to give them on the day she went home.

Home. What was that going to feel like?

As she took a last look in the mirror, everything seemed surreal: where she was; who she was about to meet. The tanned open face that glanced back at her was like part of a dream. Someone she barely knew.

Would going home make all of this rich and miraculous experience disappear, dissolve like a mirage?

No one had ever said that wanting to be with someone was convenient, or easy. Feelings couldn't be turned off like a tap. The sudden and overwhelming attraction, the sense of something new and life-affirming, but uncertain, was a new experience, alive with possibilities.

As she bounced down the marble stairs and passed the pool, she noticed the tiny orbs of phosphorescence that she now knew were fireflies.

The fireflies moved silently and Penny carried on walking. There was no message that she needed to hear. No advice or permission that anyone could or would offer her. She was the mistress of own fate, the diviner of her own destiny. If the island and the fireflies had any message at all, it was just that.

The Athena was already busy as she passed. The *Dora* was in the harbour. And there standing by the entrance to the Mediterranean's garden was Dimitris, looking cool and relaxed in a blue shirt and jeans. He raised his hand in greeting as soon as he saw her and her steps quickened for the last few yards.

'Hello.' She stretched up to kiss his cheek, as though it was the most natural and practised thing in the world, something that they did every day.

He took her hand, not to make sure she didn't trip or to help her onto a boat, but to hold it in a loving, warm, natural gesture.

She had an overwhelming sense of feeling safe, tempered with an equally strong need to protect him, to keep him safe too.

⌒

The beach was the perfect place to sit and watch the moon rise. On the sand near the dunes, all they could hear were the waves rolling in.

In Penny's head the diminishing number of days left on Corfu, which had started to feel threateningly short, were forgotten, as all that mattered now was sitting next to this man, sharing their stories, and the bliss of getting to know him better.

Pressing her bare feet into the sand, she listened to Dimitris's story of his time in London and since he'd returned home. So many small but significant things that helped her to build a picture of the man she was falling in love with. He asked her about her life in England, her dad, Bruce, the books she read, the music she loved.

The fragrant wine they'd drunk had relaxed every bone in her body. It was so easy tonight to talk. When they'd finished the bottle of wine Spiro had handed them, he had waved away their request for a bill and wished them both good health. It felt like a blessing.

She spoke lovingly about her dad, as Dimitris spoke in a similar way about his mother, each understanding the ways that loss had impacted on the other, at different times, in different circumstances. They both understood that feeling of standing in the abyss of grief, of loving and losing, then rediscovering their capacity for love and life.

There was a plan made too to visit the Snow White Villa together. To share and delight in the discovery for her, and rediscovery for him, of the island.

Dimitris put his arm around her shoulder as she talked about the impact Corfu had had on her life in such a short time, and why. Instinctively, she rested her head on his shoulder as she did so. Each tried to outdo the other in a gentle and wholly generous attempt to comfort, connect, and celebrate what they had found together.

Hours passed that felt like minutes, before they decided to walk back up to the main street.

Dimitris waited as Penny put her shoes back on.

He took her hand again, kissing it before he let it fall back to her side. '*Kardia mou*,' he whispered in her ear.

Chapter 52

It was so early in the morning that St George hadn't quite changed into its day clothes and there was still a hint of ethereal sleepiness about it.

The blanket-grey sky gave in gracefully to the golden rays of the rising sun and a porcelain-blue canopy established itself above. The shops, tavernas, and bars were silent. First breakfasts were still an hour or so away and the atmosphere was more *Marie Celeste* than a vibrant coastal village.

It was into this nearly waking world that Penny stepped, making her way slowly to the sea from her apartment. It was the earliest she'd ventured out on Corfu. Even the cats didn't stir as she passed.

She wanted to enjoy the space of a new day, alone, walking on the beach. She also needed more than anything to reflect on the last days and particularly the evening before.

Dimitris was already out with his father on the *Dora*. They had left in darkness.

Past the harbour now and onto the sands, she slipped out of her flip-flops and carried them in her left hand. Over her shoulder, the harbour and then the Athena beyond, were softly gilded shapes, slowly revealed by the new light.

Just before she reached the dunes, she dropped her sandals, sat down, pulled her knees up to her chest and hugged them. Resting her head on her knees she stared out at the sea.

All she could hear were the waves and her own thoughts.

As she did at all important moments in her life, she sat quietly playing back the film reel of her evening with Dimitris.

After they'd left the beach they'd wandered around St George, like teenagers who'd just met at a noisy party, felt a mutual attraction for each other, and had decided to escape, to spend time alone.

Walking slowly and stopping every now and again to say hello to one of his friends or acquaintances, they had ended up at a quiet family-run bar. The tables stood on a stone terrace, the sea smooth and glassy below. The candle on the table danced in its glass holder, celebrating the gentle movement of the warm night air.

As she recalled it now Penny smiled, closing her eyes to bring the memory closer: the sound of Dimitris's voice, the sea, the stars above, and a yacht on the horizon.

If she was honest, this strange newness of being with someone was combined with a growing ease and familiarity. She liked the way he almost chastised himself when he'd expressed something in a way he thought clumsy, or if he felt he'd asked something she didn't want to answer. He had not mentioned Bruce directly, but asked her how she was in a way that acknowledged what had happened the night before.

Telling him the story made it feel like history, something she'd read in a book. She found it liberating to not try to be something, someone, she wasn't.

Bruce had harvested her confidence, which she now realized had been the powerful dynamic in their relationship. All her dad's wonderful and enriching words of love and support, so uplifting throughout her childhood, had wilted under the reign of Bruce.

The thought still haunted her that if her dad hadn't become so ill, when all her instincts had been to be with and look after him, the necessary and final rift with Bruce might not have occurred.

She hoped that it would have come at some point. Being alone was better than being with someone who didn't love her – the real her.

'This is the real me, here and now.' The words sang in her head as she tried to memorize Dimitris's face.

She'd had to coax him to talk about himself. When he did, she sat back and enjoyed the time she could watch him, without feeling as though she was staring. In his self-effacing manner he dismissed his years in London as a lucky break because Theo was his uncle, rather than accepting the idea that it had anything to do with his talent or skills.

He still found talking about his mother painful. Penny could sense that he not only blamed himself for not being there when she had died, but for the fact that she had died at all. Had he broken her heart with his apparent disinterest and being away for so long? The fact that he was talking about it at all, was, Penny would discover in later days and weeks, miraculous.

She had come away to Corfu not to find herself, but to find a way to move forward, to begin living again. To experience all the tiny, but significant joys of the everyday, without grief tugging her back under the bedclothes.

There was no bartering or halfway house with death. It was a fact, a constant for humanity in a world where discussing it was often considered a taboo. That it should shock and disorientate was forgivable, understandable . . . human.

And so was falling in love. Perhaps falling in love was part of life growing around her grief now.

She hoped it was the same for Dimitris.

St George was coming to life.

The shutters on the supermarket rolled up, and the delivery van with the bottled water arrived. Two people jogging along the beach said good morning as they passed Penny.

She stood up, her mind wandering happily with her feet along the water's edge. Drawn back towards the harbour, she shielded her eyes from the already bright sun and peered across at the panorama to see if she could see any movement.

She hoped Tess would be there and they'd have time to share a coffee. She wanted to share with her some of the story of the evening before. The idea of being in Tess's company appealed for her humour, compassion, and pure likability.

Penny felt a bond with the woman, who had so subtly and sensitively taken her under her wing when she'd first arrived. She was one of those on this special island who'd held out a hand and invited her to take it, when she was still struggling in the quicksand of grief.

Pausing as she reached the Athena, Penny felt herself smiling, suppressing the joy inside, as she remembered parting from Dimitris the night before.

On Firefly Lane, watched indifferently by sleepy lizards and stalking cats, he had kissed her again. It felt like a promise, part of a journey. Its sweetness spoke of tenderness, as well as need. As she kissed him back, she was saying, 'Don't give up. Be with me and we'll be okay – we'll be more than okay'.

Looking across at the harbour before stepping into the restaurant, where she could see Tess was already making herself a coffee, she spotted the *Dora*, making her way back home across the wine-dark sea.

The Snow White Villa near Cressida, with its wide veranda, walled garden, and wild flowers, was the last of the Durrells' residences on Corfu.

Penny had always meant Kalami to be the final location of her pilgrimage, but now it felt so right to be here as her holiday came to a close. This was the place the Durrells had left from as the Second World War loomed.

It felt right too now to be wandering with Dimitris, looking for this place; a place that had more meaning, because now she felt she understood why they had loved this island so much.

The house lay behind walls and gates, private, settled in its foundations, keeping its secrets, holding to itself the memories of those who'd lived within its walls. An ornate, carved, alabaster-white edifice of beauty and charm.

'Leaving' as a word and an action now had less sting. The threat of going home felt hollow, unimportant. Penny realized that if you fell in love with a place or a person, they never really left you, or you them.

Wherever she was in the world, in her heart she would always be on Corfu and here, as she was now, with Dimitris and the Durrells.

Acknowledgements

This book wouldn't have been written without the endless love, patience, and support of my family. From the first tentative words typed out in St George South, Corfu, in May 2019, they have been there for me. So, love and thanks to my dear husband David and our children, Geoff and Lizzy.

There have been many kindnesses, from people I already knew, but also from some I haven't yet met in person. For this, I thank you and will be eternally grateful.

Love to my understanding and supportive colleagues at the XP Trust.

My thanks to dear Annabelle Louvros of the Corfu Literary Festival and the wonderfully kind and helpful Liz Fenwick.

To my friends in St George South, Corfu, much love.

To Rose, Bengono, and the rest of the team at HarperInspire, my deep gratitude and appreciation. My sincere thanks also to Gale for her brilliant editing work.

During the writing of this book, it has been a real pleasure to chat with Tracy and Nick Breeze, Margo Durrell's grandchildren. I hope they like it and feel it captures some of the spirit of their remarkable family's time on Corfu.

Finally, I would like to acknowledge the amazing work of Dr Lee Durrell, the renowned naturalist and author, and wife of the late Gerald Durrell. She has my ongoing admiration and respect. Lee was kind enough to correspond with me, so that I could share with her the story of the book.

This book was written because of a world and a time that was captured and immortalized by the Durrells. My life, and that of many others, has been richer because they were here.